Mandrake Petals and Scattered Feathers

Tales from the Forest and Beyond

MANDRAKE PETALS AND SCATTERED FEATHERS

Tales from the Forest and Beyond

David Greygoose

Mandrake Petals and Scattered Feathers

Text copyright©2021 David Greygoose

ISBN 978-1-8380247-3-4

The Author has asserted his rights under the Copyright, Designs and Patents Act 1988 to be identified as the author of this work.

This book is a work of fiction and any resemblance of characters therein to persons living or dead is purely coincidental.

Conditions of Sale
No part of this book may be reproduced or transmitted by any means without the permission of the publisher.

British Library Cataloguing in Publication Data.
A catalogue record for this book is available from the British Library.

3 4 5 6

First Published in Great Britain
Hawkwood Books 2021
This edition 2023

Printed and bound in Great Britain by CPI Group (UK) Ltd.
Croydon CR0 4YY

"I'm reading these stories on a high-speed train of steel and glass and plastic. Out the window are fields and forests, Norman towers and Saxon trackways... I glance back at this book, and feel that these tales grow from that very earth."

PAUL DU NOYER: music journalist, founding editor of *Mojo* magazine and author of *Liverpool, Wondrous Place*.

"In this atmospheric collection, characters are strikingly drawn with absorbing simplicity of style. Through sinister encounters and ominous symbolism, Greygoose breathes dark new life into the folk tale genre."

LIZZIE NUNNERY: 'Daphne: A Fire in Malta' (BBC Radio)

"Each of his characters waits eagerly in the wings for their turn to dance, dazzle and spin in a linguistic firework display with every turn of the page. Entranced."

PHIL MAY: co-writer of The Pretty Things' classic, *S.F. Sorrow*

"Strange happenings and wyrd wanderings: magical and compelling, haunting and other-worldly."

MELANIE XULU: MOOF magazine of psychedelic music and art

"David Greygoose's richly descriptive folk tales conjure up a dreamlike other-world reminiscent of the work of Arthur Machen or Mervyn Peake's 'Gormenghast' trilogy."

MIKE STAX: *Ugly Things* magazine (USA)

"The tale unfolds like a Gaelic Lay; Tale Teller Greygoose leads the way... read by candlelight if you can."

DONOVAN: 'The Hurdy Gurdy Man'

For
T.V.S.

ACKNOWLEDGEMENTS

Thanks to Eleanor Rees for editorial advice, support, encouragement and inspiration; and to Ellis Delmonte for continuing insight, enthusiasm and dedication.

Cover image by Steve Willmott from *Zeds Magazine*, published early 1970s in Sherborne, Dorset. Every effort has been made to contact the artist.

MANDRAKE PETALS AND SCATTERED FEATHERS

AT THE CROSSROADS / 1

LOWDEN'S BECK / 3

Something or Nothing / 10

THE GREY GIRL / 13

MEADOWSWEET AND THE DRESS OF GREEN / 26

A Bottle of Tears / 32

THE KEEPER OF SECRETS / 35

QUOB / 42

PHYSICIANS OF HIGH DEGREE / 51

CROW JACK / 56

Riddle-me-Ree / 69

GULL BOY / 72

The Sun and the Rain / 80

THE SHIP IN THE FOREST / 83

HAWKSTONE / 101

Mullops and the Snail / 111

WRANGLETHORN AND MARRADON / 113

A Haze of Heat / 123

ROWAN / 125

THE MELPHEN CHILD / 137

Three Apples / 145

THE HANGED MAN / 147

A Wondrous Shell / 156

THE POND OF SORROWS / 159

CHUDDERS / 168

Nowhere / 188

THE WHALE IN THE MOUNTAIN / 190

THE FEATHER IN THE SACK / 199

JINTY CATCHPENNY AND OLD JELLIMUTTS / 204

Arm Wrestling / 209

THE HORSE IN THE WATER / 210

OLD JESSUP / 219

MOON MOTHER / 224

A Necklace of Snails / 232

LANTERN AND TUMBLEPIP / 238

A GIRL WITH NO SHOES / 246

A Little Bit of Bread and No Cheese / 256

COPPEN AND THE CROOK-BACKED DANCERS / 263

MANDRAKE PETALS AND SCATTERED FEATHERS / 269

THE WAITING STORM / 278

BACK AT THE CROSSROADS / 283

AT THE CROSSROADS

Now they say that at the crossroads, when the moon is full, you can see everyone who ever passed this way. You can see them greeting one another, whether they came here yesterday or many seasons gone. You can see lost lovers kissing, you can see old foes squaring up, wrestling and fighting. You can see strangers dancing in the thunder and the lightning.

Then in a moment, before you can blink, before you can rub your eyes, it is silent again, as if none of them had ever been here. But if you look down you will see footprints criss-crossing the leaf mulch, more than could ever pass this way in a night or in a day. And you hear soft voices, just for a moment, floating on the wind. But then you turn around to catch what they are saying and they are gone, and there is only Pickapple sitting on an upturned bucket outside his hut, laughing at you.

His laughter rattles the leaves until they tumble from the trees, covering up the footprints as if they were never there. His laughter rattles the clouds to send them scudding across the moon till there is only darkness, and you are alone with the darkness, alone with Pickapple and his laughter.

Now who is Pickapple, I hear you asking? Let me tell you - Pickapple lives in a hut right next to this crossroads just outside the village. He likes to spin the sign-post around, so no-one knows where they're going. He says it is the wind, but no-one believes him, because no-one ever believes anything Pickapple tells them.

But now you are alone with him, and Pickapple starts dancing. He dances in a capering circle, plucking you up and spinning you round and setting you down till you are so dizzy it is you that are dancing and Pickapple is sitting quite still on the ground.

LOWDEN'S BECK

When the long day dawdled slowly and Rimmony grew tired of the gossip of the other girlen as they clustered about the well, she would slip away quietly and take herself down along the rutted lane then on up the track that led to Lowden's Beck. She would glance this way and that to make sure no-one had followed her, then make her way along a path so choked with weeds and thorns you would scarce know it was there unless you had been before. But Rimmony she went there every day.

Where did it lead, this path that only she knew? Why, it led to the waterfall that tumbled down the hill, rippling and splashing into Lowden's Beck. And Rimmony would sit beside it and wash her hands in the water, and sometimes her feet and then her long dark hair, for the water felt pure and soft and clean - and then she would sit on a rock and dream.

She would dream the voice of the linnet on the branch high above was singing just to her as the water leapt and danced from stone to stone. Then sometimes in the heat of the afternoon sun, Rimmony's lids would flutter closed and the voice of the linnet became the voice of a boy, talking to her as she nestled against the rock.

"I see you, Rimmony," the voice seemed to say. "I see you, Rimmony, when you come here every day. You do not see me, but I am watching. I am here in the trees, I am here in the shadows. I am the voice of the air that kisses your cheek. I am Flax Wing..."

"Flax Wing..." Rimmony would whisper in reply, in

her mind seeing the figure of a tall slim boy standing beside her at the edge of the stream.

And one afternoon, when she opened her eyes, sure as sure, he was standing there, just for a moment. His hair was long and flowing and his eyes burned amber fire; but as he raised his hand to beckon her, he vanished pure away.

Rimmony called his name, but there came no reply. She ran to the spot where he had stood, but all she heard was the water's cry. She leapt nimble-footed from rock to rock then plunged back and forth through the bushes, still calling. But all that she heard was the clamour of the birds as they swooped from tree to tree.

Rimmony sat down by the stream again and buried her face in her hands. Flax Wing had been here, she had seen him.

"I seen him and that is enough. Not to worry that he's gone. If I seen him once, I will see him again, for now I know that he is here."

She lifted her head and called again.

"Flax Wing..."

Her voice echoed through the trees.

"Flax Wing, I will come again. Wait for me here."

Next day Rimmony came back again, and the next day and the day after. She would sit on the rock by the waterfall just as she had before and watch for Flax Wing and wait, and softly call his name. But Flax Wing never came.

Some days she slipped from her mother's gaze before dawn was fully woken. She would eat no breakfast, no supper neither on her return, for her belly was filled with a wondering, a longing, as she ached to run her fingers through Flax Wing's long flowing hair.

Then half the night she sat awake, by the light of a candle until the dawnlight came: sewing moss and petals and strands of wool, the bones of small animals, straw and grass into a dress of green. Then she strung a necklace of bits of broken shell and berries she'd gathered all down by the stream

"One day," she whispered as she finally lay to sleep, "Flax Wing, I will wear these all for you."

Day after day, Rimmony scarcely ate, she scarcely slept. She slipped like a shadow to the waterfall, but Flax Wing never came. He never came when she called him. He never came when she left him gifts of food that her mother had wrapped to take with her: cobs of bread, morsels of cheese, berries and nuts.

Every night when she returned, she told her mother she had eaten them, but instead she had left them on the rock by the stream. The next day when she went back, the food would be gone and Rimmony knew that Flax Wing had been. He had slipped down from the trees and eaten her gifts as dusk light crept slowly through the woods. She told herself she was feeding him, even though he never appeared when she was there. And she turned her back on the twittering and chattering of the nut-hatches, chaffinches, great tits and linnets who descended on the morsels soon as she walked away.

One day when Rimmony headed out towards the path, she slowed her step as she heard a scurrying in the bushes behind her. She turned and caught her breath. A boy was standing beside her.

"Elmskin!" she said sharply. "What are you doing here?"

Elmskin blushed and looked away.

"Just walking to the wood," he muttered.

Rimmony stared at him.

"No-one comes this way no more. Hope you're not following me. Get yourself off back home!"

Elmskin opened his mouth to say more, but as Rimmony glowered he just grew confused, turned around slowly and walked away. Rimmony stood for a moment and watched him go, then picked her way quickly along the track to Lowden's Beck.

Each day it was the same. Elmskin got up early and hung around the pigmires, waiting for Rimmony to appear. Then he slipped along behind her, so she'd never see and followed her all along the track to Lowden's Beck. When they got to the waterfall he sat there, up on a higher ledge looking down and watched as Rimmony combed her hair and spread her skirt and scattered food all around. Sometimes she sang and sometimes she fell to calling a name: *Flax Wing! Flax Wing!* - ringing around the hillside. But Elmskin didn't know who that was and nobody ever came.

Then she'd lie and she'd sigh and she'd cry and then get up again and shake the leaves from her dress and turn around and make her way slowly home, while Elmskin followed close behind.

One morning, early autumn, Rimmony came to the waterfall same as usual, same as she ever did. Her hair was all matted for she never brushed it now. And her skin was moon-pale for she hardly ate nothing and left all her food for Flax Wing to find. But she wore a new dress, the dress of green she'd been making all this while, covered about with moss and petals and strands of wool. She wore it for Flax Wing and now she called his name loud as she could muster, though her voice was grown weak.

"Flax Wing! Flax Wing! Come see me again..."

Then as she stood and listened, she heard a voice reply: "Follow me..."

Rimmony followed. Followed with beating heart and quickening step, slipping and slithering away from the stream, following the voice which called her still, leading on till she came to a place where the hill fell suddenly away.

The voice had stopped. Rimmony looked around. Then she heard it again, faint but clear - *"Follow me!"* - echoing up from the river which gushed between dark black rocks far below.

Rimmony stepped forward.

"Flax Wing!" she called and listened again for his reply.

She heard the roaring rush of the wind all around her and the swirl of the water on the rocks.

"Flax Wing!" she shouted, one more time.

"Rimmony."

She heard a voice speak her name, not from far below but standing close behind her. She turned around.

"Rimmony..." Elmskin held out his hand.

"Oh - it's only you."

Her voice was heavy with disdain as Elmskin stepped forward and took her hand gently, but Rimmony pulled away and turned again to the edge of the drop and the rocks far below. She teetered a moment, listening for Flax Wing's voice. But there was nothing.

"Rimmony, come home."

Elmskin stood beside her and she stepped back and stood for a moment, her eyes staring one way and another. Then he took her arm and steered her gently back along the track, back towards Lowden's Beck and then on back to the village. As they walked, Rimmony said little to Elmskin's questions. Did not tell him why she went there, just gazed ahead with a far-off look in her eyes.

Each day Elmskin called at her house, to take her out walking and talk to her quietly. Then bit by bit she told him of the boy she'd seen, how she longed for him to speak to her again...

Elmskin shook his head.

"Mayhap it was only me. First off when I followed you, I always called after you."

"Oh no," Rimmony replied. "Was not you. You sound rusty as an old creaking door."

"Don't care if my voice be coarse as a goat. Don't care if the sun don't shine in my hair like this boy you think you seen. I only know I'm with you now and I can keep you safe and that makes me feel warm inside - like a fire on a cold winter's morn."

Rimmony glanced at him a moment then kissed him quickly on the cheek, but when he turned to take her hand she was staring far away, away to Lowden's Beck. Away to where the waterfall danced. Away to the edge of the steep drop, the rushing river and the rocks below.

Next day Elmskin knocked at Rimmony's door. First there was no answer but then her mother came down.

"She's already gone. Gone off in that dress of green - the one she was wearing when you brought her back."

Elmskin ran as fast as he could, all the way down the path to Lowden's Beck. He called her name, but all he heard was the rushing of the water. He called her name, but all he heard was the echo of his voice. He pushed on through dense brambles to the place where the hill fell away, high above the rocks and the frothing river. He looked all around but nothing could he see till his eyes fell on a pile of clothes folded neatly at the edge.

Elmskin held his breath and slowly took them in his arms. Rimmony's green dress that she'd spent long nights stitching, sewed from moss and petals, strands of wool and tiny bones. And lying on top was her necklace made of shells and shrivelled berries. He stared down at the rocks below, but nothing could he see there, only the surging water and a rowan tree clinging to the edge. Then he stood and listened and just for a moment thought he heard her voice, calling for Flax Wing far away.

"Rimmony!" he shouted in reply.

Then there was silence. He stood a while and waited but heard only the call of a distant linnet and the roar of the river below.

Something or Nothing

Pickapple would go out every morning while the mist swirled thick around the roots of the trees, just as the throstles were waking to sing, just as the cock was a-crowing, down at the edge of the village. Pickapple would listen and sometimes he'd mimic the sounds on his little penny whistle - or sometimes he'd keep quiet and tune his ears to the patter of rain, far off and far.

But then he would go gathering truffles, beneath the roots of the trees. They were the best truffles in all of the forest and he didn't want no-one else to know where he had found them. One such morning he came back to his hut and there he caught sight of Mullops, crouching behind a tree.

"What have you seen?" Pickapple challenged, hiding the truffles in his jacket.

"Seen nothing."

"I'll show you nothing. What is in this bag? Think it something or nothing?"

Mullops scratched his head as the bag bulged and squirmed, then from deep inside came a noise like a chicken.

"Not nothing," said Mullops. "Sounds like a chicken, and a chicken is something."

"Look inside," Pickapple instructed.

Mullops seized the bag, still wriggling and struggling, and plunged in his hand.

"There is nothing."

"But you said there was something," Pickapple reminded him as he took back the bag.

Mullops frowned as he heard a loud squawking.

"This chicken I cannot see, but in this bag I know it

must be... I've always wanted a chicken," he cried. "If I had a chicken I would feed it on corn and it would lay eggs for my breakfast every day."

He grabbed at the bag, but as he did so, the chicken began to bark. He plunged his hand inside again, but once again there was nothing.

"This dog I cannot see, but in this bag I know it must be... I've always wanted a dog. If I had a dog I could go out each day into the woods and hunt for rabbits for my supper."

Mullops grabbed at the bag again, just as the dog began to grunt.

"Why, it be not a dog but a fine pig for sure!"

He plunged his hand in the bag but could find nothing more.

"This pig I cannot see, but in this bag I know it must be... I've always wanted a pig. If I had a pig I could wallow with it all day in the mud. I could follow it into the wood to dig for truffles of my own underneath the trees. And then I could dine on bacon all winter..."

Mullops paused.

"But then if I had bacon, I'd have no pig to wallow with and I'd have no truffles at all."

"Mayhap you have no pig anyway," Pickapple reminded him as Mullops grabbed at the bag again and plunged his head full inside to look.

"There is nothing!" Mullops shouted. "No pig, no dog, no chicken. There is nothing at all."

"There is nothing but an empty head," Pickapple cried as he seized the bag and pulled the draw-strings tight around Mullops' neck and watched as he blundered off into the woods, bumping into every tree that he came to.

"If I can't see you, then you can't see me," Mullops

muttered hopefully.

"Oh Mullops, I can see you plain as plain," Pickapple cried as he opened up the door of his hut and slipped the truffles safely inside.

THE GREY GIRL

A thin dawn mist shrouded the houses as Old Shankpepper stood in his doorway and stared to the end of the street. There he saw a figure moving. He rubbed his eyes, thinking at first it was a bird lost its way. But then he saw it was arms that were flailing, feet that were skipping. A girlen lost in the trance of a dance.

Shankpepper caught his breath, then called out a name, but the girlen did not respond. He stepped from his door and hurried towards her, trying to make out her face, but she flitted away. Shankpepper stopped stock still, shook his head then rapped his knuckles on the window of a cottage across the way. There came a shuffling from inside and then the door was pulled open. Old Mother Fuskin stood there, her long grey hair spilling down about her shoulders.

"What's all this bother so early in the morning?"

Old Shankpepper pointed.

Mother Fuskin squinted down the street.

"Tis only morning mist. Soon be gone," she said.

"Priddie Tippet, I saw Priddie Tippet, my favourite grandchild of all," Old Shankpepper replied, his eyes open wide.

"Be gone with you," Mother Fuskin said. "Priddie Tippet is dead and you know it well. Drowned in the Dark Pond, deep in the wood."

Shankpepper grabbed her arm.

"Who's that there then?"

He pointed again.

Mother Fuskin peered through the clearing mist and sure enough she saw what Old Shankpepper had seen - a girlen dancing at the end of the street. A girlen dressed all in grey.

"Taint Priddie Tippet," she said at last. "Priddie's face was always smiling and she would never wear grey."

"Suppose you're right," Old Shankpepper sighed. "But just for a moment, there in the mist..."

"Mist is gone now. But this girlen ain't. Who d'you think she is?"

The two of them stood and watched as the girlen danced nearer. Her bare feet beat out a pattern like as if she was listening to a rhythm that crossed and kicked and flew. But she moved in silence, no tune could they hear.

"Mind you," said Mother Fuskin, "there's those as said they saw a girlen much like this the day your Priddie drowned."

She left Old Shankpepper standing at the door and stepped out in front of the girlen as she skipped all down the street.

"Who are you?" she demanded. "Where have you come from?"

By this time other doors had opened as the village was woken by the commotion.

"What's your name?" Mother Fuskin asked again.

But the girlen spoke not a word. She just danced on, her grey dress swaying, her hips flexing and twisting, her heels and toes skipping and skittering in a blur.

Mother Fuskin retreated to her doorstep and stood with the others, arms folded, and watched. But Old Shankpepper pushed his way forward.

"I know this step!" he cried. "I know this caper, the measure and the changes. Ain't hardly danced it since I was a young'un.

"Them was sprightly days," he grinned around the watching crowd, some of them nodding in agreement. "Every summer's night we'd dance this step, out there on the Green. Then over to Ludditch to find their girlen to join us."

A cheer went up as he stepped forward and threw away his stick. But the girl in the grey dress took no notice. She flung her arms up above her head and spun around and around as Old Shankpepper moved towards her, his feet keeping time across the ground.

A handclap started and then a stamping of feet as Old Shankpepper picked up the rhythm. But the girlen flitched away from him, moving out to the edge of the Green, circling him about till the old man took the centre, dancing faster and faster as the handclaps grew louder. Until he stopped. And sat down.

The girl still did not look at him but drew in closer, circling around and around as he sat quite still, drawing his breath. Then he scrambled to his feet and stumbled past her, returning to pick up his stick again to a ripple of cheers and applause.

Then Mullops stepped up.

"I can gain her," he said and set off straight towards the girlen in grey. Soon as he reached her he made to twine an arm about her waist, same as he would with any girlen in the circle dance. But this one slipped away, away and away, stepping merry all around the back of the crowd, leaving Mullops standing, shoulders slumped, in the middle of the Green.

Out of the cottages ran sleepy-eyed childern, their hair all tousled with raggedy dreams. They ran towards the Grey Girl and began to dance behind her, following her every step. Mullops stumbled back to join the others and led them in clapping out the rhythm while the childern danced wilder, capering and leaping as the Grey Girl led them in circles, this way and that, then up the alley and back again.

The old'uns kept up their stomping and clapping and broke into a cheer as the childern reappeared. But rather than run to meet their mothers, the childern set off again, following the music that no-one could hear as if they'd always known it, up the next alley and all the way back.

Soon enough it became a game. Each time the Grey Girl led them between the houses, the people would keep clapping and turn about and around to see where the childern would appear.

"Where've they gone?"

The clapping of the beat and the stomping of the feet.

"Which way they coming?"

"I hear them now."

"There they are!"

And the childern would swoop back into view past the cheering crowd. Then they were gone again and the stamping continued and the clapping and the laughter.

"They gone a long time."

"Be here soon enough."

"They just hiding, you see."

But then there was silence.

The childern did not come, and not the Grey Girl neither.

The birds they sang the same as ever. The early mist had cleared and now the sun broke through. In the fields the cattle lowed and the long-haired sheep shook their shanks and bleated. But the childern did not come.

"Must be hiding," Dundledrum the butcher declared, rolling up his sleeves and striding up and down the alleys, peering into shadows and tipping over barrels.

"Must be hiding," said the others, scuttling all round

the village, peeking and prying into every nook and cranny where they thought the childern might be, calling each and every one of them by name.

Mothers rushed indoors to check the beds of their other youngsters, those that hadn't woken early - dragging them out onto the Green and setting them to look for the others.

"Might be in the wood yard," one of the youngsters suggested.

"Told you never to go there."

"But we do - just you don't know. That's the best place to hide!"

Dundledrum and Fitcher rushed to the wood yard at the back of Old Shankpepper's cottage. Piles of timber all stacked up, all higgledy pickledy. Fine place to hide. Fine place to get trapped - the mothers always warned, for the timber was known to fall and young Fallowfield had been under it, years ago, so they said. Knocked flat on his back by a beam on his head then the whole pile came a-tumbling down. Never found him till three days later.

Dundledrum and Fitcher tore at the stacks, tossing slats and beams aside, shouting out the names of each of the childern. Then Dundledrum stopped, breathing heavy, sweat on his brow,

"They ain't here," he said. "Ain't here at all. If they had been we'd have heard them by now, giggling and shrieking like it was a bit of fun."

Fitcher looked at him and nodded grimly. Tugged at one last timber, kicked it with his boot till the rest of the stack came clattering down.

"This ain't no game no more," he muttered.

The two men turned and walked slowly towards the Green. All the others had drifted back there too, their eyes dull and dejected in the brightness of the morning sun.

"They've gone," said one mother flatly.

"They've gone," another echoed.

"They've gone," went up the cry with a sobbing and a wailing and a ripping of aprons and shawls.

Dundledrum and Fitcher paced to the end of the village, following a trail of footprints in the dust and the mud.

"Soon find'em now."

But when they got to the path that led to the wood, the footprints stopped. Dundledrum stood and scratched his head. No sign at all. No broken twig, no dropped kerchief.

Next day and next and all through the nights they searched the fields, the woods and the streams. They took long poles to prod the ponds, they dug down deep into foxes' burrows. But the childern were gone. They knowed it true. The mothers bore it like a bitter stone, buried deep inside them. Sisteren and brothers played games of chase and catch that made no sense without the missing ones.

Little Marvisty Vetch fingered the hem of her sister's second dress and wondered if she would ever wear it now, but knew deep down that she would never want to. She only wanted her sister back, her sister who would pinch her and punch her and cheat her. Her sister who would steal all her tatties at the table when her head was turned. Her sister who would tell her such tales in the upstairs room while they waited for sleep to come. She wanted her back. She wanted her back so bad that she took to wandering the lanes away from the others. And sometimes she might see a flutter of white away in the bushes and fancy it was her sister's kerchief. But no, it was only an old goose feather lost on the breeze.

But her brother said nothing. Said nothing of how he missed their sister. Would go every morning straight out to the woods and stay there all day and never say what it was he did there. But he didn't roam with the other boys no more and when he came home he would spend all his time just sitting on the window ledge, staring out.

Then he took to playing his drum. An old drum made of an earthen pot with a skin stretched across. He would tap out a rhythm but then he'd stop, like as if he didn't have it right. Then he'd start up again and tap some more and stop again and start.

Marvisty listened. She knew she knowed that rhythm. Searched her head for where it came from, and then one night, just as she was drifting off to sleep and the moonlight stole through the window, she knew what it was. Was from the story her sister always told her, about an old woman who came through the woods and came a-knocking, a-knocking on the door. And she'd always tapped it out, on the dresser or the headboard. And that's where Marvisty had heard it before.

Next day her brother didn't go to the woods. He just sat at the window, tapping and a-tapping at his drum. Marvisty came and sat beside him. Didn't say nothing. Just watched his hands and the patterns that they made, shadows blurring across the drum's tight skin.

And then he'd stop. And start again. She watched his face. He didn't look at her. Just staring and staring, away and away. He played the rhythm again and again, but it still wasn't right. He cast down the drum. Marvisty sat and watched him. Then she knocked, knocked on the old gnarled oak of the windowsill, just as their sister had knocked when she told them the story of the old woman in the woods.

Her brother said nothing, but he began to play along with her knocking, playing out the rhythm till they kept time together, over and over, again and again.

Then her brother leapt up and ran out into the street, his drum tucked under his arm. He sat on a tree stump in the middle of the Green and he played the same rhythm, over and over. Old Shankpepper came out from his cottage to see what the noise was. He stood rooted in the middle of the Green as he watched the boy playing and then began to tap his foot along with the beat.

"This is the jig the Grey Girl danced when she came among us that day. It's the same jig I danced when I was a lad..."

"It's the jig the Grey Girl danced when she come to take the childern away," Old Mother Fuskin muttered as she came to stand and watch.

"We weren't there then," Marvisty reminded her. "Me and my brother were both still a-bed."

Old Shankpepper was on his feet again, capering away to the rhythm of the drum. And soon they all came, old'uns and young'uns out on the Green - and if they didn't know the rhythm already they picked it up soon as soon.

But some didn't want to dance.

"Tis the tune the Grey Girl used to take the childern away," Old Mother Fuskin repeated.

"So mayhap if we dance it now, they'll all come back again."

They danced and they danced, but nobody came. No childern running down the alleys. No Grey Girl drawn back by the rhythm. But they danced all the same. Danced to forget what they were dancing for, though the alleys stood dark and silent. No laughter shifted through the shadows. No footsteps approached from the depths of the wood. And then the drumming stopped. Marvisty's brother sank to the ground. His fingers were blistered and bleeding, his arms they were aching, his wrists could not move any more. And so the dancing stopped. One by one they realised that all they were hearing was the clatter of their own feet and not the drum that had summoned them.

All that could be heard was one blackbird, high in the tree, singing out shrill and clear as could be. But then the bird stopped as it heard no more of the hubbub below. It sat with its head to one side as it watched, watched the noonday sun swing round to light the shadows of the alleyway. Watched as the crowd on the Green looked around to see the lost childern coming towards them, threading their way back just like the day they had vanished. And just like that day, a look in their eyes as if they were seeing a place faraway.

The mothers stood rock still, not wanting to believe. But then a gasp and a cry as they rushed towards their young'uns and clutched them tightly.

"Where have you been?"

"Where did you go?"

"Where is the Grey Girl who took you away?"

But the childern said nothing and the mothers looked again at their faces, and they were old, old as Old Shankpepper or Mother Fuskin, as if they had been away not for weeks but for years. And now they'd stopped dancing they could dance no more, their limbs all a-spindle and their faces lined with wrinkles.

"Where have you been?" Marvisty's mother demanded.

But Marvisty's older sister said nothing, only pointed.

Pointed to the edge of the Green and beyond, down the lane that wound its way through black fields, raucous with crows. Pointed the way to the woods.

They all made their way there, old'uns and young'uns, sisters and brothers, some clamouring and chanting, some sullen and silent. Mothers fussed around the ones that had gone missing, still mithering them with questions.

"What did you do there?"

"Where is the Grey Girl?"

"What did you eat? Where did you shelter?"

But the childern only told them how good it felt to be back and never dropped a word about where they had been as they reached the wood so lush and green. Thrushes shrilled their warning song while squirrels and rabbits scampered away as the procession straggled between the trees.

"Which way? Which way?"

The lost childern led them.

"Ain't never been this way before."

They plunged deeper into the undergrowth till the track seemed like no track at all as they struggled through nettles and bindweed and beneath their feet a slush of mud.

Flies buzzed dully all around as they staggered out of the bushes and near straight into a stagnant pond. Crows clattered through the branches of the overhanging trees as one of the childern let out a cry -

"There she is!" and pointed across the pond.

Old Shankpepper pushed his way to the front.

"Is it my Priddie Tippet, come back again?"

Mother Fuskin hauled him back.

"No, you old fool. I told you she's gone. And watch your footing else you'll slip in this foul pond."

"Then who is that?" Old Shankpepper exclaimed, his hand shaking as he pointed across the water.

But it was not his favourite grandchild of all, it was not Prinnie Tippet but the Grey Girl sitting alone in the middle of a circle of trees. Her mouth was stuffed with straw, dead flowers clung to her hair. Her face was streaked with lines of clay and her eyes were wide as the moon.

The crowd fell silent and stared across the water as the Grey Girl stared back, though just as when she had first danced to the village, she seemed to see nothing at all.

Then she spat away the straw. She opened her mouth and sang:

> *You give me little*
> *And I will take plenty.*
> *Your bellies are full*
> *While my plate is empty.*
>
> *I'll take your sons*
> *And I'll take your daughters*
> *To come and live with me*
> *Down by the water.*
>
> *The trees they are tall*
> *And the forest is deep.*
> *They'll taste the cold moonlight*
> *Before they find sleep.*

The gathered crowd shivered as her voice soared pale and clear. She began to sing the tune again and this time the childern she had lured all joined in as they linked hands and danced slowly all around the pond.

When they reached the Grey Girl she stopped singing.

One by one they plucked the flowers from her hair and flung them to the ground like as if they were a shower of snow.

Then silence fell. The people watching scarcely breathed and the birds all ceased their singing. The Grey Girl slowly toppled and lay in a bed of darkening mulch. The childern took up her song, quiet at first then louder as they watched her skin shrivel, frail as leaves in winter. Her very flesh faded as a soft wind blew till only her bones lay stretched in the mire.

And the mothers watched as their childern's faces grew young again and they danced once more to the rhythm that Marvisty's brother beat out on his drum. And as they danced, they sang:

> *The trees they are tall*
> *And the forest is deep.*
> *We've tasted cold moonlight*
> *But we cannot sleep.*
>
> *We are your sons*
> *And we are your daughters.*
> *We came here to live*
> *Down by the water.*
>
> *We gave her little*
> *But she came and took plenty.*
> *Our bellies were full*
> *While her plate was empty.*

The trees they are tall
And the forest is deep.
We've tasted cold moonlight
Now we wake from our sleep.

MEADOWSWEET
AND THE DRESS OF GREEN

Elmskin took the green dress, the dress that Rimmony left behind, the dress he found lying all out by Lowden's Beck. The dress that she had made with her own busy fingers, every stitch and every button, every tuck and every line, all the trims of moss and petals, strands of wool and tiny bones. And beneath there was the necklace made of shells and cherry stones.

He carried them back home and next day he woke and folded the dress into a bag and without a word to his mother, set off into the fields, out to the dell of bluebells where he always dreamed that he would walk with Rimmony beside him, laughing and talking and watching the sun as it climbed slowly through the sky to touch the distant hills.

Now the dell was as he knew it, filled with the trilling of the birds, the stone-hatch and the brambling thrush, the linnet and the chaffinch. Elmskin spread the dress out gently on a soft bed of moss and there he lay beside it and stroked the cloth and touched the folds as if Rimmony lay beside him and was not lost at Lowden's Beck.

The sun grew warm as the day rolled on and Elmskin's eyes soon closed. His fingers fondled the fabric still, so soft and green as moss. He dreamt he was with Rimmony, walking on through the woods to another hollow he had never seen before. All around white flowers grew, their petals sweet as snow though the sun sang through the branches which wrapped them all around till they were rocked like in a boat and drifted far away.

He heard a girlen giggling then all rippling through the trees and woke to see if it was Rimmony, laying close beside him. But Rimmony was gone. Elmskin sat up straight and stared about the dell. The green dress it was gone as well from where he'd laid it on the ground. The sun beat down still warmer than it ever had before. And the girlen he still heard, laughing in the distance and the cracking of dead bracken as she skittered through the trees.

Elmskin shook his head and rubbed his eyes. Then he put his hand in his pocket. The necklace still was there, the necklace made of shells and cherry stones which Rimmony had left all out at Lowden's Beck.

Late that day, dusk came crawling out from the grey wood beyond, calling him from his mother's kitchen to stand there at the door. A skein of geese flew low towards the darkened fields and drew him like a thread down towards the well.

There the girlen were gossiping, clapping hands and whispering. Soon as Elmskin came into sight they stopped and clustered all around one girl who was giggling, but they kept her hidden from view. Elmskin stood before them as they stared silent back at him, then suddenly they moved aside and pushed the girlen forward.

Elmskin's mouth opened wide. She was wearing Rimmony's dress of green and for that moment in the twilight he was with her in a dream. The others said nothing, covering their faces as this girl slipped quietly away.

Elmskin followed as she walked, slowly first then

quicker, all down the darkened lane. She did not turn her head to see if he was following, but follow he surely did, his heart beating hard in his chest, his feet stumbling eagerly through the rutted mire. He lost sight of her at the bottom, turned a corner and she was gone.

"Rimmony!" he called soft in the moist night air.

But there was no reply, only the lowing of the cattle in the fields and the hoot of an owl in the woods. Then a ripple of laughter from inside a byre at the side of the track, all filled with clean straw. He stepped inside and there sat the girl, her long hair spilling over the dark green dress.

"Rimmony," he said.

But then she laughed and turned to look him straight in the face.

"Not Rimmony at all," she answered him, "but Meadowsweet."

He stared at her. Stared at the green dress Rimmony had made with her own nimble fingers. Stared at Meadowsweet's long flowing hair, so like Rimmony's own. Stared into her eye as she smiled, and picked at the buttons which Rimmony had stitched.

"Beneath this dress," she said, "I am fox, I am blood, I am musk, I am bone. I am spit, I am heat, I am claw. I can give you all that Rimmony never gave, and more..."

Elmskin stood silently.

" ... let me show you."

She grabbed Elmskin's hand but he pulled away.

"You are not Rimmony," he said. "Her eyes were grey as waking dawn. Her smile shy as a shivering lamb as she walked across the Green."

"Rimmony never smiled, never spoke to anyone and now she is gone," Meadowsweet taunted, " - but I am here."

Elmskin turned away and walked from the byre all up the muddied track and back to the well where the other girlen were still lounging, watching and waiting.

Next day, Elmskin rose early. Outside the birds were singing, but as he looked through the window he knew he would never see Rimmony as he once had every morning, making her way all by herself down the lane to Lowden's Beck.

He pulled on his boots and jacket, wrapped a hunk of bread inside a napkin then slipped his hand beneath his pillow till his fingers reached Rimmony's necklace made of shells and cherry stones. He held it for a moment, then tucked it in his pocket, crept downstairs and stepped out into the cold morning air. All at once he was trembling. He wanted to set one foot in front of the other - but suddenly his knees were weak. He just wanted to sit down and stay right where he was. But the sunlight was mottled, the birds they were calling and so he set off down the lane till the village was behind him.

He made his way into the woods to the place where the four roads meet. There he stood a while, staring at the sign, trying to reckon out which way Rimmony might have taken. Then a shadow fell across the track. Elmskin looked up. He knew who it was.

"Pickapple," he mumbled under his breath.

"Pickapple indeed," came the reply. "Which way are you going? Which road do you seek?"

"I don't know," said Elmskin as he shuffled from foot to foot. "Have you seen a girlen come this way, three days before?"

Pickapple stared at him.

"Girlen come. Girlen go."

"Last time I seen her she was up at Lowden's Beck.

Left her clothes all behind and went diving in the river by the dark black rocks."

Pickapple shook his head.

"That I might remember," he said, then continued: "One road is dark and dreary, the other long and hard. One looks like it is bright and green but will trick you on its way."

"Which one is which?" Elmskin asked. "Here at the crossroads they all look the same."

"Can't tell you that," said Pickapple. "Can't tell you that unless you give me summatt to help me remember."

Elmskin pressed his hand in his pocket and ran his fingers along the shells and shrivelled berries of the necklace hidden there.

"Ain't got nothing," he grunted.

"All boys got summatt in their pockets," Pickapple reckoned, "be it a penny or a blown egg or a key. What you got there? Mayhap you are hiding some trinket from this girlen... some keepsake she has left you. Let me see."

He made a grab for Elmskin, but Elmskin skipped away, then tripped and found himself sprawled in the mud with Pickapple capering around him. He kept one hand gripped tight on the necklace in his pocket while with the other he shoved the kerchief of bread under Pickapple's nose.

"Here," he said. "It's all I got."

Pickapple unpicked the kerchief and peered at the crust inside.

"Wasn't what I wanted," he said. "Wasn't what I wanted at all. Doesn't glisten like no girlen's trinket."

He paused, staring askance at Elmskin, who gripped the necklace in his pocket even tighter.

" - but see you here," Pickapple continued, "no girlen's trinket tastes as sweet as a crust of bread dipped in dew."

Elmskin sat up and watched as Pickapple scoffed the morsel of bread and wiped the back of his hand across his mouth.

"Which road should I take?" he asked.

"Please yourself," Pickapple giggled as he skipped back into his hut. "Go where you think your girlen went - it's all the same to me."

Elmskin ran fast as he could, off down the first muddied track. Soon as he was away from the crossroads he put his hand in his pocket to draw out the necklace again. He pressed the shrivelled berries hard against his cheek and felt the shells brush his lips like as if they were kissen. Then he opened up his jacket and plunged the necklace deep inside the lining where no-one would ever find it.

He strode on down the lane, and the brambles they were silver grey and all the leaves hung lush and low and the path it was smothered over in moss so the light was tinged with green as it flooded in between.

As he looked back one more time before walking quickly on, he thought he heard Rimmony's voice, calling out his name. But then he heard a ripple of laughter that sounded more like Meadowsweet. And so he ran, he ran and ran till his boots near dropped from his feet.

A Bottle of Tears

Most days Pickapple sits in his hut, just waiting. He waits for the moon, he waits for the stars. He waits for the leaves which blow in wild circles all about the signpost which stands at the crossroads. And some nights Pickapple turns it around and around so that in the morning strangers do not know which road to take.

And Pickapple tells them. He tells them right, he tells them wrong. He tells them wise, he tells them sly. He watches them go, knowing in the end they'll find their way. For some roads lead over the hill and never come back and some roads wind all around and around until you're right here again, standing at the crossroads next to Pickapple's hut. And he will shuffle out and greet you with a grunt and a nod and you will remember that you have come this way before. And you will remember what you forgot the last time, to press a gift into his hand to thank him for his help.

Inside Pickapple's hut are jars of tarnished coins and buckles. Bits of feather and curious stones. A hat and a belt and the head of a snake. A set of dusty yellow bones. Red pebbles fetched from the belly of the river. A crow's foot, a badger's paw and a rusty twisted key. All laid out in lines or hanging on the wall.

One morning a child came passing by and knocked on Pickapple's door and asked him for a glass of milk and a knuckle of fresh-baked bread. Pickapple gave her water and a fistful of mouldy oats. And then he saw. Her face was covered in thorns. Her arms, her legs and her hands.

"How do you come to look like this?" Pickapple

asked the girl.

"My mother said she made me this way so that none would ever kiss me. But at night I curl up in a ball and my own limbs do prick me."

"Where is your mother now?"

"She left me to ride to the market. She left me all alone. She left me sleeping in a bucket of clay but still she has never returned."

"How long gone?"

"A night and a day and a night and day more and the long slow slip of the moon from the depths of the river to the high hill-top through the eye of the wintering storm."

"How will you find her?" Pickapple asked. "The ways they are hard and long."

The Thorn Girl smiled.

"I will wait for a while and a little while more, for *she* should look for *me*. But she went to market with a tall fine man with a hawk on his shoulder and money in his hand. I know that she has gone."

Pickapple slipped inside his hut and came back with a dark bottle filled with clear liquid.

"Drink this," he said and the girl obeyed.

"It tastes of long dead rivers," she said. "It tastes of the deepest sea."

"It was given to me by a traveller," Pickapple replied, "who said it was given to *him* by a child who lived in a cavern far beyond the reach of the sun. And it was not rain that filled the bottle and was not drawn from the river and was not fetched from the sea. It was her very own tears, and now you have drunk them, why you have set her free. The sun will rise again for her and she will leave the cave.

"And if you travel down that road," Pickapple

pointed, "and walk for a night and a day - then you will find her walking toward you. And you will give her the bottle and tell her that her tears are gone, for they are inside you now."

"What will happen then?"

"Why then that girl will kiss you."

"No-one can kiss me," the Thorn Girl said, "for my mother has made me this way."

"This girl will kiss you," Pickapple repeated. "Look at your hands, touch your cheeks - for by the drinking of her tears, now all your thorns are gone."

THE KEEPER OF SECRETS

The Keeper of Secrets lived in the hollow of an old tree. There he would sit and listen to the mutterings of a raddled old rook, a fox with three legs, a stub-footed pigeon and a one-eyed frog. And the hedgers, bodgers and ditchers would come and the charcoal-burners too. And the girlen who tended the geese and the old'uns and the potswills and those that had forgotten they ever had secrets at all. They would come to the tree and Old Snick, for that was his name, he would listen. But truth to tell, he did not keep these secrets well, for he would whisper them to the wind and the leaves as they fell and the babble of the nearby stream.

But he would whisper them to Herristy too - who would come and see him at twilight and she said that she would tell no-one, but soon enough the whole village knew of the man with the fox's tail and the boy who kept rats' eyes in a bag, the spider who spins silken rainclouds, the girl who dances naked when the moon is full and the boy who speaks like a dog... till all of the people whose secrets these had been didn't go to Old Snick no more.

"Might just as well tell everyone down on the Green," they said.

But little Binnie did not hear them and she had a secret she could not share and felt so she was bursting. So she went out one morning, all out to the wood and walked till she came to Old Snick's tree where he was sitting alone, for no-one came to see him no more.

And she sat herself down on a tussock of grass and

whispered into the hollow of the tree. Old Snick sat up startled, for truth to tell he was sleeping.

"I have a secret to give you," she said. "Can you hear me?"

"I am listening," said Snick with a grunt.

"At night when I sleep, I dream," she said. "I dream I am lying inside an egg. I can feel the shell all around me when I reach out and touch with my hands. It feels soft as gauze but it is strong and will not break and through it I can see colours breathing and shapes dancing all about."

"What do they look like?" Old Snick asked.

Binnie paused.

"Look like they are flowers and stars..." she said.

"Go on," said Snick, the Keeper of Secrets, "I am listening."

"Good," said Binnie. "I lie there and I can hear voices."

"Whose voices are they?"

"I do not know. But a man comes. I can hear him roaring and shouting. I hear him banging tables and beating his fists on the walls. Then I hear my mother screaming, then laughing, then crying."

"What then?" asked the Keeper of Secrets.

"Then it all goes quiet," said the girl, watching as a spider crept towards the tree. A blackbird landed beside her and gazed at it curiously.

"Then a great wind comes," said Binnie suddenly. "A great wind comes and blows all through the house. Then I hear the man laughing and climbing up the stairs and a window opening and closing. Then he is gone."

The spider had gone too. Binnie fancied the blackbird had eaten it, till she saw it again, crawling up her arm. Old Snick reached out and picked it up betwixt his finger and his thumb and cradled it in the palm of his hand.

"Then what?" he asked.

Binnie's eyes grew wider, watching the blackbird as it hopped all around.

"Then the house is quiet. Can't hear nothing at all till mother comes scurrying, going from room to room, picking up vases and dusting them, laughing and singing. Then I hear the door open and she comes into my room. I'm still lying there, inside the egg like I told you before. And mother comes and strokes the shell all soft and gentle. then harder and faster and she's not mother no more but a hawk-sparrow beating her mottled wings. Then the shell breaks open and she is mother again bending over me, wiping the sweat from my head.

"'I heard voices,' I tell her, 'voices and banging all loud in the night.'

"Then she pats my hand all tender and tells me was only the wind as she closes the casement and I go back to sleep."

"So, was a dream," grunts the Keeper of Secrets, watching the spider dance in his hand.

"Strange dream," said young Binnie, "for next morning I woke to find a clutch of brown hawk-sparrow feathers strewn about the floor."

At that moment the spider let itself down from Old Snick's hand by a thin twining thread. Just as it landed in the damp of the grass, the blackbird swooped and scooped it away.

Next day and next Herristy came to the tree and whispered to the Keeper of Secrets:

"It's me..."

Old Snick woke then and sudden, wiping the crumbs from his chin.

"Which 'me' is this?" he mumbled.

"It's me, Herristy," she said as Old Snick popped out his head through the hollow of the tree.

"What have you got to tell me?" he asked. "What secrets, what gossip, what juicy news?"

"Nothing much," said Herristy. "Nothing much at all. Wranglethorn is thieving eggs, but that ain't nothing he's never done before."

"Don't know about that," said the Keeper of Secrets. "No-one ever told me..." he mused, hastily covering a clutch of eggs with a handful of whiskery straw.

"So what's in the wind?" asked Herristy, leaning in close to the tree.

"Truth to tell, a strange story," said Snick, scratching his head. "Little Binnie came to me and told me of her dream."

"Tain't a secret then," said Herristy, sucking on a piece of grass.

"Not secret, no - but not sure if it's a dream."

"I dreamt Spoonbender took me walking once," Herristy sighed, "all out across the fields. And there he picked me a garland of flowers as white as fallen stars."

"Wasn't like that at all," said Snick. "Was a dream of a man come to her house and throwing everything about and making her mother to laugh and to cry."

"Does she know who it was?"

"Binnie didn't say. Never saw his face. Never knew his name. And her mother said tweren't no-one at all, only the wind in a dream."

"Tweren't no dream," said Herristy suddenly. "I know who it was!"

"How you know that then?" Snick asked inquisitively.

"It's that Spoonbender. Every night I beg him to come and see me, to come and keep me warm. And he says he can't, he wants to stay home. Why would anyone want to stay home stead of spending time with me? It must be him. I knowed all along. He's visiting Binnie's mother. That's what she heard in her dream..."

"Binnie dreamed she slept in an egg," Snick reminded her.

'Herristy leaned inside the tree and snatched up the fistful of grass.

"Think you know more about eggs," she said, "than a Keeper of Secrets should tell!"

Next night they went, Old Snick, the Keeper of Secrets and Herristy who could keep no secrets at all - they went all down to Spoonbender's cottage, down in a dip away from the lane to see if he be really there or up at Binnie's house, a-visiting of her mother. They crept up quickly through the dusk and hid behind a wall. The cottage nestled low in the hollow, grey pigeons rattling in the eves, their eggs dropping down to land soft in the moss below, while dark spiders wove their webs of gauze all about the door.

"He is there," said Herristy. "See how a candle flickers in the window."

"If he is there now," Old Snick sniffed, "won't be there long, for if what you say is true, why soon he will creep away all up to Binnie's mother's house high on the hill and climb in through the window."

And so they watched and so they waited and still the candle flickered in the window and as the sky grew darker and a pale moon opened her eye, so they saw Spoonbender's shadow passing back and forth.

"He's taking his time," Old Snick complained. "Mayhap he's dressing in his finest shirt and neckerchief special for Binnie's mother."

"Binnie's mother wouldn't care what he's wearing.

She's not going to sit round gawping at him from what I've heard you say."

"But he's still there," Snick muttered. "He's in no hurry to go out and see her."

"Mayhap he's waiting for when Binnie will be all tucked up asleep in bed..."

"... dreaming she is an egg."

Still no-one came out and no-one came in through Spoonbender's cobwebbed door.

"Mayhap he is not there at all," Herristy muttered anxiously. "Mayhap that shadow is his cat, going back and forth."

"Spoonbender don't have no cat," Old Snick grunted.

"Mayhap he's got one now, just to trick us. Just to make it look like someone's in when all the while he's up at Binnie's mother's window."

Snick cleared his throat.

"Mayhap we should look closer," he said.

They tiptoed slow from behind the wall, ducking low so Spoonbender would not see them picking their way through the pigeon eggs. Then Herristy peeked through the window.

"What is he doing?" asked Snick.

"Shshsh," said Herristy. "He's at a table in the corner. He has his back turned. Wait - he's moving now."

She ducked down again as Spoonbender walked towards the window, glanced for a moment through the glass and then turned back. Snick looked at Herristy as she knelt, her mouth hanging open.

"Well? Tell me - what is he doing?"

"He's making... a huge egg woven from a web of gauze, covered all over with flowers and stars."

"So that's why he does not go out."

"But... he's making an egg of gauze... "

"So you said."

"He's making it for me."

"How do you know this?"

"I told him. I told him that was what I wanted to place upon my mantle-shelf so all the village would wonder at it when they called by for their bit of gossip. I told him he should come and see me and bring with him an egg of gauze."

Snick scratched his chin and looked at her.

"So now you know why he ain't been to see you yet. He didn't want to come till the egg was finished!"

Herristy bit her lip and nodded. Then she spoke again.

"But if Spoonbender ain't visiting little Binnie's mother, then *who is it?*"

Binnie was asleep. She did not hear the knocking at the window. She did not hear her mother's step on the stair. She did not hear the window open.

She did not hear the muttered words as Snick, the Keeper of Secrets, climbed into her room.

"I'm glad that you've come," said Binnie's mother. "I have so much to tell you. Every night my daughter has a dream..."

QUOB

The lane became a tunnel of green, with brambles writhing either side. It had always been there, though Elmskin had never come this way before. He knew about it, of course. He'd heard the girlen talking and they always seemed to know. And the old'uns would mutter and whisper in corners. But he'd never seen it, didn't know where it might take him. He took a breath and ducked his head to make his way through when a wizened nut-brown figure swung down from the bough above. He stood half as tall as Elmskin, yet firmly blocked his path.

"Who are you?" Elmskin challenged.

"Who am I? I am Quob. What do you want, a-coming this way?"

Elmskin felt the stranger's strength, powerful as the sap which seeped through every living tree, as he slithered in the bed of moss and woody pilth that oozed between his boots. Quob seized his elbow and dragged him closer, leering up at him squinty-eyed.

"There be snakes down here. Snakes and slugs and water rats."

"Gnats and the midges too," Elmskin complained as he batted away a swarm of scurrying wings with the back of his hand.

Quob shrugged.

"Midges don't bother me," he said. "Know'em all by name."

"Midges don't have names," Elmskin protested.

"I know they do. There's Bartholomew and Ratsucker

and Pretty Penelope Parsnip..."

"They're mighty big names for mighty small creatures."

"Got to make them feel good about themselves," Quob declared. "Why - they're as important as me and you."

"How so important? What do they do?"

"Bite you for a start."

"What good's that?"

"No good for you - but it's good for them. Soon they'll gobble us up. Soon enough the world'll be filled with giant midges."

"If they're giants they can't be midges," Elmskin reasoned.

"How so? How so?" Quob puffed out his chest. "Look at me - I am small but mighty - but they are mighty small."

"Not that mighty," said Elmskin. "What can you do?"

"Can stop you coming down this lane."

"Can you so?" Elmskin pushed at him, but Quob stood firm.

"Can true. Don't need no push and shove neither. I stopped you just by talking to you this past while."

Elmskin shrugged and turned away.

"Mayhap I don't want to come down your damp smelly lane anyway."

He began to walk off.

"Oh, please do," Quob pleaded. "No-one ever comes this way. No-one stops and talks to me."

"I'm not surprised," said Elmskin. "I'm not surprised at all."

Quob stood aside and bowed, ushering Elmskin into the seep of shimmering green. All about the chiff-chaffs and bullfinches were chirruping and yammering so Elmskin thought his ears might burst. He felt Quob grip his elbow, guiding him on then suddenly pulling him back. Before them lay a girl all curled up, half hidden by a spread of mulching leaves. Her body was covered in a furze of green moss.

Elmskin stared at her.

"Is she dead?" he asked.

"Dead asleep, more like," Quob snorted. "Besides - nothing here be dead, anyhow. One thing rots into another and then it grows again This is just Mallow Musk who lives in the mulch and the mire."

At the sound of their voices the girl sat up and stretched, blinked and stared around. Her hair was ragged and tangled and knotted all with thistledown.

"I dream I am all filled with sap..." she whispered. "I dream the worms they burrow through me and in my gut they writhe and turn, for my belly is filled with flocks of birds who wheel and fly and sing and cry and drive me this way, drive me that, drive me in circles till I know not which way I am facing. And so I nest here, deep in this burrow."

"So Quob may keep you safe?"

"Quob do not keep me safe at all. Each night he comes and fills my sleep with a roaring and a calling for he will not let me be."

"That is my singing," Quob broke in.

"Then he smother me over with oils and potions..."

"That be to cure you of all that ails you."

"Then he smother me about with kisses so free..."

"Pah," Quob spat. "Rather kiss the knotty bark of this here tree."

Mallow Musk ignored him, then smiled as she turned to Elmskin. He smiled back, but for a moment her eyes burned ice-cold.

"What do you feel?" Mallow Musk asked.

"Feel all shivery," Elmskin said. "Shivery like I'm about to get me a fever."

"Tain't no fever," Mallow Musk smiled again.

She stroked his hand.

Elmskin trembled. He could see her lips moving, but there were no words. He looked around. Quob was laughing, but he could hear no sound. The birds had stopped singing. The insects ceased their droning and buzzing. Elmskin stared, reaching out to touch Mallow Musk, but though he could see her, she suddenly seemed so far away. Quob was laughing still, but his weathered face was fading. Elmskin's heart beat quickly. Mallow Musk and Quob were nowhere to be seen, only the damp cling of moss and the rustling trees as the sunlight filtered through the leaves all mottled green.

Elmskin stopped shivering. He felt warm again as he heard a shimmer of foliage behind him and turned to see Mallow Musk slipping back from behind a tree. She was laughing at him, her face almost covered by the tangle of her hair.

A cloud of midges buzzed about Elmskin's head and he tried to swat them away.

"I was cold," he said. "but how could that be? Here it is so warm..."

"I too am warm," Mallow Musk replied dreamily, twisting a strand of thistledown between her listless fingers. "I nestle here. I wake. I sleep."

"Come with me," said Elmskin suddenly, grabbing her hand, but Mallow Musk pulled away.

"I must stay," she sighed.

Quob stepped suddenly from a tangle of brambles, bunching his fists and puffing out his chest.

"She must stay here," Quob declared. "It's *you* that must go."

"But you brought me here," Elmskin objected.

"Brought you here, caught you here. Maybe I *fought* you here if you don't be careful. Quick now - before it's too late. Now's the time to go!"

"Too late?" Elmskin enquired, looking around. "Too late for what?"

"Too late for this."

Quob stood squarely in front of him, but Elmskin peered over his shoulder to see Mallow Musk slide deep into the undergrowth, leaving a trail, a slither in the moss, shedding her skin behind her like as if she was a snake. Elmskin watched as Quob leapt forward to crouch over the membrane, stroking it and caressing it, kissing where cheek and lips had been.

Elmskin turned away, then stopped.

"Wait! Take me with you!" he cried to Mallow Musk.

"I go to a place where you cannot follow...." Her voice came from deep in the grass beneath the tangle of nettles and thorns.

Quob was advancing foot by foot through the oozing sludge, nudging Elmskin back to the way he'd come in. Beyond the entrance the blackbirds sang and a lark climbed high to a speck in the sky. Elmskin sat down, then heard Quob creep up behind him and mutter:

"Where is it you're going?"

"I have to find Rimmony," Elmskin explained. "She left our village a moon ago but I see her every night in my dreams. I got to give her this necklace she made, the necklace she left behind."

He hunted in his pocket and pulled out the string of berries and shells. Quob studied it carefully, passing it gently through his gnarled fingers before handing it back.

"It's well-crafted," he said. "Keep it and guard it well. You may need it soon."

"How so?" Elmskin asked.

"You'll need it when you meet Raddlewick," Quob continued, placing a friendly arm around Elmskin's shoulder.

"Who is Raddlewick?" Elmskin clutched the necklace tightly.

"When you reach the end of this forest, you will come to the lake. It is deep and it is dark and only Raddlewick can guide you safely to the other side. And she won't take no-one cept if you bring her a gift..."

Elmskin walked quickly, picking his way beneath the over-hanging branches of the trees. Then sudden he broke out and stood alone beneath the towering sky and before him lay the lake, just as Quob had told him, its surface grey and silent, one solitary heron beating low along the shore-line. And then there was Raddlewick, come out of nowhere, blocking his path, her hair long and wild and her eyes a-blaze.

She looked him up and down.

Elmskin stopped, his feet fixed to the ground, his legs a-tremble though all he wanted to do was run. He caught his breath and shifted one foot, but then Raddlewick gripped him by the arm.

"You're a young'un, to be sure," she said, running her hands all about his body like as if she was setting him a-fire.

"What are you doing, coming this way? Who sent you here?"

"Qu-quob," Elmskin stuttered.

Raddlewick flung back her head and laughed.

"Quob, to be sure. What is he doing sending me no more than a slip of a boy?"

"Please," Elmskin begged. "I have to find Rimmony. Have to give her this..."

"This what?"

Raddlewick clutched him tighter.

"... this necklace."

The words stumbled out before Elmskin could think what he was saying.

"What necklace? I like necklaces. Quickly boy, show me."

Elmskin hesitated.

Raddlewick gripped him harder.

"Where is the necklace? Show me now!"

She jerked his shirt open and Elmskin felt his heart beat faster as the necklace fell into her hand. She stared at it a moment. Stared at the shells and the berries which Rimmony had gathered and threaded all together.

"What's this?" she screeched and spat upon it, threw it to the ground.

"Thought it might be silver. Thought it might be gold." She gripped him again. "What else you got?"

"Got nothing," Elmskin confessed, hanging his head. "And this that I got is meant for Rimmony, the girl I see every night in my dreams."

Raddlewick snorted and shook her head.

"Most who come this way gave up their dreams a long time ago. Put away your necklace, little man. I will take you..."

Raddlewick glanced across the surging water to the shoreline waiting on the other side.

"... tell me, how would you like to ride?"

She rolled up her sleeves and hitched up her skirts.

"I can carry you on my back. I can hold you in my arms. Or we can rock slowly side by side in this old craft of mine."

She nodded towards a boat, half submerged, filled with brackish water. "Please," said Elmskin, edging away to gather up the cluster of berries and shells from where they lay in the mud. "Please. I think I'd sooner swim. I can go all by myself. Don't need no help."

Raddlewick shook her head and gripped him tight again.

"Can't go alone. The current is fast, there are whirlpools and serpents. I will come with you."

They swam then side by side, Raddlewick and Elmskin. The waters roared, the waters surged and sometime Elmskin thrashed and cried but Raddlewick caught him and held him and bore him with her through the rapture of the rhythm until they gained the soft white sand of the shore on the other side.

Elmskin lay there, gasping for air while Raddlewick knelt over him, her long hair sweeping across his face. Then he sat up sudden.

"Where is Rimmony?" he cried.

Raddlewick stroked his forehead.

"Hush boy, there is no-one here."

"But I saw her, plain. Saw her across the water of the lake."

"There is no-one here," Raddlewick said again. "Only me."

Elmskin scrabbled in his pocket, then pulled out the necklace again.

"Suppose you want this now," he muttered.

"No boy, you can keep it. Rimmony will be grateful when you bring it to her."

She drew the darkness around them and rocked Elmskin in her arms.

"Now you must sleep," she said. "Now you must sleep..."

And as he slept, Elmskin dreamed of Rimmony how he always remembered her, walking out to Lowden Beck wearing her dress long and green. Then he dreamed Raddlewick riding with him, breasting the dark black tide. But when he woke he was all alone. Raddlewick had gone. He saw her footprints in the sand, leading back to the lake.

He quickly reached into his pocket again and pulled out the necklace that was nestled there, ran his fingers around the berries and the shells, stroked them soft and gentle, while all about him the chiff-chaffs and bullfinches were chirruping and yammering so he thought his ears might burst.

PHYSICIANS OF HIGH DEGREE

Pickapple and Mullops set out one day to find themselves an adventure.

They gathered strands of dry grass as they went, which Pickapple teased between his fingers till it hung loose and limp. Soon they came upon a farmhouse. Pickapple set his eye on a fine tall horse standing in a field.

"Come," he said, and led Mullops to knock at the door.

The farmer opened it, a short stooped man, his eyes blinking in the sun.

"Good sir," Pickapple greeted him. "We are Physicians of High Degree. We can fix bones and cure the canker. We can drive away any plague. Why we can near raise a man from the grave, but our speciality is horses."

The farmer stared at the two shabby wretches who were blocking his doorway.

"I have a horse, name of Drubben - and a fine horse he is too."

"We have seen your horse," Pickapple informed him. "We took the liberty of looking him over before troubling to knock on your door. And I have to tell you, your horse may not be so fine as he seems."

The farmer shuffled nervously.

"Whatever do you mean? Drubben is all I have, but I can tell you true that he is strong enough behind the plough and rides each week to market scarcely stopping for breath."

"Good sir, you say this - but can I show you?"

Before the famer could reply, Pickapple hurried over to the field where Drubben was quietly nibbling at the grass, vaulted the fence and approached the horse. The farmer scurried after him and Mullops trudged up behind till the three of them clustered around as the good-natured animal whinnied and blew through its nose.

"See - this is a fine specimen of a beast," the farmer declared. "What was it you saw when you examined him?"

"I looked with all the training of my eye," Pickapple told him. "And though he might seem fit and strong, when I felt behind his ears, this is what I found."

He plunged his hand into his pocket and pulled out a fistful of shrivelled fungus.

"Bits of truffle," Mullops muttered under his breath, but the farmer did not hear him. He was too busy scratching his head and peering at the crumbling fragments in Pickapple's hand.

"Rain Rot!" Pickapple declared. "I scraped it away careful."

The farmer tutted and shook his head.

"Never seen that before. Are you sure? Allus fed him the best oats mixed up with dandelions."

"Dandelions would be the problem," Pickapple nodded wisely. "See here."

He reached towards the horse's mane and tugged. In his hand appeared the tousled clutch of dried grass he had gathered on the way. He shoved it under the farmer's nose then crumpled it quickly and flung it on the floor.

"No good at all, that. No good at all. Why his mane is thin as a handful of straw."

The farmer looked down just as Mullops placed his boot across the wispy strands.

"Your horse is very sick," Pickapple surmised.

"What am I to do?" The farmer's face fell in dismay.

"Don't worry," Pickapple reassured him, as he stroked the horse's nose.

But only Mullops noticed that Pickapple had slipped a peck of pepper into the palm of his hand.

The horse sneezed.

The farmer recoiled in astonishment.

"Never done that before. Never done that."

"Truly sick," said Pickapple, patting Drubben's nose again.

The horse sneezed a second time, reared up then set off at a merry trot towards the far end of the field.

"Done it now!" the farmer cursed.

"I'll fetch him," cried Pickapple, springing away.

He raced on down to the end of the field and leapt upon the horse's back, this time slipping him a lump of carrot. The horse turned around and cantered towards the farmer. Pickapple winked as they came. Mullops took the hint and swung up to sit behind him.

"Drubben - come back!" cried the farmer.

"Never fear," Pickapple called over his shoulder as they galloped away, "we will cure him for you. Remember we are Physicians of High Degree and our speciality is horses!"

They rode on till they were out of sight of the farmer's field. Pickapple had tight hold of Drubben's mane while Mullops bounced and buffeted at the back.

"Tis a mighty bumpy business, this riding," he said. "Would be more easy to walk."

"But walking is slow," Pickapple protested, "specially as you go no quicker than a snail."

"Snail has no reason to go nowhere fast," Mullops complained, but at that moment Drubben's pace changed from a gallop to a trot to an amble. Then he stood stock still.

"Let's get down," moaned Mullops. "My bones are shook and sore."

"Then let's go for a dip in the river," Pickapple suggested. "Soon have you right again."

And he tugged and twisted at Drubben's mane to point his head towards the water. But Drubben, he had other ideas and set off at a mighty canter back the way they'd come.

"No - go the other way!" Pickapple cried.

But Drubben plunged on faster and faster as Pickapple and Mullops clung on tight as fear. Trees and hedges flashed by in the shadows and a raven swooped low across the fields.

"Where are you taking us? Where are we going?" Pickapple gasped as they galloped on.

But he knew, sure as sure, that Drubben was heading back to the field he had come from. There he came to a sudden stop, throwing Pickapple and Mullops clean off. Then the horse it heft them both a mighty hoof, before ambling away to crop at tufts of juicy grass as if this adventure had never happened.

The two of them fell to the ground, knocking their noggins against one another. They sat with their heads all a-spin, until Pickapple leapt up as sudden as he could when he saw the farmer strolling in through the gate.

"Good sir!" he cried. "Your horse, we brought him back. See, he is cured now. The Rain Rot is gone and his mane is fine and strong - so now, as Physicians of High Degree, we must discuss our fee."

The farmer laughed and looked at the pair of them and the bumps on their heads.

"If you be such fine Physicians," he said, "first you

must heal yourselves!"

CROW JACK

Crow Jack slept beneath the tangled bushes of the old wood that crouched in the shadow of the hill. By day he lurked out in the low slanting fields where no-one came near him. Farmers paid him odd coppers to scare the crows away, but seemed like he done a better job scaring off the poachers and hawkers, small boys and quick-fingers and any of the girlen who might wander out that way.

But as he stood in the field, his twisted stick shoved deep into the dark earth to hold him steady on his hobbled leg, those crows they flocked to perch all along his shoulders and his out-stretched arms and squatted on the slouch black hat that sat a-top his head.

They talked to him, the crows did, and he talked back in his harsh raw voice. Asked them where they came from, where they were going. And the crows they all told him of the ponds and the ditches and the marsh of the goose meadows down by the river.

Crow Jack listened then said how he'd been scavenging for carrion meat himself. Dead squirrels, rabbits, finches... crows. But the crows paid no notice, squawking and flapping all about Jack, his coat tattered black and his boots of ragged leather, his face cracked and creased from every season's weather.

A clatter of wing beats rattled upward in a squall of feathers as Crow Jack stumped off across the furrows of the field. His coat it swung open to reveal rows of dead rats, moldewarps and ferrets hanging bedraggled inside his lining. He marched on, muttering and cursing until he came to the road where he scrambled over the broken-down fence and stood, arms outstretched in the path of a cart that was trundling towards him.

"Stop!" Jack commanded, his voice rough and harsh. "Stop and get down."

A pale-faced traveller sat tight, gripping the reins as his weary horse shuffled uncertainly, the weight of the cart already sinking into the ruts of the road.

"Get down from your perch," Jack muttered again.

The traveller reached over to fetch up a cudgel till he caught sight of the glint of Crow Jack's knife. He got down and stood a moment, blinking at the unfamiliar fields around him.

"Your load looks too heavy," Crow Jack hissed. "Let me help you."

His blade darted quickly in the sun, cutting loose the money pouch which hung from the traveller's belt. It dropped with a clunk into Crow Jack's outstretched palm.

He smiled and tilted his hat.

"You can go now," he said and lurched away till he was lost from the traveller's sight in the gathering gloom.

"In the midden I sleep, and then in the mire," Crow Jack mumbled as the darkness smothered him.

The coins from the money pouch weighed heavy in his pocket.

"Out in the damp fields and mayhap in a barn. Out with the owls, the foxes and the vermin."

He tramped on, till in the distance he caught sight of a glimmering light.

Gentian sat by her window, gazing out past the spluttering flame of a candle into the gathering shadows.

She squinted down by the pigmires, fearing each twitch of a branch, the rattle of a lid come loose from its pail, the dull moaning of the wind. Fearing it would be Scarberry again, come rapping at her door.

Scarberry would come in the morning, would come at the noonday, would come just as daylight dwindled to dusk. Always the same, wanting to pester her, wanting her to go out a-walking with him, all down by the river where the water runs dark.

Gentian never spoke to him. She always closed her door and clambered quick-footed up the stairs to her room and sat on her bed, afeared to look down into the yard in case he still stood there. And often-time he did, moping about the slop-pens till at last she heard his footsteps shuffling away.

And then she would hold her breath, listening in case he came back again, for sometimes he did. One time she was sure he had gone and was bustling about the house, making herself busy, till she flung open the door to let in the light and let out the dust which billowed from the pillows where she had been beating them to drive away the dreams which haunted her sleep each lonely night. She flung open the door and there he stood, his hand raised in midair, about to knock again.

And she closed the door. And she waited and she waited and then she screamed. Screamed long and loud so the cockerel crowed and the pigs they snorted and heaved and the chickens they fell a-clucking and a scuttling all about.

But Scarberry had gone. Sometimes he wouldn't come for three moons or more, then sudden he'd appear. But sometimes as a tinker, sometimes a knife-sharpener, sometimes a peddlar man. They all looked different, but she knew it was him.

Gentian gripped the poker tightly in her hand, then plunged it into the ashes, raking and scraping until the last embers died away before she blew out the candles on the dresser. Outside in the darkness of the yard a low wind moaned as she groped her way up the stairs to wrap herself in an eiderdown and sleep in her cold narrow bed.

In the morning she woke to the crowing of the cock and the chattering of the starlings who scrabbled and bickered along the fence around the midden. She clambered down slowly into her parlour, her hair still loose and wild and her nightshirt clasped around her. She tugged apart the curtains to reveal the stone grey sky and then she slipped back the bolt on the front door and eased it gently open.

On the step sat a stranger, black hat tilted over his face, a gnarled stick lying at his side with one gangrenous leg thrust straight out before him.

Gentian gasped, but the stranger continued his snoring.

"Who are you?" she cried, reaching for her broom.

"I am Crow Jack," came the answer as he opened one eye.

"What do you want with me?"

Gentian gripped the broom handle tightly.

Jack pulled himself to his feet, shook his head, saying nothing.

Gentian peered at him closely.

"Sure you're not Scarberry?"

She peered at him again, trying to see under the shadow of the brim of his hat, but the stranger thrust her gruffly out of the way and then strode inside.

"I know it's you, Scarberry. I told you before, don't want to see you no more. You can't come here. You must go!"

Crow Jack cast his eye about the parlour, then before

Gentian could stop him, swung himself, stick and all and a jingling leathern bag, up the stairs to her room.

Gentian ran out into the yard, still clutching her broom, screaming to the grunting pigs, screaming to the strutting cocks, screaming to the puzzled pigeons who fluttered up onto the roof.

"Scarberry is here. Scarberry has come back. He's in my house. He's gone up to my room!"

The pigs fell to grunting even louder, pushing each other about in the mud and the mire, while the cockerels they crowed like dawn had broken again as her words echoed off to the far hills and back.

Then Gentian turned around, marched back into the house and slammed the door. She stood with the broom in her hands and glared up the stairs. She was about to shout up, but then thought again and stood quietly and listened. She could hear nothing but a loud snoring and so she set to scuttle about the parlour, polishing tables and dusting shelves. Then she picked up each of the straw dolls which lined her dresser, peered into their dried berry eyes and twisted their arms and tweaked their legs then set them down in lines again, straighter than they had been before.

She sat down and let the clouds of dust she had disturbed slowly settle across the furniture. She sat and she waited and she listened, but all she heard was the snoring from atop the stairs. So she busied herself about, putting on her coat and fetching up her basket and then she set out across the yard, leaving the door on the latch.

She spent all day down in the village, talking to the wifen, swapping tales and chit-chat, moving slowly from one house to the next and never once mentioning the stranger she had found on her step that morning. As the sun sank lower, she sauntered back, as slow as she could go, until at last she reached her own house. She paused and looked up. The curtains of her bedroom were drawn. She opened the door and stepped into her parlour and listened.

Upstairs she could hear a stomping, a dragging of a foot and a stamping. And a low voice droning, somewhere between a muttering and a singing. But she couldn't hear no word he was saying.

Gentian sat down again, but then she knowed she was hungry and so she did what she always did when she got back from the village. She took off her coat and pulled on her pinny and set about cooking herself a good rich stew of parsnips and tatties, singing to herself as she chopped and then stirred to drown out the voice from upstairs. But the more she listened, though she tried not to, the more it seemed that the voice upstairs was singing along with *her*.

She stared out of the window some more, then went out to throw scraps and peelings to the pigs and scatter some grain all about the yard. When she came back the stew was bubbling all good and hot and soon enough she ladled herself a bowlful and gobbled the lot. But then her belly was full. She had eaten all that she wanted even though there was another portion left in the pot.

"Don't usually make so much," Gentian muttered to herself, shaking her head.

Soon enough she fancied to take a walk outside and wander in the twilight, listening to the barn owls swoop across the fields and the last chatter of the starlings perched high in the trees. Then she grew frighted as a bat flew by, nearly catching itself in the strands of her hair, so she scuttled back inside and tilted up the lid of the pan on the stove to find it had all been licked clean. But up above in her bedroom the voice was singing gruff and warm, the voice of someone who had just dined well on a bowlful of parsnips and tatties.

Gentian sighed and she lit all the candles and stroked the heads of all the straw dollies whose eyes seemed to watch her as she picked up her sewing and busied herself with her needle and thread till it was time to go to bed. But her limbs were too weary to climb the stairs. And the stranger was still there. She had no words to say to him. She didn't know what she could do. And so she slept the long dark night away, sitting upright in her chair, still clutching tight to her broom till the grey light of dawn crept into her room.

Then with a muttering and a grunting and a stumping down the stairs, the stranger crept in too. He glared all around. Gentian clutched the broom handle tighter still, but he seemed to stare right through her. Mayhap this wasn't Scarberry at all. She knew Scarberry too well. He would be wheedling, begging and reasoning. Mayhap this man *was* Crow Jack after all.

Crow Jack sat down at the kitchen table. Then he stood up again, opening cupboards and pulling down pots and jars from the shelves till he'd found himself a loaf of bread and a scrap of ham and a tuppet of cheese to spread all over with last winter's pickle.

Soon as he'd finished he wiped the back of his hand across his mouth, left his plate and his crumbs where they sat on the table and stamped out into the yard where he pulled him a bucket of water from the well, sluiced his face and shook himself then drank down all the rest.

Gentian watched to see what he would do next. To her relief, Crow Jack glowered around then set off through the gate, mumbling to himself.

But he came back. Crow Jack came back every night and

every night Gentian let him in, though he walked straight past her as he came through the door and seemed not to see her as he climbed up the stairs. And every night she let him sleep in her bed while she sat downstairs all alone by the window. And he ate the food she put out for him and came and went much like he was a cat gone hunting, though he never brought anything back, cept himself, and he never uttered one word to Gentian, nor ever spared her a glance.

But she got used to him, she said to herself. She got used to his stench of dull ditchwater and the rot of decaying leather. If he was late coming back, she'd sit at the window and watch for him. And he made her feel safe, for Gentian realised all the time Crow Jack was there, Scarberry never came back no more.

And some of the wifen in the village would smile and nod when she went by and one of them even made so bold as to say,

"I see you got yourself a new man."

But Gentian said nothing, only lowered her eyes and blushed and hurried off back to her house.

She was nearly home when she saw Scarberry. Not thought she saw him, but truly saw him, ahead of her on the track. Only one way he could be heading - her house out beyond the woods. There he was, lolloping along in that way he had, like as if he was a lost dog, panting and mooning with that look in his eyes like all he wanted was to be took in and given a home.

But Gentian had always said 'no'. Gentian thought he was just a great larrup, and would only be a nuisance, cluttering up the place. And she told herself he wasn't kindly at all, nobody ever was. She knew that look in his eye - soon as he got over the doorstep he would change.

Gentian paused, hoping Scarberry hadn't seen her. But he just carried on, loping through the trees.

"He'll get there before me and find I'm not in. But he won't go away, he'll wait round there all night - then how'm I going to get in?"

She clutched at the key in her pocket. Then she looked up and saw of a sudden, Crow Jack coming on along another track. Soon enough he met with Scarberry and they stood toe-to-toe on the path.

"Where'm you going?" Crow Jack demanded.

She couldn't hear Scarberry's reply, but saw him nod towards her house. With that, Crow Jack burst into a foul-mouthed rant, calling Scarberry all manner of names such as she'd never heard before. She covered her ears, but still he went on, roaring and cursing till she looked up and saw Scarberry turn back, heading towards her down the track.

Quickly Gentian hid herself behind a tree, watching as Scarberry went on his way, his face so sad and down she almost felt sorry for him. Almost called him back. But she knew Crow Jack would be waiting, for he couldn't get in through the door to her house till she came along with the key.

That evening Gentian sat with Crow Jack and poured him a bowl of dandelion tea.

"Where do you come from?" she asked.

Crow Jack just grunted and jutted his head towards the fields and the woods outside.

"Why'd you come here?" Gentian continued, almost reaching out to touch his hand, but pulling quickly away.

Crow Jack scowled at her, then finally looked her straight in the face.

"Vittles," he said. "Vittles and a bed."

Gentian lowered her eyes.

"What do you do? What did you do for food before you came here?"

Crow Jack grunted and pulled an old rabbit and a mole from inside the lining of his coat.

"Catch'em," he said.

Gentian's nose wrinkled as she stared at the two dead creatures already turning rancid.

"You could cook'em," he said, but she pushed them away to the edge of the table.

"How do you catch them?" she asked instead.

"Make a noose," Crow Jack said. "Simple - see?"

He gestured with his large cracked hands. The knuckles were hairy, Gentian noticed, and his fingers were stunted but strong.

"I've hanged men, too," he said suddenly, staring out of the window. "When somebody pay. That's what I do. Make a noose. String'em up. Let them drop."

He slammed his hand down flat on the table. Gentian jumped.

"Hanged a girlen once an' all. Only a young'un. Sad little thing. Eyes as grey as ᴛhe dawn."

Gentian paused. Shook her head.

"What had she done?"

"They never tell me. I don't ask. I just hang'em, then they pay me. I'm not the judge."

Gentian raised an eyebrow, but Crow Jack gazed down, shuffling his boots.

"Do you think about it after?" she asked.

"Don't think at all," Crow Jack grunted. "Best way. Else you start seeing their faces. Seeing their eyes. Seeing their lips move one last time. Listening for what they're saying. I'm the only one as would know."

He leaned close to Gentian. She could taste his breath

at the back of her throat. Crow Jack's voice was dark as his eyes. Outside the window the night was drawing in. A cold wind rattled.

"So, no - I don't think," he said. "Don't think at all. Would you?"

Gentian shook her head.

"Lost one once," Crow Jack coughed. "He hung right enough but his neck was too strong. Left him dangling near through the night. Had to cut him down in the morning. It were blear cold. Fingers near too frez to hold the knife. But hold it I did. This 'un!"

Crow Jack whipped the steel from his belt. Gentian shrank away. He flicked the blade back and forth.

"I cut him down. And he landed there on his feet and just stared at me. 'Ain't no-one can hang me,' he said. And twere true. Least ways, I couldn't. Never lost no-one before. Never have since."

"Where did he go?"

Crow Jack shrugged. Pared at his nails with his knife.

"Dunno. Just let him go."

"Did they still pay you?" Gentian asked.

"Cause they couldn't pay me. That was the worst of it," Crow Jack recalled. "Job wasn't done."

"Wasn't your fault his neck was too strong."

"My job to set it all up proper. The noose, the drop. Got to be right..."

There was a long pause. Gentian stared around the room at her straw dolls set out straight and neat, just the way she put them.

"Thank you," she said at last, again wanting to touch Jack's hand, but holding back as he glowered at her.

" - Thank you for stopping Scarberry from coming here. I don't ever want to see him again."

Crow Jack spat on the floor.

"Don't thank me," he muttered. And then again, louder. "Don't thank me. Don't no-one ever thank me!"

He rose to his feet and trudged up the stairs to fetch his slouch hat and the leather pouch of coins. He hoisted his coat about his shoulders and walked out the door into the gathering night.

That night Gentian slept in her bed, the bed that Crow Jack had been sleeping in. She could smell him all through the room, the smell of dead moleskin, the smell of damp leather, the smell of his body hot between the sheets.

But Gentian liked it. Made her feel warm. Made her feel safe. And soon she slipped into a deep dark sleep.

She dreamt she followed Crow Jack out into the fields. She dreamt she followed Crow Jack all down the darkened lanes. And then she was with him everywhere he went. She helped him scoop up water from the cold brackish pools. She helped him tie the snares for the rabbits and the moles. She helped him snap their little necks and skin their hides with a sweep of his knife.

She dreamt she lured travellers as they came all down the track. Waited till Crow Jack rose from the ditch and then he cut their purses and they shared the glittering silver.

Then she dreamt she saw Scarberry again, shuffling down the path. Dreamt Crow Jack stopped his way and cussed him out and bound his hands and took him to the hanging tree. And then he slipped the noose all about his neck and left him there, his eyes a-bulging. But then as she watched, Scarberry slipped the noose and walked away. Crow Jack was gone and only Scarberry now, walking and a-walking all the way to her house. There he fell to knocking, knocking at her door.

Gentian woke to knocking. She sat up in bed, shaking the dreams from her head. Stared and watched the cold dawn slipping in through the window. But the knocking did not stop. She gathered a shawl all about her and trod slowly down the stairs.

"Tis Crow Jack come back," she told herself.

But as she opened the door, twas not Crow Jack at all, but Scarberry who stood in the dawnlight. At first neither spoke. The cock crowed sleepily at the far side of the yard and one pig grunted then rolled over again.

"The house is empty now. Crow Jack has gone," Gentian said quickly.

She turned and stared into her tiny parlour, the rows of straw dolls all lined up straight, the stairs Crow Jack had trod up to her bed.

Scarberry thrust his hand into his pocket and pulled out a new doll, its eyes dark cherry red.

Gentian opened the door wider.

"Better come in," she said.

Riddle-Me-Ree

Pickapple sat in the clearing, twisting his head this way and that, watching as Littleberry came jigging along with her hands tucked behind her back. He tiptoed quick behind a bush, then sprang before her, skipping from one foot to the next.

Littleberry smiled.

"I knew you were there," she said.

Pickapple looked crestfallen.

"No-one ever sees me come and no-one sees me go. I am here and there. I am hop and twitch. I come to steal shadows. Now tell me plain - what's that you're hiding behind your back?"

"Hiding nothing at all," Littleberry said, frowning straight ahead.

Pickapple leapt towards her.

"Let me tickle your elbow," he said, "then we will see."

Littleberry slipped behind a tree, giggling as she ran.

"Oh no, Pickapple," she declared, "you'll play no tricks on me."

Pickapple frowned and scratched his head.

"But I have played one trick already, for I have made you smile. Now I'll play another - just answer this riddle-me-ree. What falls to the ground yet soars high as a tree?"

Littleberry laughed.

"Why, that's simple. Tis an acorn."

Pickapple shook his head.

"Could be an acorn, true. Acorn soars high when it grows to an oak. But 'a corn' grows in a field. You have three guesses and guesses three - what falls to the ground yet soars high as a tree?"

Littleberry laughed again, then frowned.

All the time Pickapple circled about her, trying to spy the bag she clutched behind her back.

"Why then, tis a squirrel, for a squirrel soars high when it climbs up a tree."

Pickapple leapt and spun around.

"Tis never a squirrel, for a squirrel may soar, tis true and may climb as you say. It may leap, it may jump, it will float, it will glide - but a squirrel will never fall to the ground."

Pickapple snatched at the bag. Littleberry pulled it away, then stamped her foot.

"Why, now I am tired of your riddle-me-ree."

"You have one guess more," Pickapple reminded her, leaning over and around to peer at the bag again which Littleberry tucked quickly behind her back.

"Why then, tis a stone. Throw a stone in the air it will soar to the sky and then fall to the ground."

Pickapple sneaked behind her back.

"Stone is too easy, but this riddle's too hard," he cried as Littleberry spun around and around.

"I have given you answers and answers three. Now tell me the end of your riddle-me-ree!"

Pickapple stood still and closed his eyes, then opened them again.

"Tis a fish," he blinked.

Littleberry shook her head in disbelief.

"A fish can be caught and fall to the ground from the end of the line, tis true," she said. "But no fish can ever climb as high as a tree."

"From the bottom of a lake to the top is the measure of any tree. I said it soared *high* as a tree. Didn't say the fish climbed up in no tree."

Littleberry smiled and tutted as Pickapple twirled around, then quick as a flash snatched the bag from her hand.

"Give it back!" she protested as he capered away to the other side of the clearing, then quick as quick slipped in his hand and quick as quick pulled out a plum.

Littleberry burst out laughing again.

"Pickapple stop! You cannot eat that plum for it is ne'ery ripe. Give it back to me and I will take it home and when it's round and plump why then I'll bake a pie."

Pickapple gave back the plum with a sigh.

"But will you share the pie?" he asked. "Will it be sweet and soft and the juice run down my chin?"

Littleberry shook her hair and scurried quick away.

"Your mother was a rum'un," she shouted over her shoulder. "A rum'un always roaming. Don't know where she got you. Think she found you in a basket by the stream. And your mother's mother was a bluebell who went a-lummin with a fish!"

"Hippety hop!" cried Pickapple. "A fish and a bluebell I be. Knowed it all along..."

He bent down suddenly and scooped something from the grass.

"You can run as fast as you like," he cried, "but you have lost your plum. And I will eat it up, whether tis ripe or not..."

And he licked his lips and pinched the fruit betwixt his finger and his thumb.

"You may chase me all you like," she said, "or you can wait and wait - but you will never know when you'll ever taste the pie!"

GULL BOY

Old Grindle lived in a croft he had built of loose stones and driftwood at the bottom of the cliffs, at the edge of the beach. He had lived there all his years, watching the waves and listening all night to the squalls and the gales, the blustering and blowing of the wind and the skirl of the gulls who called him to pitch his small boat out into the grey running tide and furl his nets overboard to trawl the waters for the spin of the fish. His hands were hard and horny and his face was dark as rock as he scanned the surface, tracked the currents till the time came to drift back in with his catch.

Then each night Old Grindle would light a fire of stacked timber and sit and stare into the flames that gnawed the heart of the whitened wood; and he would warm his hands and warm his bones and listen to the roar of the ocean which he could not see in the shadows beyond, though he could feel its turning in his blood. Other nights, when the moon was high he would follow its shimmer as it danced across the water and then he would fall to mending his nets.

But one night such as this he looked up from the knots and the weft and saw one pale gull skim along the moon's path over the waves, swoop down around him, circle about his cottage and then cut away into the darkness.

Other nights, when the chill of the winter came and Grindle was sitting inside by his fire, he would hear the gull come a tap-tapping at his window and he would hasten to the door and open it. First the bird would swoop shyly away, but then soon it would wait for the door to open and sit there on the step, its head on one side, watching.

One night, when the wind blew bitter with a storm brewing up all across the bay, Grindle heard a crash against the window and raced to the door. He found the gull lying there frozen on the ground, its eyes wild and haunted, a dark trickle of blood smudged across her breast.

Grindle caught her up in his arms, wrapped a cloth around her, brought her in where she could feel the warmth of the fire, then laid her gently on the bed.

The bird lay still, but soon enough she began to stir, her eyes fluttering open as her breast rose and fell. Grindle sat beside her, stroking her feathers and then she nested down the night with him and all next day she stayed while the storm beat on about them.

Three days on, the gale ceased its howling and Grindle ventured out to gaze upon the shore, to check his boat and check his netting while the gull remained inside, flapping down from the bed and strutting slowly round the kitchen till when he came back she was standing there, a glint back in her eyes and her wings stretching wide and strong.

Grindle nodded.

"You can go now," he said. "You'll be safe. The storm is gone."

He left the door open wide so she could fly away but she took no notice and scrabbled back into the room, close to the fire's warm glow, close to Old Grindle's chair. Close to his bed.

She stayed a long night and a long night more, the gull who never flew away, who nestled close to Grindle as they kept each other warm, all through the dark nights and then the hard days too. When Grindle set out onto the sea again, his boat pitched and tossed by the waves, all the while the pale gull circled up above to see he came to no harm, to see he steered safely home.

Then one day the boy was born, the boy whose legs were strong as strong, his body supple as any child, but his head was raked with feathers pale, a bone-hard beak set in his face, eyes that glistened ocean-bright. A gull's head sure, like his mother.

But his mother was gone, away and away, back across the ocean, keening and wailing, back to the blackness, back to salt wind, back to the storm which had borne her.

And so Old Grindle reared his son. Showed him the ways to farm the fish, to trawl the seas. And the boy was quick, his eyes darting down to catch a flash of silver deep beneath the waves.

Some days the boy would wake early while his father was still snoring. He would creep out through the door, out into the dawn-light just spreading along the shore and he would run up and down, stumbling across the pebbles and flapping his arms, trying to fly until he was too tired to run anymore. Then he would sit down on the cold stones, his shoulders aching, his legs shaking and he would cry one tear as he peered out to sea, staring at the gulls as they wheeled and turned, wondering again if his mother would come home.

But she never came. She never came and his father grew older and older. His hair turned white and his beard hung long and his hands would shake and his back stooped over till he could take the boat out no more and he would sit all day at the door of his croft watching the sea; and the boy hoped he was watching for his mother as well, though he knew that truly the old man looked at nothing at all, only the rolling tide and the rising of the moon.

And came the day when his father died and the boy was left all alone and alone. He knew that he should put out to sea in the fishing boat, just as his father had shown him. But that night there came a storm, wild as the storm which had driven his mother to this door and when he woke next morning the boat was no more, smashed into pieces all along the shore.

Mavroc the Gull Boy sat on the rock each day, watching the dull grey sea, watching the dull grey sky, trying to find the place where air and water met, wishing he could swim there, wishing he could fly.

He tried again, loping awkwardly up and down the beach, his feathered head twisting this way and that. But he just slipped on the wet seaweed and landed flat while gulls dived and screamed around him.

Mavroc sat and mumbled to himself. Some days a stranger appeared on the shore and he would call out in a voice raw with loneliness, a stream of words he learned from his fisherman father. But the stranger took this for cursing and turned quickly away.

And so he took to sitting again, passing the long days by. He left the cottage door open wide, hoping another gull might fly near, but none of them came. He scanned the horizon for passing boats and cried out to them, but they took no notice for his voice on the wind sounded no more than the call of any other gull.

He pecked dejectedly at the seaweed on the rock, its long red strands rich with iron and salt. But Mavroc craved the fish which he and his father had brought back in the boat and he longed to soar and to fly and to plunge into the waves and rise again with the flash of a fish as he saw the other gulls do.

One day, one misty day, when the sea spray rose in a silver haze, Mavroc looked up and down and saw a lone figure coming towards him. She walked slowly, picking her way across the rocks. Mavroc turned his head away. He knew that once she'd seen him she would walk away, just like all the rest. No good to get up now, no good to run and so he just sat there as the figure came up close to him.

She touched him on the shoulder and as he turned he could see droplets of moisture sparkling like jewels in her long straggled hair. He waited for her to flinch away when she saw the feathers, the beak, the staring eyes. But she gazed at him steadily and then she smiled.

"You have fine feathers," she said.

Mavroc tried to turn away but she touched his arm lightly and sat down beside him.

"I wish I had feathers fine as yours. I been collecting them all along the sand."

She opened her hand to show him a fistful of feathers, scrawny and broken as bits of dried leaves.

"What you want them for?" Mavroc asked. His voice was rasping and slow.

The girlen looked at him again.

"My name is Rimmony. I have no cloak to keep me warm. I need feathers to knit together to keep out the wind and the rain and the weather."

She shivered and turned away.

Mavroc leaned his head towards her and as he did so, one of his feathers slipped loose and drifted into her lap. Rimmony plucked it up quickly.

"This can be my first feather!" she cried, tossing the others aside. "These are no good."

Mavroc looked at her.

"Want to help to keep you warm," he said.

"So you shall!" Rimmony exclaimed, but then she leapt up and danced away, back into the mist, clutching the feather high above her head.

Next day Mavroc woke in his cottage by the beach. He thrust open the door, same as he always did, and went to sit on the rock on the shore, same as he always did. But then he fell to thinking of Rimmony and wondered if she'd come again. He gazed at the sea, he gazed at the sand. He peered along the tops of the slippery rocks. He was so busy looking, he didn't hear Rimmony creep up behind him, till she clapped her hands over his eyes.

"Guess who this is," she teased.

"You are Rimmony," Mavroc said slowly.

Rimmony dropped her hands, giggling.

"How did you know?" she asked.

Mavroc shrugged.

"Nobody else comes to talk to me. Had to be you," he replied.

"Sit with me," she said.

They sat together, a while and a while, staring out at the sea.

"Do you wonder where it goes?" Rimmony said at last.

"Goes to the ocean and way beyond to islands where fish jump into your net."

"How do you know that?"

"My father told me."

"Where is your father?"

"My father is dead," Mavroc grunted.

"I'm sorry," said Rimmony.

Mavroc said nothing, then laid his head on her shoulder. Rimmony gently stroked his feathers.

"So soft," she said. "Soft but strong. I can feel the oil that keeps out the water and the wind."

Mavroc nodded.

Then Rimmony quickly tweaked out one feather.

"Got two now," she said, pulling the first from a pocket in her skirt.

Next day and next day when she came again, Rimmony would stroke his head, but then quick as quick she would tweak out more feathers. Mavroc smiled, he didn't complain. He liked it when she came and wanted her to be warm.

"Soon have enough for a whole cloak of feathers, just like you wanted," he said.

But soon enough a bald patch appeared on his head where Rimmony had pulled all the feathers away. She rubbed it gently.

"Don't *you* feel cold?" she asked.

Mavroc touched his own hand to his scalp.

"It is good to feel the cold and the wind," he replied. "I do not want my feathers. Take them all."

He laid his head in Rimmony's lap. Slowly she plucked away all the rest of the feathers, from the sides of his head and from his face, gathering them into her pocket.

"I don't want to hurt you," she said as drops of Mavroc's blood spilt onto her skirt.

"Not pain," he said.

She worked quickly, her nimble fingers plucking away every last feather, then the soft fluffy down beneath to reveal the face of a raw lummin-boy, pale and blinking, his cheeks and chin fresh-shaven.

They stood and stared at each other then Rimmony took his hand and they walked together along the sand, dropping the feathers in a trail behind them.

Mavroc stopped suddenly and looked back.

"Wait!" he exclaimed. Above them in the sky a pale bird wheeled and dived, then turned away. "Don't you want the feathers to make a cloak to keep you warm?"

Rimmony shook her head and slipped an arm around his waist.

"You can keep me warm instead," she said.

The Sun and The Rain

As Pickapple opened his eyes, the sun was shining cauldron-hot, the birds were singing honey sweet and the flowers were swaying all hazy bright and yellow. Pickapple rushed to the door and flung it wide, then he remembered it had not rained for days. The grass around his hut lay parched and brown. The leaves drooped limp and sullen from the boughs.

Pickapple smiled as he wondered if he could trick the sky. Wondered if he could make it rain. And so he thought his saddest thoughts, that the moon would never rise again, the milk would sour in the churns, the truffles would be buried too deep to find.

Pickapple sat and cried. He cried till he could cry no more, then he peeked out between his fingers to see if the sun was crying too. But no, the sun was beating down, making the very dust to dance. And so Pickapple smiled again. And then he laughed at the sky.

"You have tricked me," he said. "You have tricked me, but I can't trick you. Can trick Mullops and sometimes trick Littleberry. But can't never trick the sky."

Pickapple shook his head.

"Reckon I'll just have to be happy instead."

And so he was....

And the next day when he woke, Pickapple was happy still as he remembered the sunshine and all the bright flowers he'd seen the day before. He sat up and listened for the birds chirruping and tweeting, but all he heard was a dark gloomy silence.

He groped his way from his narrow bunk and pulled open the shutters to peer outside. The forest was sodden with dull heavy rain. Not a bird was in sight and the sun was hidden behind a wall of grey cloud.

Pickapple opened his door and stood to watch the puddles deepen, seeping up to his step.

"Now how'm I to get out," he muttered, "without the rain soaking through the holes in my boots?"

But then he remembered.

"This was what I wanted. I wanted to trick the sky. I wanted to make it rain!"

And Pickapple closed the door and sat on his bed and smiled and smiled. But the rain fell on, all that day and all the next day too, till Pickapple fell to shivering and boiling kettles of water till he'd run out of nettle tea.

"Not to worry," he said at last as he threw open the door again. "All I got to do is laugh at the sky and the clouds will roll away."

So he sat in his doorway on an upturned bucket and he laughed and he laughed till the tears rolled down his chin. But twas no good at all, the rain came down harder than before.

"You tricked me again," Pickapple complained. "Got to remember, I can trick Mullops all of the time and I can trick Littleberry some of the time, but can't trick that old sky at all."

Then he cried sad tears to join all his happy tears till the puddle round his boots nearly came up to his ankles.

Then he smiled.

"No good crying for the sky, not one way nor the other."

And as soon as he smiled he looked up to see the clouds all roll away and the sun come creeping out.

"I done it at last!" Pickapple laughed as he capered into the woods. "I tricked the rain, I tricked the sun... I tricked them both and now I even tricked the sky!"

And then he slipped and fell flat on his face, still grinning as he sat up again, covered all over in mud.

THE SHIP IN THE FOREST

Cummonly wore a skirt blue as the ocean to hide the web which bound her legs. These legs, if legs they be, were covered all over in scales, and at night she dreamt of the sea. Dreamt of waves and coursing currents, dreamt of winds and sweet salt air. Dreamt shoals of fish gliding around her, rainbow tails flicking, mouths opening and closing, singing their greetings.

Not here. Not here in the forest where dull-eyed crows flapped darkly as they swam squawking between the trees. Here were no golden beaches, there was no sweet sea breeze. Only the stench of decaying moss and rotten leaves where Cummonly sat in her glade, fingers sifting a clutch of beechnuts and acorns which she pierced and threaded to hang about her neck like as if they were shells from the depths of the ocean.

In her head grey gulls wheeled, wailing their sorrowing pain. She wove her long tresses with dock leaves and briar, like it might be bladder-wrack, and bit her lips to taste the salt that surged in tides through her veins, her body rocking as if she swam strong and free.

One bright morning she woke, stretched her arms and looked up to see a ship that trawled slowly atop the trees, its sagging sails breathless for wind, its anchor dangling loose through the branches, snagging on rooks' nests and a tangle of ivy and thorns, while the crew lolled sullenly over the side, tossing curses and empty bottles to lodge morosely in the bushes below.

Cummonly could hear them singing, deep songs, dark songs, dirty songs that stank of the sea. Stank of bilge and rotted fish. Stank of scurvy and festering storms. Stank of ill-fortune and hollow words.

The captain traipsed the deck with a rolling swagger, her face worn and weathered by the whip of the wind. Her hair was silver and knotted in braids that hung across the shoulders of her grimy yellow coat. Her tongue lashed her crewmen in a low rasping voice, sending them scuttling back to their posts, to haul the ropes, to trim the sails, to continue their precarious voyage across the forest's ocean.

Cummonly watched as the ship plunged and tossed till it pitched up sudden against a great oak. She heard the captain screaming and cursing, barking frenzied orders to the crew who scuttled side to side trying to right her. But it was lost. The ship keeled over and sank down through the branches till it came to rest in the undergrowth.

Cummonly levered herself towards the vessel, her belly rubbing sore against the pilth of broken twigs, snagging nettles and thorns. She gripped the keel and the planking, heaving herself up hand-over-hand until at last she hauled herself onto the deck and lay panting, her blue skirt flapping like as if she was a fish just pulled from the water.

Nobody saw her. Cummonly peered around, then edged slowly to hide behind a stack of crates and watched as the captain strode past, cracking nuts between her teeth as she went and spitting out the shells. Then a calloused hand grabbed Cummonly's arm and pulled her quickly into the shadows.

"Stay here," a coarse voice warned. "Stay here else Griss will see you. She'll rip your throat out soon as look."

The man was squat and wiry, his body scarred and weather-worn. He stared long at Cummonly.

"What are you?" he said at last. "I have travelled many oceans and set foot on many an island and birthed up in many a port. But I never seen a creature like you before."

She lowered her eyes, then looked at him again.

"I am Cummonly," she replied. "And I have never seen any like you, for I am grown used to the boys of the woods. Tell me, what is your name?"

"I am Helmscuttle."

"Then Helmscuttle, I will stay with you and you can tell me tales of the sea, for that is where I long to be."

"I long to be there too," Helmscuttle grunted. "The wind has blown us astray. We sail this dark forest day after day and never see the ocean no more, never hear waves beating on distant shores."

Cummonly rocked back and forth.

"Your words are sweet as sea breezes to me," she cried. "Tell me more..."

"Not here," said Helmscuttle. "Griss will see. Come with me."

He grasped her arm. Cummonly slithered, crabbing and awkward, pulling herself along on her elbows as she dragged the tail of her legs, scaled and webbed as they were.

Helmscuttle heard footsteps striding across the planks.

"Tis Griss," he hissed and grabbed at Cummonly, bundling her down through a hatch.

She fell. Breasting the darkness, flailing her arms. To land in a mass of blue.

"Tis the sea!" she cried, staring around. Her hands grabbed fistfuls of hard blue husks. She peered at them close.

"They are blue," she said, shaking her head, "but they are not the sea."

She sniffed at one curiously then tried it between her teeth. It cracked open, white and salty inside.

"They are seed," she smiled. "Seen the like before, but never so blue. Mayhap they are seeds of the sea."

She scooped up a handful, stuffed them in her mouth, but spat them out again. Then a scrambling thud and Helmscuttle was beside her.

"Don't touch," he warned. "Don't let Griss see. This is her cargo. Nobody supposed to be down here."

"You are here."

"Came to see you."

"Why'd you want to see me? Nobody else ever do."

"Got to keep you safe from Griss."

"Why? - what will she do?"

Helmscuttle closed his eyes and shook his head.

"Don't let her hear you, that's all. I'll bring you food. Just keep quiet and wait."

"But..."

But he was gone, shinning up a ladder at the far end of the hold.

Cummonly sat in the darkness, sifting the blue grain between her fingers. As it shifted, the sound was alike to water on a beach. Cummonly closed her eyes. She could hear gulls calling overhead, feel the pitch and plunge of the prow as they drove between the waves. An island floated into view where strange birds flew, brighter than any she had ever seen before and their cries were like to childern who had been locked away behind walls.

Then Griss on deck, screaming orders for the boats to be lowered to go ashore. Cummonly could hear her pacing, rattling the timbers overhead. Then someone shook her. Was not Griss but Helmscuttle.

"I brought you food," he said.

Cummonly smiled and opened her eyes. She reached out hopefully as he pressed a bowl into her hands. She peered in to see a fistful of dried biscuits and sighed.

"In the forest I eat berries and mushrooms and fresh roots. Pick'em myself all shining with dew."

Helmscuttle scowled.

"This the best we got."

Cummonly broke a piece of biscuit, touched it to her lips then placed it on her tongue. It was dry and bitter. She winced.

"Go back to the forest then," Helmscuttle growled.

Cummonly shook her head quickly.

"No - I want to be here. I want you to take me to the sea."

"Can do that," said Helmscuttle. "Just have to wait. First we got to get this ship righted."

"How long will it take?"

Helmscuttle shook his head.

"Could be days. The trees have twined their branches all round us like as if they were arms. You'll have to stay here till we're free."

Cummonly looked at him.

"I'm cold," she said. "Won't you keep me warm?"

Next morning Cummonly stirred in her bed of blue seed. Outside she heard the singing of the birds and the swaying of the trees, same as they always had been though somehow different now. She picked at the last crumbs of biscuit in the dish and wondered when Helmscuttle might come again. She could still feel his warmth as she lay back and watched the light filter through the hatch of the hold.

Up above she heard raised voices. It was Griss. She was shouting at Helmscuttle. Cummonly sat up, trying to make out the words.

"Where... why?... liar!"

A blow struck sharply.

Silence.

Then Griss shrieking again.

"You are *my* crew man. You do not desert me. Tell me again, where have you been?"

Silence.

Another blow.

Cummonly cowered down, burrowing into the swirl of seeds till her blue skirt was covered all over and it was like as if she was drowning, with no legs at all.

Another commotion above. Boots running harsh across the boards. Then the rattle of the ladder at the far end of the hold. Cummonly shut her eyes again and waited till she felt a sharp pain in her back.

She looked up.

It was Griss.

It was Griss gripping Helmscuttle tighter than manacles.

It was Griss who hissed,

"Is this her?"

Helmscuttle said nothing. He would not even look at her. But Cummonly looked at him.

"Yes, it is me. Please - Helmscuttle meant no harm. He brought me food. He kept me warm..."

"That food is crew's food. Are you one of the crew?"

Cummonly shook her head.

"No - but I could be so if you wished it. I wish to sail to the sea. Please - take me with you."

Griss snorted impatiently.

"What *good* can you do?" she sneered. "Except

lounging here befouling this cargo with your stench."

Cummonly floundered as she tried to lift herself from the shifting mass of blue seed. She saw Helmscuttle turn in alarm at the sound of more feet descending the ladder. His crewmates shoved him aside and grabbed at Cummonly, dragging her up.

"She cannot..." Helmscuttle tried to explain as the men stared in puzzlement at the scales on her legs as she struggled to wrap her skirt around her. And then she fell.

They dragged her up again, urged on by Griss who was cursing out orders as they bore her up the ladder. She caught a brief glimpse of familiar trees, heard the rattle of rooks in the branches, before they tossed her over the side.

She landed face down in a bed of nettles and turned to see the ship looming above her, the faces of the crew-men peering down, hurling grotesque insults, goaded on by Griss who had scaled up the rigging.

Cummonly wept. Tears as salt as any sea. But she blinked them away and wiped her eyes with the back of her hand before crawling off, hauling herself by her elbows back into the shelter of the bushes.

All that day she watched the ship. Listened to Griss barking orders at the crew as they hacked away the branches that gripped the vessel and hauled on the ropes, trying to right it, and angled the sails to catch fresh breeze. One moment she thought she saw Helmscuttle leaning over the side, peering into the trees. She fancied he might be looking for her, but did not dare to make herself known as she burrowed down deeper into the rank dark mulch.

Then a crack and a creak and the ship was upright, soaring again to the tops of the trees. The sails billowed and the crew-men cheered as Cummonly watched sadly, for she knew her chance of reaching the sea would drift away with this craft. And she knew she'd never see Helmscuttle again.

Except at that moment a shadow flashed down, over the rail of the ship. Came crashing, splintering through the branches to land, legs shaking, just an arm's length away from where Cummonly was hiding.

She reached out.

Helmscuttle fell into her arms.

"You're shivering," he said.

"Thought you were lost to me."

"Come, let me warm you again."

Again they were warm and again they were cold as night followed day till the dawn again.

"Why did you stay?" Cummonly asked as she cooked fresh-picked mushrooms on an open fire.

"Stayed to be with you."

"But you'll miss the sea."

"The forest is an ocean. You have shown me."

Cummonly looked away.

"But I wanted to journey to the sea," she said. "That was why I climbed aboard."

"But then you found me."

"Found you, yes - but not the sea. The sea is in me. It flows through my veins. It has to find me."

"I have found you."

"You are Helmscuttle. You keep me warm. But you are not the sea."

Helmscuttle sat in silence for a moment, then from his pocket he pulled a leathern bag.

"What is this?" Cummonly leaned over.

"Wait - I will show you."

He picked at the draw-strings then pulled open the bag and tipped into his hand... blue seeds.

"Same as in the hold of the ship," cried Cummonly. "Same as I slept in. Same seeds as gave me dreams of the sea."

"Dream more," said Helmscuttle.

Cummonly watched as he took one seed betwixt finger and thumb and placed it upon the tip of his tongue. Then he closed his eyes. He rocked back and forth.

"Can feel the water," he said, "the suck and flow of the tide."

Cummonly grabbed at the bag.

"Let me try!"

Helmscuttle opened his eyes.

"Hush," he said. "Be slow. Let the sea come to you. You cannot steal the sea."

Cummonly sat quietly.

"Open your mouth," Helmscuttle instructed.

Gently he placed one seed on her tongue.

"Do not swallow," he said. "Just wait."

Cummonly waited. The seed tasted sweet yet bitter. A warmth spread through her limbs. She began to smile, but then her legs felt numb. She held out her hands but her fingers would not move. She stared at Helmscuttle, who sat smiling.

"What...?" she tried to ask, but her lips were frozen.

She closed her eyes.

Ice flows drifted all around them as the boards creaked, the rigging froze. The voices of the silence screamed in urgent torment. Pillars of green light unfolded across the sky. Cummonly's limbs would not move in the stillness, save for her teeth which rattled in a language she did not know.

"There is no sleep here, there is no waking..." She

heard Helmscuttle's words in a slow hazy slur.

"Keep me warm," she murmured, as she tried to reach out to him, but he did not move, he could not hear.

When they woke their eyes melted to the forest's lush green, the tang of red berries and the drone of hovering flies. Cummonly stretched.

"I saw the sea."

Helmscuttle nodded. He held out another seed.

"Can see it again."

Cummonly shook her head.

"No, wait. This sea was harsh and cruel and cold."

"Next time might be warmer."

Cummonly looked at him cautiously.

"We might drown."

They waited. Let the day drift by in a dream of stolen berries and hazy kisses. But when the light drained away from the clearing, Cummonly held out her hand.

"Let us go to the sea again."

Helmscuttle smiled, unpicked the string of his leathern bag and shook out one seed, nestling sharp and blue in his palm. He picked it up betwixt finger and thumb, just as before, and placed it on the tip of Cummonly's tongue.

She closed her eyes. She smiled the smile of far-away islands, heard the waves ripple gently across amber sands. She sighed as she swam in deep balmy water, shoals of fish brushing close against her body as she floated, as she writhed, as she spiralled through the tides.

Cummonly laughed and she heard Helmscuttle laughing too. She could feel his body's warmth without touching. Could feel the ripple of the current carrying their movements one to the other.

And so each day they ate the seed and wafted away on new voyages. They forgot to eat, they forgot to drink. Their thirst was quenched by their dreams.

One morning, Cummonly woke and reached out sleepily.

"Where are the seeds?" she asked. "One more to take me back..."

There was no reply.

"Wake up," she muttered, prodding at the bed of leaves where Helmscuttle slept. It was empty. He had gone.

Out in the woods, Helmscuttle wandered. He clutched at the bag of blue seed, though it was near empty now. Each clearing he came to seemed a new place to dream, but Helmscuttle strode on until he happened upon a tumbledown hut at the side of a crossroads. A hunched figure sat at the door, puffing on a pipe of pungent herbs. When he saw Helmscuttle he rose.

"My name is Pickapple," he said. "Which way are you going?"

Helmscuttle peered this way and that.

"I am going to the sea."

Pickapple scratched his head.

"Ain't no sea around here. Leastways none I've ever seen. There's an old brook down by that-aways. But sure there ain't no sea."

"I know this," said Helmscuttle. "I spend my days in the woods over there, telling tales of the sea to Cummonly."

Pickapple raised one eyebrow.

"What do you tell her?"

"Tell her of dogfish and dolphins and whales. Tell her of beaches filled with white sand. Tell her of islands and faraway lands."

"I like this," Pickapple grunted. "Take me with you."

Helmscuttle shook his head.

"Can't take no-one. I lost my ship."

"Have you nothing you can show me," Pickapple

stepped closer, "that comes from this wondrous sea? Mayhap a gull's feather, or a tooth of a shark or a piece of rotted timber from a ship?"

Helmscuttle frowned.

"I have nothing like this."

Pickapple squinnied his belt.

"What is tied in that leathern bag?"

"It's nothing," said Helmscuttle quickly.

"Can't be nothing," Pickapple reasoned, "else why do I see it has weight at the bottom. Nothing don't make a bag bulge."

Helmscuttle looked flustered.

"Ain't nothing special. Tis only old seeds."

"Where do they come from?"

"They come from the sea."

"If they come from the sea then special they be for I ain't heard of no seeds that grow in an ocean. What colour are they?"

"Blue," Helmscuttle replied.

"Ain't never seen no blue seeds before. Show me."

Helmscuttle put his hand on the bag.

"These seeds are special."

"Thought you said they were nothing."

"These seeds are special to me."

"If'n they are so special then I will give you something special in return. Wait there."

Pickapple disappeared inside the door of the hut. There was a great rattling and banging and then he returned and produced a piece of folded paper all mildewed and mouldered and pressed it firmly into Helmscuttle's palm.

"What's this?" Helmscuttle grunted indignantly. "Don't look nothing special to me."

"It's a map," Pickapple told him. "It will take you to

the sea."

Helmscuttle grabbed at it eagerly but Pickapple stayed his hand.

"Do not look at it till you need to. To start any journey you must follow your own nose."

Helmscuttle's eyes narrowed but then opened so wide it was like as if the ocean was already in his gaze. He held out the bag to Pickapple.

"If this map will take me to the sea, then I do not need these seeds, for they are only dreams and not the true sea at all. Spend half the day sleeping and all the night too. Never get nowhere that way."

Pickapple smiled and handed him the map, then took the leathern bag and hid it in the corner of his hut. When he came back out, Helmscuttle had already gone.

Helmscuttle walked on out of the forest through the damp and the drizzle, the sunshine and the misty dusk, until he came to another crossroads. There was no sign there to point the way and still no sight of the sea.

Helmscuttle turned around and around.

"If I go left there is mountains, and if I go right there's a stream. If I go straight on there's tangle of brambles, but if I turn around I'll be back where I came."

He thrust his hand in his pocket, his fingers scrabbling around for the map which Pickapple had given him.

"*Do not look at it till you need to* - that was what he said. Well, I need to now, right enough."

His fingers picked at the edge of the paper, so wrinkled it seemed almost bonded together. He peeled back the corners, holding his breath, afeared that he might rip it, until he had the map open at last - but then he scratched his head. The faded paper had no roads at all, no mountains, no forests. No sign of the sea. Helmscuttle smoothed it flat. All that he saw was one black arrow, etched in fading ink.

"Pickapple has tricked me. This ain't no map at all!"

He was about to screw it up and toss it away when he looked at it again.

"The arrow is pointing straight on. Maybe not such a trick at all, for straight on in the distance I see a river - and whichever way a river flows, sure it will lead to the sea... so this is the way I must go!"

Next night as Pickapple was sleeping, came a knocking at his door.

"Who is there?" he cried.

Again the knocking came. Pickapple rubbed his eyes and stretched, then lifted the latch.

"Just as I thought," he said, "there is no-one here at all."

"Let me in," said a voice. "I am cold."

Pickapple looked down. There on the ground was Cummonly where she had crawled out of the wood.

"Not much warmer in here," Pickapple muttered. "Not with the wind blowing under the door. Better come in. The fire is out, but put this blanket about you and sit until you get warm."

Cummonly nodded and shivered and watched while Pickapple brewed a pot of comfrey tea. Then she sat with the cup clasped in her hands and gazed all about by the flickering candle flame. Pickapple followed her eyes as they lighted on the leathern bag lying in the corner. He saw her fingers twitch, her lips moisten.

"See something that interests you?" he asked.

Her eyes rolled suddenly.

"I need to reach the sea. I need to be in the water. I need..."

She lurched towards the bag.

"Wait," Pickapple's voice stilled her. "Sit quiet. See - you have spilt your tea."

"Keep me warm," Cummonly pleaded, casting her arms about him, while all the time her eyes were fixed on the leathern bag in the corner.

Pickapple eased away from her.

"Let me get it for you," he said and crossed the room to fetch the bag.

Cummonly was shaking, her eyes filled with salt tears. Pickapple tugged at the string of the bag and shook one blue seed into the palm of his hand. Cummonly sighed and her lips opened wide. Pickapple placed the seed on her tongue. She smiled and slithered forward, clutching him sleepily.

"I feel the tides of the sea inside me. I smell the sea. I taste the sea... but I am cold," she murmured, "...keep me warm."

Pickapple returned from trudging the dew-laden paths of the forest to find Cummonly still curled and sleeping, just as he had left her. He rattled a pan on the hob and she began to stir, stretching her arms and rising.

"I'm brewing nettle tea," he told her.

Cummonly smiled.

"Give me seed."

Pickapple shook his head.

"It will only make you sleep again," he told her.

"I need to feel the bite of the breeze. I need to taste the salt."

"You need to drink this tea," said Pickapple tersely. "Only way you'll get to the sea is to set out and find it."

Cummonly sat cradling the cup in her hands.

"Come with me," she begged, "in case I get cold."

Pickapple shook his head.

"I have to stay here. Who else will trick good folk on their journeys?"

Cummonly looked at him.

"Would you trick me? Would you send me the wrong way to find the sea?"

Pickapple shrugged.

"How can I trick you? Don't know where the sea is myself. If I don't know the right way, can't tell you the wrong."

"If you won't come with me, then give me the seeds."

Pickapple paused, then held out the bag.

"May as well take it," he said. "It's no use to me. I tasted one seed after Helmscuttle left them. He said they were precious. Not precious to me, just bitter and hard. Give me a belly ache. Didn't see no sea."

Cummonly took the bag and clutched it to her, then slithered slowly out through the door.

In the dark depths of the forest, Cummonly sat. In her lap she clutched the leathern bag which held the seeds. But there was only one left now, shimmering blue. She picked it up betwixt her fingers and touched it to her tongue. Closed her eyes, but then she spat it back into her hand.

"Only one more, but then no more. My journey is long and still only a forest of endless trees. No matter how much I swallow the seeds, the sea does not come to me."

Last night she had dreamed herself marooned on a shore. No tide, no gulls calling. Nothing more. She dropped the seed back into the bag and drew the string. Dug her fingers into the leaf mulch beneath her and stared at green nettles and the lingering mould. Then she untied the bag, drew out the seed and pressed it into the ground.

"It will grow," she whispered. "If I wait, it will grow. I may never reach the sea. I may never see Helmscuttle again. But I will have new seeds. I will have my dreams."

And so she slept and dreamt of nothing at all.

When she woke a blue bush grew beside her. Its flowers were turquoise and hues of deep marine. Cummonly reached out to touch one. Its scent was as salt, the salt of the sea. Its petals opened wider and in its throat there was formed a tiny fish. Cummonly held out her hand to catch it as it flapped out, newly birthed. But then another and then another from all over the bush. She tried to catch and kiss them all, but they flew past her, swimming up towards the sky to perch on the branches of the trees and sing, like as if they were birds.

Cummonly listened to their song and joined in, and as her voice rose to meet theirs, so she rose to stand on her feet. Her webbed legs were shaking but she swung her arms upward and swam through the air up to where the fishes were waiting. Soon as she reached them they left the shelter of the leaves and they swam all together with Cummonly, into the wide blue of the sky.

They swam as a shoal, wheeling and turning, crying out to each other as they swirled on and up, over the green of the forest.

Pickapple stepped out from his hut and looked up into the sky at the clouds scudding slowly over the tree tops. His eye lit on one which looked so it was a ship, its sails all a-billow. Then it broke up till each wisp was like a fish swimming, and he fancied he saw the shape of Cummonly high in the sky. Then they merged again to become all as one and the edges smudged with grey and it started to rain.

A slow rain, a drizzle, nothing more, soft and blue. Pickapple held out his hands then touched the moisture to his tongue and smiled.

It tasted of salt.

The salt of the sea.

HAWKSTONE

All Elmskin could hear was the rushing of wind and the desolate cry of distant birds as he walked along a winding track far from the forest, up into the hills. Then the path was plunged into shadow as the sun slipped behind a cloud. When it appeared again, Elmskin looked up to spy a hawk hovering high above him. The bird circled slow and lazy, dropping ever closer, its wings scarcely moving, only the very tips feathering the wind. But from the harsh jut of its beak and the hunger of its eyes an eerie silence spread. Elmskin did not move, nothing around him moved. Not a mouse, not a beetle, not a shrew. All were frozen to the spot as hard against the midday sun, he saw the shadow of the hawk cast beside him on the ground. And there in its centre lay a small grey stone.

The hawk shrieked again. Elmskin looked up and it was gone, drawing its shadow away from him, scudding across the ground. Elmskin bent down to pick up the stone. He felt that it was warm as he cupped it in his palm. As he watched, its grey skin shivered and then cracked through like it was an egg. Elmskin gaped open-mouthed as a long grey flower sprang out from its shell.

He placed it slowly beside the road and wondered as it grew and grew as tall as him but spindly still. And then it was a flower no more. Its drooping head became a face, its petals arms, its leaves were hands. Its scrawny stem a trembling body, shivering in the cold grey wind.

Elmskin stared at this boy whose face was long and pale. His ill-fitting clothes, the colour of cloud, hung loosely from his shoulders. He stared back at Elmskin, blinking slowly, and then spoke in a hoarse whisper.

"Who are you?"

Elmskin held out his hand and introduced himself. The boy stood expressionless, watching him and yet not watching him at all, staring beyond him to the line of distant hills.

Elmskin repeated his name. "Now you must tell me *yours*."

The boy stared around.

"Where did I come from?" he asked at last.

"Come from a hawk," Elmskin replied. "From a stone in its shadow."

The boy frowned and looked away.

"Then I am Hawkstone," he said.

Elmskin stared again at the boy's skinny fingers, his lank straggling hair, then set off down the hill, and turned to see Hawkstone still standing at the top, a furrow of confusion crossing his face. Elmskin raced back and grabbed his hand and dragged him along.

"You're hurting," Hawkstone complained.

Elmskin loosened his grip and allowed the boy to shuffle behind, gazing all around at the sun, the sky and the dark circling birds. Soon enough dull clouds swirled above them, grey as Hawkstone's eyes. A fine mist of rain wrapped around their shoulders. Elmskin shivered as it soaked through his jacket, soaked through his hat and sank deep into his marrow. He turned to look at his companion, but Hawkstone was dancing, as dry as straw, a smile on his face as he flapped his long fingers.

"Don't know what you are, to be sure," muttered Elmskin, "but whatever you be, you better come with me."

And so they trudged on, mile after mile, with nary a

word and nary a smile. Each time Elmskin turned to make sure Hawkstone was still there, it seemed like he was floating slowly through the air.

"You might not be tired, but I surely am," Elmskin declared as he flopped to the ground. "Your belly must be empty, and so is mine. But vittles I got none."

Hawkstone sighed and sank down. Elmskin sat beside him and they both stared all around. Night was falling fast and a chill wind gnawed their bones.

Elmskin peered through the gloom and nudged his companion in the ribs, then wished he hadn't, the thin figure seemed so frail.

"What's that over there?"

Hawkstone turned to squint at a light in the distance.

"Tis marsh gas," he whispered. "I seen it before."

"When you seen marsh gas?" Elmskin asked. "You only just grew from that pebble."

Hawkstone shrugged.

"I come and I go."

"Well, I seen marsh gas too," Elmskin declared. "Tis nary marsh gas but the light of a house. And if there is a house, then there is vittles."

He leapt to his feet.

"Quick, come with me."

But Hawkstone stayed where he sat, staring the other way.

"Suit yourself," Elmskin shrugged, and set off by himself.

"All the more vittles for me," he called back over his shoulder, but Hawkstone was still sitting gazing at the head of a thistle and stroking its feathery down.

"Can't live off air," Elmskin muttered as he trudged on towards the flickering light.

With every step his boots sank deeper into the waterpudge till he came at last to a clutch of trees. On the far side a light glimmered and he could hear a fire crackling inside the walls of a ruined cottage. Its roof gaped open to the sky and branches twined and tangled, thrusting out through the empty windows.

Elmskin could hear a woman singing and peered inside to see her poking at the fire. She squatted in the darkling light, a cloak of leaves wrapped about her shoulders, then turned as Elmskin ducked in under the ivy-choked lintel.

"What do you want?" she demanded, as she raked at the embers again.

"Want vittles," Elmskin declared. "Me and Hawkstone, we lost our way and now we're mighty hungry."

"That's a shame," the woman grunted. "Ain't no vittles here."

Elmskin peered at a tray of pies set out beside the fire. The woman followed his gaze.

"Ain't no vittles here," she repeated and covered the pies with a cloth.

"Ain't no food, only fire. I have to keep this fire alight, day and night."

Elmskin looked at her again. The leaves of her cloak were shrivelled, her face and her hands full pale.

"Must have fire to keep me warm. See - it is dwindling now. That's cos you've kept me talking. You can help me, seeing as you're here. Break me some more twigs off those old dead branches."

Elmskin turned. All through the cottage, trees had grown, thrusting up through the floor and out through the cracks in the stone of the walls.

He stood quite still.

"If I help you gather wood - then will you give me a pie?"

"Ain't no pies," the woman said. "And if there were - they ain't for the likes of you. Make these pies myself from the berries you see all around."

Elmskin reached out to touch the clusters of purple berries hanging from a bush which sprouted in the corner.

"Don't touch," the woman said quickly. "Them berries is poison."

"Then how can you eat them?" Elmskin retorted.

"Don't eat the berries," she replied. "I stew 'em up and sieve off all the juices. Then I bake the pulp into pies."

"Thought you said there was no pies." Elmskin stared at the pans and the dishes stacked up by the fire.

"Ain't no pies for *you*," the woman muttered, prodding again at the embers. "Quickly, don't just stand there. Fetch me more wood."

Elmskin obliged. He turned and snapped the dead white twigs which had grown from the twisted branches. Suddenly he felt the lash of a bough as its thorns snagged into his neck. He pulled away, his fingers dabbing at the trickling blood, to find the woman standing close behind him.

"You bit me!" he challenged.

The woman smiled and shook her head.

"You bit me," he accused again.

"I am Night Ash," the woman said, "and it was the thorns as bit you, not me. Look what you done now with your bothering and fuss - the fire is near gone out. You supposed to be fetching me wood."

Elmskin clutched his knotted kerchief against the side of his neck.

"It's cold," he complained.

"Be colder still if this fire goes out. Fetch me kindling, quick as quick."

Elmskin snapped off more twigs and thrust them into

her hands. Night Ash knelt before the fire, prodding and poking, then she seized up a pair of leather bellows and set to puffing and blowing, but the flames would not respond.

"All your fault," she grumbled. "This fire were fine till you came along."

A wind blew up around the cottage, howling with the voice of the mountains, wailing with the darkness of the night.

"Hawkstone will be waiting," Elmskin exclaimed.

Night Ash seized his waist. "Hawkstone chose not to come. He sent you here to meet me, now you must keep me warm."

"The fire is out," Elmskin replied. "Mayhap now we can eat the pies."

"Told you before, them pies not for you. Lie still here by the embers and let me wrap us around."

Night Ash grabbed twigs from the thorn bushes, not caring if they snagged at her hands. She wound them this way, she wound them that, till they were wrapped all snug, and then she began to sing:

My fire will feed your fire,
My heat will fill your veins.
Taste the tongue of my desire
And you won't leave here again.

> *The night is cold and empty,*
> *The wind holds us in its arms.*
> *Though we be tired and weary,*
> *The dawn will bring no harm.*

*My fire will feed your fire,
My heat will fill your veins.
Taste the tongue of my desire....*

Her voice trailed away.

"But the fire is out," muttered Elmskin.

He stared at Night Ash, but she had fallen deep asleep.

"*Won't leave here again...* - Won't I?" he declared. "I'll be out of this tangle quick as quick."

Elmskin turned and then he turned again but was stuck as fast as he could be. He looked into Night Ash's face, watching as her eyes rolled beneath her lids. Her lips moved as if she was speaking, her cheek twitched as if waiting to be kissed.

He tried to guess her dreams from her sobbing and her sighs. He dreamed she must be dreaming of riding a wild white horse through the forest and away, up into the mountain till she gazed down from the top at the rivers and the valley below. Then turned into a raven and plunged down and down. He could tell it from her calling, her voice cracked in her throat. He could feel it from her strength as she clenched her fingers and spread her arms.

She wrestled with the thorns that bound them, though they did not seem to hurt her. Elmskin clung close beside her until suddenly she broke free. Yet she was still sleeping, there in the deserted cottage, and the night it came howling down through the broken roof.

Elmskin turned and seized the tray of pies that sat by the sullen ashes. He plunged away through the open door, blundering through beds of nettles while behind him he heard Night Ash singing still:

"*My fire will feed your fire, my heat will fill your veins...*"

As Elmskin ran, the voice grew fainter: *"Though we be tired and weary, the dawn will bring no harm..."*

Dawn broke as Elmskin staggered from the woods and stumbled across the marshy dreck, still clutching the tray of pies. He felt the wind howling as he tottered forward. He heard the sound of hoof beats behind him, pounding closer and closer, like as if it was the horse escaped from Night Ash's dream.

He ran on all the faster, as still it came closer, could feel the hot smoke of its nostrils breathing down his neck.

Elmskin clutched at the pies as they scattered this way and that, but though he tripped and landed on his knees, scrabbling around to try and gather them, the horse came no closer, did not rear up its hooves, did not come crashing down upon his head. Yet he heard its frantic whinnying and Night Ash's voice a-calling:

"You won't leave... you won't leave... My fire is low and you must feed it. My thorns are sharp and leave me bleeding. My wounds are deep in need of healing."

He slowly turned around. There was nothing there behind him, only the empty marsh leading to the wood. But then he saw a mist rising, a white cloud surging, shaped almost like the horse he thought he'd heard. He watched till suddenly it was over him, and then dark rain came falling, soaking through his shirt.

Elmskin gathered the sodden pies from where they had fallen, their crusts all crumbling, bruised and broken, their juices oozing red as blood.

When he reached Hawkstone, he was sleeping. He shook his shoulder to make him wake.

"Hawkstone, Hawkstone, got you pies," he cried and thrust one at him as Hawkstone blinked his eyes.

His face was pale, his fingers shaking.

"Need vittles to warm you," Elmskin cajoled.

Hawkstone blinked again and pushed the pie away.

"My belly is filled with thistledown and rain. This crust will weigh heavy as stone."

"I have pies enough for two, for three. If you won't eat'em, there's more for me."

Hawkstone rolled onto his back, gazed happily upwards then let his eyelids shut and lay quiet, his mouth slowly opening and closing while Elmskin devoured the first of the pies, the blood-red juice tricking down his fingers to gather sticky around his wrists, clinging to his cuffs as he munched.

"The pies are not for you..." he heard the voice of Night Ash again as he chewed and swallowed, swallowed and chewed.

The pie was sweet, the pie was bitter, savoury and delicious, succulent and sour. Elmskin shook his head and brushed the crumbs away. His belly felt warm, his belly felt full. He licked his lips and grabbed another.

"The pies are not for you..." he heard Night Ash's voice again, but he took a bite, just the same.

Then he stopped. Hawkstone was snoring. Elmskin watched his rolling eyes staring up towards the stars. As he followed his gaze, Elmskin felt a pain at the base of his belly. He gripped beneath his shirt to find a tree sprouting outwards, trunk and branches and leaves pushing lithe towards the sky.

As Elmskin watched, twigs and green leaves spouted, wafting this way and that, reaching towards the white silence of the rising sun. Then in its branches a small bird alighted, hopping and beckoning and fluttering her wings, all the time singing a pleading song in a voice that was Rimmony's own.

Elmskin called out to her, but the bird sang on,

ignoring him as he climbed, scrabbling through the branches of the soaring tree. He could hear Rimmony's voice as he drew even closer, but as he reached out to touch her, the little bird flew away, high into the lightening sky, her song spiralling fragile as laughter.

Elmskin slithered back down through the knotted boughs and found himself sitting at the root once again and watched as the tree shrank back into his belly from where it had come.

Hawkstone was snoring still.

Elmskin shook him roughly.

"Get up," he chided, and dragged him to his feet.

"Get up now. We got to go."

Mullops and the Snail

Mullops had nothing better to do and so he came out to see Pickapple in his hut at the crossroads to pass the time of day.

Pickapple held out his fist for Mullops to see.

"Is this a stone or a snail?" he quizzed, opening his hand quickly then closing it again.

"Why, I think it is a snail," said Mullops.

"You think too much. It is a stone," Pickapple responded.

But he kept his fist clenched tight.

"Let me see," Mullops demanded. "It seemed like a snail to me. I saw its neck and the horns upon its head."

"Well then," said Pickapple, "if you saw all this, mayhap it is a stone with horns and a neck."

"There's no such thing," said Mullops.

"But if you declare it has horns and a neck, why then it must have horns and a neck. And if it be not a stone, why it must be something else. Mayhap it is a cow that's strayed from the pasture."

Mullops scratched his head.

"You could not hold a cow in your hand."

"My palms are broad, my fingers are long. I can hold many things. And besides, when I eat one of Old Granny Willowmist's good meat pies, why then I hold a cow in my hand."

Mullops shook his head.

"I would sooner believe it was a stone," he said.

"So it is a stone, if you believe so," Pickapple retorted. "I told you all along."

"Stone or snail, snail or cow, we will only know if you show me. Open your hand."

Pickapple smiled and opened his hand slowly. A bright scarlet butterfly fluttered away. Mullops watched its shimmering wings as it landed on the bushes over the way. As he ran across to take a closer look, Pickapple dropped a snail onto the path beside him and quickly walked away.

WRANGLETHORN AND MARRADON

There was a girl as lived in the woods. She had not eaten for a year and a year, only cobwebs and sips of dew. She dreamed of a mountain where nested a bird who laid pure white eggs laced through with gold. She dreamed of a valley where a lone flower grew, its petals as black as the raven's dark hue. She dreamed of a city of hunched stooping streets where shadows slipped slowly through air rich with smoke.

But all she had seen was the forest leaves and creatures who scurried and burrowed and scampered and came sniffing right up to her, nibbling at the matted ends of her hair, licking her cheek and nuzzling her ear. And she knew them every one, though she did not give them names, for to name them would be to steal them from the worlds they had made in the mulch of fallen leaves.

Truth to tell, she had no name herself, for there was no-one there to name her and she had no need to, for she was a shadow in this world of rustling and shuffling, shifting and crawling. But the old'uns in the village knew of her, though they never told how she came to be there. And the young'uns too - some of them said that they'd seen her, or heard her there in the woods, singing or whispering in words they could not tell.

But the old'uns said twas only the wind, or fox that was lost or a fallen bird - and that she was not there at all, though they knew... they knew that she was. And they called her Wranglethorn.

Now one day Wranglethorn tired of dining on cobwebs and dew and she pulled herself out of the mulch, a long skirt trailing its hem in the mud as she made her way along a wandering path to the very edge of the wood. And there she saw the fields, and the smoke of the village rising far off and far. And there she saw too a sky filled with clouds of red as the sun dipped slowly down.

So she took deep breaths, all the while whispering and whimpering to herself as she crossed the first field of roughly dug soil and then another and then another more. Then she stopped with a start as she saw a scarecrow stood in the middle of a field. She stepped towards it cautiously and tapped upon its skinny shoulder till it swung around and toppled down into her arms. She clung to it and gazed upon its shrivelled face and its eyes carved deep and its lips cut all jagged and rotting. Then she kissed it sudden but the scarecrow creature did not stir as it sagged in her arms and she dropped it to the ground and left it to lie there, all alone and alone in the middle of the field as the crows came back and flapped all around and followed her down till she came to the village.

Now it was dusk. Shadows crawled out from the crouching buildings, drawing her down the dark crooked street, the alleys lurking with a leech of moss and a stench of dull rot which followed her as she flitted from window to window, staring wide-eyed at the firelight flickering inside.

But no-one came out and no-one came in and the street waited empty as she listened at each door to laughter and coughing, drab voices grumbling and a song which leaked and spluttered as if it had been spilt across the cold stone floor.

Then at an upper window she saw the shape of a dark

bird watching her, its eye a golden yellow, its beak sharp and long as a silver blade. It flurried this way and that, its silhouette filling the frame, black wings beating like a billowing cloak, trapped in that attic room. Though she could not hear its voice, Wranglethorn knew it was calling and she called back, a muted cry, like a bird herself.

Nobody heard, not the bird at the window, nor anybody else in the silence of the street. Wranglethorn called again and the bird at the window flapped its wings and beat its silver beak against the glass so hard that it seemed it must break.

Wranglethorn knocked at the door, rattling the latch till she heard footsteps approaching inside. The door opened and the bird appeared, all bedraggled in black almost like she was a girlen, and clung tight to Wranglethorn's shoulder as they clutched each other, sobbing, their muted cries echoing about the street.

But still no-one came and lights they went out at the windows till the street flowed about them, a river of night, and Wranglethorn led the bird-girl away, back across the fields, back towards the trembling shadows of the wood.

Next morning as the sun rose pale and misty above the sullen cottages, an old man and an old woman came shuffling down the street. They came up to the house where the bird-girl had been at the window the night before. They spied the open door and stepped inside, calling out her name:

"Marradon, Marradon..."

There came no reply and so they hurried up the stairs, but the tiny room was empty.

"Our daughter," the old woman wailed, "where is she

gone?"

"Someone has took her," the husband muttered. "See her bed is not slept in and her coat is still here."

The mother cast her eyes about in despair.

"She has gone a-wandering again, wearing no more than that black dress of hers covered about with glittering stars. See - even her shoes are here."

"Shoes here, sure. But not that silver blade she has, shaped like a sickle moon. Always brandishing it about, don't know what she thinks."

"She carries it to keep her safe. You know that, you know."

"None is here would do her harm. They just watch her come and go, flitting here and flitting there."

"Someone done her harm now. Someone carried her away."

"But she got her sickle blade to protect her."

"Mayhap some beast has come - stronger than she'll ever be. Anyways, she is not here. Our daughter she is gone!"

"She is gone!"

"She is gone!"

The cry set up all about the village.

"Marradon is gone."

Some looked in the sloppens, some looked down the well. Some looked in lofts and nettle beds. Some looked asquint at the young boys grown as tall as men, who wandered about doing nothing much at all except lifting stones and looking asquint at each other.

"Who was it saw her last?"

"Who was with her in the orchard?"

"Who was with her by the shadow of the wall?"

"Wouldn't go nowhere with her at all. With that long black dress that hangs like wings and the sickle blade she carries everywhere she goes."

"That blade ain't nothing. She won't do you no harm. That blade is for cutting down mistletoe, that's all."

"Mistletoe to kiss you..."

"Kiss you and more..."

"Never mind that now. Where is she gone?"

"The old'uns want to know."

"Weren't none of us now. Never saw her last night at all..."

"We knowed who it was..." they heard the old'uns say. "Twas Wranglethorn. She who lives all out in the woods. Tis she who comes whenever a wrong has been done."

Wranglethorn had led Marradon away from the village, all back across the fields and into the wood. They sat in a hollow twined round by roots under the bough of an old gnarled oak. And in the dark all you could see was their eyes. In the dark all you could see was the stars that glistened on Wranglethorn's dress. And in the dark all you could see was the sickle blade glinting silver as it rested in her hand. And all you could hear was Marradon's voice as she so slowly sang:

> *I bring you spit,*
> *I bring you fire*
> *to light your endless night.*
>
> *I bring you spit,*
> *I bring you fire*
> *to quench your fear of flight.*
>
> *My beak is sharp,*
> *my talons strong.*
> *My eye is quick, now hear my song...*

Her voice trailed away. High above them in a tree a blackbird woke and took up the melody for a fleeting moment before the night's aching silence swallowed the sound.

There they lay till dawn, which slipped about them like a cold misty breath till the sun wrapped them in its arms to keep them warm.

Marradon woke and stared at Wranglethorn.

"What do you do in the woods?" she asked.

Wranglethorn stirred slowly.

"I dream of mountains I have never climbed," she murmured. "I dream of a valley dripping with dew. I dream of a city with a shadowy eye."

Marradon stared back, then rolled away from her, smoothing the skirts of her long black dress.

"Been to the top of the mountain," she said, "and found me this pure white egg."

She reached her hand inside her dress and there sure as sure was an egg laced through with gold.

"Been to the dip of the valley and found me this flower dark as night..."

There in her hand it sprang then grew, with petals black as the raven's dark hue.

Wranglethorn shook her head but Marradon smiled again.

"Been to the city too..."

And from her sleeve she drew a bottle, filled to the top with dark swirling smoke. She pulled the stopper and let the vapour escape as she began to circle about the glade, cutting the air with her silver blade.

"But how have you been to these places?" Wranglethorn cried. "These are *my* dreams. How do you know of them?"

Marradon sat down beside her, stroking the edge of the

knife with her long slender fingers.

"Grith takes me," she said.

"Who is Grith?" Wranglethorn asked.

Marradon gazed high into the swaying branches of the tree.

"You do not see him," she said quickly. "But he is strong and he is wise. He walks with me through the waking hours and sleeps by my side at night."

"Last night *I* slept by your side," said Wranglethorn ruefully.

Marradon shrugged her shoulders and paced about the glade again, swaying her long black skirt so the stars upon it glittered and shone.

"Only because you brought me here and took me away from my home. But Grith will come looking for me because Grith is *mine*."

"But the dreams are *mine*," Wranglethorn clenched her fists. "You knew nothing of these places until I told you! Stay with me here. We can dream and dream again and travel wherever we choose."

"I don't need your dreams," Marradon muttered. "I have my own."

"You have nothing," Wranglethorn hissed. "Don't even have Grith. Where is he now? He's so strong and wise but he's not come to find you."

Before Marradon could reply, Wranglethorn made a grab for the egg, for the flower, for the bottle of smoke which lay upon the ground. But Marradon snatched them away and tucked them in the pocket of her dress.

Then a blizzard's brood, a nightmare howl, a rending of feathers, a sullen eye, a sunken scowl, a scarred dress, a blinded thigh. Ranting words and panting breath. Clutching fingers, tearing of a nest of knotted rage. A sobbing cage of wounded dreams. The salt caress of sweetened blood.

Wranglethorn lay sprawled in the mulch of rotted twigs, gazing up at Marradon who stared down at her.

"I go to Grith whenever I choose," she spat. "The dreams will take me to him and I will meet him there."

"The dreams are mine..." Wranglethorn repeated but swallowed the words as she caught Marradon's eye.

"... how will you get there?" she asked instead.

"Will fly," Marradon replied proudly.

"Sure they say your dress do look like wings and your sliver blade a beak."

"Many say that," Marradon shrugged, slipping the long black dress from her slender shoulders. She sliced the air once more with a sweep of the silver blade, then cast it to the ground before lifting her arms to the sky. For a moment she shivered, her lips parted eagerly, her nostrils flared and then she rose effortlessly, high above the trees, high through the willowy mist, her palms outstretched to caress the rising sun.

Wranglethorn waited a moment and watched until Marradon had gone, melted into the hazy veil of the clouds. Then she turned back to where the long black dress lay all rumpled on the ground. She picked it up and pulled it over her head, stepped this way, stepped that, trying it for size. She plunged her hand in the pocket to find the shattered shell of the egg cracked open, a shrivelled flower lying limp and lifeless and a broken bottle tarnished with soot. Wranglethorn threw them aside and plucked up the sickle blade from where it had pierced the soft earth. She held it aloft and circled it once about her head, just as she heard a commotion of voices coming through the wood.

"It is her!" they cried. "It is Marradon. We have found her again."

"Where is Wranglethorn?" one voice snarled. "We know she took Marradon from us."

The young girl stepped forward to greet them, the rising sun behind her as she stood in the long black dress, the sickle blade glinting in her hand.

"Wranglethorn is gone," she said.

"Tis not her. Tis not Marradon," the father whispered at the back of the crowd.

"Hush," said the mother. "Tis good enough. We lost our daughter Marradon long ago. These folk believe she's found again. We cannot say them 'no'."

They took her back then, to the village and opened up the door of the house where Marradon had lived. They led her gently up the stairs and into a narrow room. Its ceiling was low. The window was squint. Wranglethorn gazed out into the street.

And down below, the young boys grown as tall as men looked up and saw her as a bird with long black wings and curved silver beak and called to her once again.

"Come to the orchard," they shouted. "Come with us to the shadow of the wall..."

At the window, Wranglethorn sliced her silver blade, but not for mistletoe.

> *My beak is sharp,*
> *my talons strong.*
> *My eye is quick,*
> *now hear my song:*
>
> *I bring you spit,*
> *I bring you fire*
> *to feed your foolish fight.*
>
> *I bring you spit,*

*I bring you fire
to ride you down the night.*

A Haze of Heat

Pickapple sat in a haze of heat while flies buzzed all about him and the sweet song of the blackbirds danced in his ears. He felt so his head was filled with stacks of hay and his tongue was as dry as straw. He lolled like a dozing donkey and thought of nothing at all.

Then sudden, Mullops was beside him, saying -

"Let's walk to the pond and slake our thirst with the pure clean water."

Pickapple shook his head.

"It's too hot," he replied lazily. "Get even hotter just walking there - and besides, the pond's not clear, it's clogged all up with weeds."

"Then let's climb to the top of Barestone Crag," Mullops suggested. "Least it'll be cooler there and we can feel the breeze."

"That breeze'ud blow us back again before we ever get there," Pickapple complained as he flicked away the flies.

"Let's go and see Snuffwidget then," Mullops implored. "He were there before, down in the village, cleaning out his barrels. Said he had one last scoop of brew and he were saving it for me, for when I came back."

"What good's one scoop shared between two?" Pickapple complained. "Why not just come and sit here beside me and we can watch the tiny ants running in and out."

Mullops grunted and sat down, gawping at the ants as they busied all around.

"Do you know ants are so strong they could pick up that stone?" Pickapple informed him.

"Why don't they then?" Mullops challenged.

"Maybe there's not quite enough, "Pickapple mused. "Maybe it takes a hundred ants and then a hundred more to pick up a stone that size."

"So how many ants do you reckon is there?"

Pickapple scratched his head.

"Don't know," he said. "Don't know at all. Maybe you should count them."

"Maybe and I should," Mullops agreed. "Nothing else to do here, sitting in the dust."

"Go to it then," said Pickapple and slowly Mullops started."One - two - um - seven - three - four... what be after 'four'?"

"Five," Pickapple replied.

"Oh - I knowed it. Five - six - seven. Oh no, I done 'seven'. Nine - it must be 'nine'. These ants they do run around so. Sure I counted that one before... Pickapple... Pickapple?..."

Pickapple was starting away down the track.

"Where you going now?" Mullops demanded.

"Going to the pond to sit in the shade then mayhap I climb to the top of Barestone Crag to feel the cool breeze. But first I'm off to find Snuffwidget. Don't want to waste the last of his brew."

"Wait - let me come too," Mullops begged him.

"No," Pickapple called back over his shoulder. "You got to stay there till you counted all them ants."

"So I have," said Mullops. "But now you made me lose count. Where was I? Oh - I know... one... two..."

ROWAN

Elmskin trudged slowly through the snowy woods, his eyes scanning the scraggy bushes for any red berries left hanging there. But all that he saw were shrivelled and shrunken.

"Not enough for a handful," he mused. "Won't taste of nothing but mildew and mould. Not even if I boil them in a pan of melted snow to make them bright and sweet."

Then his eyes lighted on drops of scarlet and he stumbled towards them, thinking they must be a trail of berries. But weren't no berries, no. Twas spots of blood glistening brighter than any berry could be.

Elmskin was cautious. He glanced around. But he was curious too. Whose blood could it be? He followed the trail that led fresh towards a thicket of trees. There he stopped, peering round again, and then through the shadows he caught glimpse of a fawn.

Elmskin paused. Such a beautiful creature, its coat all dappled in the winter sun. It sniffed the air, then its nostrils flared. Elmskin knew that she had sensed him. Before he could move, the creature bolted away across a field ploughed for winter, drops of blood still spilling onto the snow blown light across the furrows.

As Elmskin set off in brisk pursuit, he saw the fawn did not run quickly. One foot hung limp and he realised the blood spilt out from a wound. As her pace slowed, the fawn kept glancing back over her shoulder till Elmskin fancied she was looking to see if he was following on.

The cold air caught his chest as he tried to run faster,

tried to catch up, but the fawn stared back at him again then suddenly sped off, running straight to the dense cover of a wood.

Elmskin stood in the undergrowth. Birds squawked all around him between the creaking branches. He could not see the fawn but followed the trail of blood, gleaming against the darkness of leaf mulch and the shivering whiteness of snow.

Then she was there, sitting on a cushion of grass, patiently waiting. Her wide eyes stared shyly at Elmskin as she stretched one slender leg towards him. He could see the gash in her ankle, wet with scarlet blood. The fawn leaned forward and tried to lick the wound. Elmskin crept closer to look.

"It is a bite," he said. "Who has done this?"

He moved to touch the fawn's leg, but she reared up suddenly and bolted away, heading through a tunnel of overhanging branches. Still the blood, like scarlet berries, dashed against the leaves. Elmskin ran, his heart all pounding, but the fawn was lost from sight as the path twisted and turned out of the wood, across a field to where the snow was piled thick all around a wattle hut. Elmskin looked about but there was no sign of the fawn. Then he saw that her footprints led to the small hut's door. As he approached, a girl stepped out. He gazed at her ragged dress and down at her trembling legs. Then he saw her ankle was bleeding.

He turned away, pointing at the droplets that were spilt across the snow.

"Is this your blood?" he asked.

"Yes," said the girl. "I was bitten."

Elmskin looked around.

"Where is the fawn?"

The girl shook her head.

"There is no fawn. Only me... I am Rowan."

"You're sure you haven't seen a fawn? I followed the trail of her blood. She had a wounded leg... like you."

"That was my blood," Rowan insisted. "I was bitten."

"What bit you?"

"A dog."

'"But the fawn...?"

"I saw no fawn. They come and go, so quickly. Quick as shadows. But you must be cold, come in," she said, her dark eyes opening wider.

Elmskin ducked through the low door. The only light inside the hut came from the embers of a dying fire. Rowan smiled, watching Pickapple as he gazed all around. Half hidden in the smoky shadows he saw, patched together from bits of leather and scraps of cloth, the masks of dogs, of foxes, of wolves hung from the slope of the roof. Rowan reached up and touched one, spinning it round and around, its eyes blazing, glowing red. Elmskin peered close and saw each was a berry set at the sides of the head.

"How do they shine?" he asked.

"I brew the apples when they fall," Rowan replied, "then dip the berries in the juice. Keeps them bright as any eyes."

"Bright as any blood," Elmskin remarked, staring at her ankle's raw wound.

"Dog bit me, like I told you," Rowan explained, then turned away.

In the flickering light Pickapple stared at her arms, scored with red weals and a mesh of white scars.

"Not the first time," he said.

Rowan turned back and sighed.

"Not the first time at all."

"Let me help you," said Elmskin. "I can bathe the

wound."

She winced as she twisted her ankle towards him and he wiped the blood from the gash.

"What sort of dog did this?" he asked.

"Just dog," said Rowan, gritting her teeth as Elmskin looked around for something that would make a bandage. Rowan ripped off a piece of her scarf which Elmskin saw was already bloodied and frayed. He wrapped it tight around her ankle and gazed again at the shadowy masks suspended from the ceiling.

"I make them to keep away harm," Rowan explained.

"Don't work so well." Elmskin nodded at her bandaged ankle.

"Make other things too," Rowan said quickly. "Been making a broth. Would you like some?"

"Thought you'd never ask," Elmskin grinned. "The smell from that pot been tormenting me ever since I came in!"

"You must be hungry," Rowan said softly as she hobbled towards the fire.

Elmskin nodded.

"True enough. No berries left on the trees."

"Maybe I got them all!" Rowan winked, pointing up at the eyes of the creatures that stared down from the ceiling.

"Maybe you have an'all," said Elmskin. "All that's out there is snow and a dog. But I never seen him. Seen a fawn though. Fawn that led me here. Wonder where did it go? Seemed to vanish soon as I came to your door."

Rowan turned away, her hair hiding her face as she tended to the pot.

They sat and drank in silence. Outside branches creaked under the weight of newly fallen snow. A fox howled in the distance. The wind sighed sleepily.

Elmskin was sleepy too. He stretched his arms and nodded gratefully towards the empty bowl.

Rowan smiled.

"You may sleep here," she said, indicating the matting strewn on the floor before slipping behind a curtain which she drew across the centre of the room.

Elmskin slept. He slept dog sleep. He slept howling. He slept back itch and wet nose. He slept the long hunger. He slept smell of wattle and candles and straw.

The red eyes of the masks watched through the darkness as he woke and crawled towards the door. Outside fresh snow had fallen again. Elmskin stretched. He knew Rowan was not awake yet for he had not heard her stirring. His limbs were frez. His nose was sharp with the whip of cold. He set his head towards the wood to go and fetch kindling sticks for the fire.

But then he saw paw-prints close to the hut.

"Dog was stalking all around," he muttered. "Come up to the door and gone off."

He followed the trail across to the wood, his own boots crackling through the frosted waste. No colours now but black and white. The drops of red blood that had led him here were all covered over in the drift of snow.

Between the trees the tracks led on till Elmskin came to a pond. One paw print in the mud at the edge, but then nothing more. Elmskin stared all around then heard a rustling, a scurrying through shadows. Then glimpse of dog - a black bulk, hulking, then gone.

Elmskin scurried after. But the brambles, the nettles, the low hanging branches all bound together as if they were kin. And they beat him back and the dog was lost and Elmskin returned to find Rowan wide awake and singing as she lit a fire.

"Where have you been?" she asked.

"Been to get kindling," Elmskin replied.

"Just as I need," she said, holding out her hand.

Elmskin hung his head.

"Didn't get none," he said, "but saw dog."

Rowan looked startled.

"Where was he?" she asked.

"Saw his trail outside the hut. Tracked him into the wood. But then lost him - he was gone."

Rowan frowned and bit her lip.

"I don't want to see him. I don't want him round here no more," she cried, her eyes wide, her face turning red with anger then pale with fear. She gazed long into the fire, watched as the glow of the kindling faded, the slow smoke dwindled and the spark was extinguished.

"Want you to go seek him," she said.

Elmskin nodded.

"What should I do when I find him?" he asked.

Rowan spun round and looked him in the eye.

"Want you to kill him," she said.

Elmskin paused, gazed up again at the eyes of the dogs and the foxes and the wolves hanging from the ceiling.

"He is big," he said. "Near as big as me. Why kill him? What harm has he done, wandering up to your door? Plenty of other creatures been here. I seen their trails. A stoat been a-slinking, a robin, a fox. None done you harm."

"This dog done me harm."

"How so?"

"You know. You seen. Look how he bit me. Told you it was dog."

Rowan ripped away the bandage that Elmskin had tied the night before. The wound was still raw and wet with blood.

"And here," she said, drawing up her sleeves to show

her arms all meshed with scars.

Elmskin drew his breath.

"Not all," Rowan cried, unbuttoning her dress and rolling it down to show the weals bitten into her back.

Elmskin touched them gently.

Rowan turned.

"You must stay with me here," she said, "to tend my wounds and bring me fuel for my fire. You may share my food. We can keep each other warm."

Elmskin nodded.

"True it is warmer here than wandering the woods in the wind and the snow."

"Then stay with me," she pleaded.

As Elmskin embraced her, he could feel her trembling until suddenly she moved away.

"But now you must go and find this dog," she said, "else it will come and kill us both."

Elmskin snatched up his hat and reluctantly stepped towards the door. But then he turned back.

"I will not find him in the wood. I must wait till night when he will come sniffing round the door again."

Rowan turned away as she buttoned up her dress.

"Do what you please," she said.

"I please to keep you warm!"

Elmskin reached towards her but she pushed him away.

"If you want to be warm," she said, "then go you back out into the wood and fetch more sticks for the fire."

With that she retreated behind the curtain which divided the hut, picked up another dog mask and set to sew in its eyes. Elmskin cursed and grumbled and shuffled out the door to spend his day chasing after sticks like he was a dog himself all out in the snow.

That night Rowan slept but Elmskin sat up and kept

watch, listening for the pad of feet outside. After a while he near dozed off, peering at the embers of the dying fire that glowed bright as the eyes in the shadowy masks that hung above him.

Then sudden, a slithering of feet, a snuffling, a whimpering. A low, dull howl. Elmskin sat up and gripped a stick and then flung wide the door.

There was the dog, a dark hulk against the white snow. Elmskin hurled himself at the creature but it ran off, snarling. Elmskin pursued it and dived at it again, wrestling its weight to the ground. Flurries of whiteness stung his eyes, filled his mouth, his nostrils as they fought, as the tussled, as they wrestled, rolling over and over in the moonlight.

The dog growled as Elmskin pinned him down. Then whimpered. The moaned. More alike to man than any dog. Elmskin looked. His face *was* man. His hands were man. His feet kicked hard as any man.

Elmskin gripped him.

"Who are you?" he snarled between gritted teeth.

"I am Lithran."

"Thought you were a dog."

"I can be dog."

"Did you bite Rowan?"

"Bit her, yes. But bit her as a dog. Would never bite her as a man. Would never harm her at all."

"But you bit her as a dog."

"Dogs don't bite like men. Don't always mean they want to hurt. Human-kind don't understand."

"Understand you bit her many times. I seen the scars."

"How you seen them?" Lithran growled suspiciously.

"She showed me. On her arms. On her legs. Drawn blood. That's doing harm."

"Not for dog. Dog would bite just to play. Just to stop

her running away."

"She'll run from you if'n you bite her."

"Like I said. Only bite to play. To run with her. To take her to the woods."

"So you turned to dog?" Elmskin snorted.

Lithran nodded.

"Dog can run down any fawn. She led me a chase, through the woods, over streams. But I know these woods well, better'n her. Caught her in the dark glade, her legs all shaking. That's when I bit her."

Elmskin frowned.

Lithran held up his hand.

"Not to hurt her," he said. "Just to stop her running. Wanted her to stay by me."

"Why would she stay if you bit her? Didn't want you as a man. Why would she want you as a dog?"

"Dog's different. Different in the forest. The lush green grass. The musk of summer sweat. Fawn would understand. Only a nip, it weren't no bite."

"If'n it weren't no bite, how come she got all the scars?" Pickapple responded.

"Fawn skin softer'n a girl's. Marks easy. But the marks are meant as a message. Not to hurt..."

Lithran shook his head.

"She didn't understand," he said.

"I don't understand," Elmskin replied.

"Want to be with her. Want to be close. Don't want her to run."

"She'll only run if she thinks you a dog," Elmskin explained. "Why don't you come to her like you are now? Why don't you come as a man?"

That night as Rowan slept again in her space behind the curtain, Elmskin gazed up at the smoky ceiling. Gazed at the mask eyes of the wolf, the fox, the dog.

"Mayhap if I can be dog too, then we can reason, Lithran and me."

He crouched and felt the dark wind howl through him. The room sucked and bellied, and the air was filled with a searing smell of putrid rot, of sickening sweetness, the swim of sweat, the clench of gall, the rolling of the moon.

Elmskin padded slowly, placing his feet with care as he stepped into the night outside the hut. The wind blew wild and he began to howl to chase it away. Howled to see if Rowan would wake. Howled to see if she would come out and drag him inside to stop his howling. Would bed him down beside the fire and rub his back and stroke his ears and keep him warm.

But the door burst open and Rowan flew out, her eyes ablaze. Not girlen no more but wild cat, feral, back arched and tail raised. Her claws flailed quick and sharp, ripping at Elmskin's flanks.

He cowered away.

"You have cut me," he said. "Now I am bleeding."

"You want to be dog," Rowan spat. "You run on all fours. You whine and you howl. Now you are bleeding. Now you know how it smarts, how the blood seeps red as fire!"

"But I am not no dog, you know that," Elmskin objected. "Let us go inside. It's cold out here."

But Rowan stood her ground, tail still bristling, blocking the door.

"I am not Lithran who you fear as dog," Elmskin continued. "And he is no dog neither, but a man true. You know this. Let him come to you."

"I do not want to see him," Rowan spat.

"Let him come at night," Elmskin pleaded. "You will not see so much in the shadows. He will not come as dog to bite but as man to be tender. And you must be woman true, not fawn or cat as I see you now."

"I cannot wait," Rowan hissed. "Every night I sit, hoping that he will come. Be he dog or man I do not care. I only want to feel his warmth."

"He will bite you," Elmskin reminded her. "He will take your skin between his teeth. Drops of blood will spill to the ground like berries from a tree."

Rowan smiled.

"He only teases. That's what you told me. Remember?"

As she stepped back into the hut, Elmskin followed her and watched as she gazed to the masks on the ceiling, their red eyes burning as she yowled and wrestled and rolled, till she was girlen again, pulling a shawl around her shoulders and touching her wounded foot.

"I cannot wait," she said again. "Come, let us go and look."

The field was crisp with new fallen snow, but they scarce felt the cold as they trudged together towards the wood.

"We'll find him here," Rowan whispered. "I know where he comes."

They pitched into the sudden darkness and picked their way towards the pond. The moonlight flickered on the water where the thin skim of ice was broken. Then Lithran pointed. There on the surface a shadow floated.

It was the dog.

Elmskin gasped.

Rowan grasped his hand.

"He's gone," she said.

Elmskin watched as just for a moment the dog's face turned to Lithran as man. Then the moon slipped behind the clouds.

"What can I do?" Rowan cried.

"Hush," said Elmskin. "I can stay with you. I can still keep you warm."

Rowan looked down and shook her head.

"He was the only one who could ever bring me warmth."

"But you were frightened of him."

"Not frightened at all. I am not cat nor fawn nor girl. Look to me and you will see."

Elmskin turned.

Rowan had gone.

In her place was a trail of leaves that lead like footprints back towards the pond. The water was still and empty. Then by the light of the moon, Elmskin found a crouching tree, its branches hung with berries glowing bright as drops of blood.

THE MELPHEN CHILD

On winter nights they saw her, wandering the lanes and out across the moor. They called her the Melphen Child, like wisps of snow she was, entwined with ice, breathing mist upon her poor numb fingers.

Her footprints skittered across the frost like a bird or a clutch of broken twigs. Some nights no-one saw her at all but they heard her singing in a muted voice as she came knocking at their windows, crying "Let me in, I'm a-freezing. Let me in."

But they turned their faces to the fire and tugged their shawls about their shoulders and muttered to each other, "Hush, it is only the wind."

And the Melphen child would slip away to sleep in their stables and dung-yards, pulling thin straw about her to bring some warmth through the long dark night, before creeping off at dawn.

Late one evening, Lallenday rose from her hearth and shuffled out into the yard. There she found the tell-tale footprints leading up to the door of her out-house. She prodded it open and there lay the Melphen child, her eyes all a-blinking, straw clinging to her shivering shoulders.

"How long have you been here?" Lallenday asked, but Melphen's teeth could only rattle and her lips were pinched numb with cold.

"Come inside," Lallenday bade her and reached out a hand towards the girl.

The Melphen's fingers felt cold as death might be, but

she rose and followed back across the yard and in through the door of the squat grey house. Here a fire was lit and bread and porridge pudding laid out on the table.

"Sit you down by the hearth and bring the blood back to your bones," Lallenday urged.

Melphen smiled gratefully and stretched out her fingers towards the flames. She drank a cup of warm milk that Lallenday pressed into her hands and after a while her limbs stopped their shaking, though her face was still pale as the snow from where she came.

Next morning Lallenday woke to find the Melphen child had risen and was rattling at the latch on the door. Soon as Lallenday opened it the girlen ran all a-flutter across the yard, her hands outstretched to catch the falling snow.

"Stop!" called Lallenday as she reached the out-house.

Melphen paused, looking round, her eyes darting this way and that, startled as a sparrow.

"Stop," said Lallenday again, catching her breath as she reached the child.

All around was frozen still, icicles dangling from the dark guttering, snow slithering down from the roof.

"You may stay," said Lallenday warmly.

Melphen looked away.

"You may stay and help me. I will give you shelter."

She opened the out-house door. In the shadows lay a stack of rough timber and fallen branches. Lallenday picked up a small axe.

"Here - you can chop for me while I cook more porridge. Then we will have logs for the fire to keep us warm."

Melphen chopped. She chopped until her hands were so warm she felt so they would melt. But then the axe grew heavy and her arms grew heavy and her head grew heavy too and she felt so she wanted to sleep. But each time she sat down to rest herself a-top the pile of wood she heard Lallenday's voice call across the yard, soft and sweet:

"I do not hear you chopping. Are you alright? Keep on chopping the wood for me or we will have no logs for the fire and then there will be nothing to eat."

So Melphen knew she must continue and swung the axe again and watched the spiders as they scuttled away and the beetles who scurried from the wood chippings. She began to dream of bowls of soup and plates of stew and scoops of bread till she grew quite faint and sat down again, but then she heard Lallenday's voice once more.

Her fingers shook as she seized up the axe, thinking she would be bidden to work again. But this time Lallenday's voice came, sweet and pleasant as before:

"Come you in. You have chopped enough. You must be getting cold."

Melphen dropped the axe in the corner of the out-house and scurried quick as she could across the yard. Lallenday was waiting to greet her at the doorway of the kitchen. Melphen dashed inside, her eyes darting all about, hoping at least for a pot of gruel. But the stove was not even lit and instead Lallenday handed her a broom.

"Go you now," she said, "and brush down all the stairs."

The Melphen Child sighed and seized up the broom and climbed to the top of the house. Then she clunked her way slowly down, raising clouds of dust all around while Lallenday sat and watched with a smile upon her face and a twinkle in her eye.

"You work so well," she said at last, "that I have more for you, for I see you like it and it keeps you warm. Why, the colour is almost come back to your face."

All day Melphen dusted wainscots, polished candlesticks and scrubbed cold stone floors. All day she listened, hoping she might hear the sound of pans bubbling in the kitchen, the aroma of herbs and maybe a shank of salted pork. But all she heard was Lallenday singing and Melphen was so hungry she forced herself to join in for fear that otherwise she might faint away.

"I hear you are happy in you work," Lallenday broke in. "You have a fine voice and you hold a good tune. Come sing with me in the kitchen."

Melphen threw down her broom and rushed straight way to the kitchen, hoping Lallenday might at last be preparing food. She stopped in the doorway. Sure enough a meagre scrag of mutton and a clutch of vegetables were set out on the table ready to be cooked, but nothing had been started.

Lallenday smiled.

"Come child. Sing to me more. Sing to me while you make ready the supper."

Melphen sang.

"Louder, child. Louder. I can hardly hear you. There - pick up that knife as you sing and chop the meat and mix the stew."

The Melphen child seized up the knife in her hand. She gripped it tightly, hunger knotted in her belly. A thin wind blew outside. Pale light glinted on the blade as she brought it down.

"Sing, child, sing. I do not hear you!"

So she sang as she chopped as she sang, the rhythm of the knife slashing through the bone. She tossed the screws of flesh into the pan and followed them with a fistful of tatties. Then she boiled the water and she sang. She stirred the pot and she sang. She went to the cupboard and fetched out the one bowl that waited there. And she sang. And one tarnished spoon to sit in that bowl. And she sang.

Then when it was cooked all through, she poured out the stew and watched as Lallenday drank every drop, scraping her spoon around the side of the bowl till all of it was gone. And the Melphen child sang, and she sang, till she could sing no more.

Lallenday sat and looked at her.

"Why, child you are tired. You must be cold. I will find more work for you to do."

And so this went on, dawn to dusk and dawn to dusk again. The Melphen child polished the plates and the pans till she could see her pale face staring back at her, but ne'ery a scrap did she eat from them. She chased the chickens about yard and collected up their eggs, but Lallenday saved them all for herself. She washed all Lallenday's shawls and wraps till her hands were red raw, but never once was offered to wear one herself.

"The work will keep you warm," Lallenday told her, all the while smiling and singing.

And Melphen smiled with her and Melphen sang but beneath her thin garments her bones were hungered and cold.

Every evening Lallenday would climb a set of steps to an attic room and there she would sit with a pillow stuffed with straw propped up on stool. Across the cushion was a spread of lace with the threads all dangling down. At the end of each thread hung a bobbin so white it seemed as though it must be carved from ice. And Lallenday's hands moved quicker than a bird, shuttling the bobbins back and forth so that the threads meshed and twisted and the lace grew longer and fuller each night.

The Melphen child scarcely saw this, for Lallenday quickly closed the door, but she would pause outside to listen to the clatter of the bobbins before returning to sweeping the floor. Then she crept down the stairs to try the latch but the door was always firmly locked. Her nimble fingers picked at the catches on the window frames, but again they would not budge. She even wondered if she had grown so thin that she might slide like a shadow under the door.

Some nights she could peck at the crusts and the crumbs that Lallenday had left, before sluicing the plates in a bucket of cold water. She wept as she watched the moon ride by through the frosted window, but from upstairs in the attic room she only heard Lallenday's singing and the rattle of the bobbins light as hollow bones. Then the click of the door as Lallenday closed it and Melphen heard her feet on the stairs.

"There, my child," she would say, ruffling Melphen's hair. "The work has warmed you. Now it is time for bed."

But Melphen could scarcely sleep. All night she lay on the cold kitchen floor and listened to the howling wind and the wrack of the snow till dawn came to claw at the window again.

One evening Lallenday touched Melphen on the shoulder, still smiling broadly as ever.

"Come child, let me show you."

She took her hand and led her up the steps to the attic. Melphen gasped as she gazed around. The room was filled with billowing lace, stiffened white by the frost. In the corner hung a shimmering dress.

"It will make me young again!" Lallenday declared, running her fingers down the sleeves.

Melphen stared at her curiously.

"Don't doubt me. Here, I will show you."

Lallenday lifted the dress from its stand and slipped it over her shoulders, flouncing out the folds. She paused for a moment, then turned slowly and finally pirouetted. As she came to a stop, she thought she saw Melphen's lips move, as if she was mouthing out words.

"Speak up," she said, "I cannot hear you."

"No," Melphen muttered at last. "You look like an old woman in a lace dress."

Lallenday's face darkened. The smile had gone.

"So that is what you think, you ungrateful child, after all that I have done for you."

Before Melphen could move, Lallenday grabbed her by the hair and locked her in another room, scarce bigger than a cupboard.

"There you will stay till you *are* grateful. Will be no work to warm you. Only your loneliness for company."

Melphen stood on tiptoe and stared out of the window. She watched the stars so pinprick bright burning through the darkness. She watched the dawn creep up, swathed in a blanket of snow. She watched fingers of ice form on the guttering so close that she could reach out and touch them if only she could open the window. But the window was locked tight as all the others and Melphen could only shiver and shake with silent sobbing, while in the room next door, on and on, she heard the rattle of the bobbins. She pondered what Lallenday could be making now, then turned back to stare at the frozen fields where she used to roam.

Nights went by, then the bobbins fell silent and Melphen fancied that Lallenday must be sewing, for she heard the rustling of lace. And then she started to sing again, her voice clear and pure as the frosted sky.

Melphen joined in, her voice rising to meet with Lallenday's and they twisted in harmony like as if they were sisters, though both were shut in separate rooms.

Then one day, when Melphen was near sleeping on the hard wooden floor, she heard a key turn in the lock and then Lallenday's voice.

"Come see, child," she said, "what I have made for you."

Melphen shuffled slowly through to the other room, then stood back and looked. There in the corner hung a dress of lace, same as the other Lallenday had made before, only smaller.

"It will fit you," Lallenday smiled. "Try it on."

Melphen reached out and slowly lifted the dress. It was cold to touch, as if every stitch was frozen. She slipped it over her shoulders and stood, sullen faced, while Lallenday gazed at her.

"Now you look as I did when I was young," she declared.

But as she watched, the Melphen Child's face grew frail till she looked old and then grew older still. Her cheeks pale as snow, her fingers fragile as ice. Lallenday stepped close and threw her arms about her, but as she did, Melphen slowly melted away, till all that was left was the dress of lace, lying on the floor.

Lallenday picked it up and held it to her as she skipped and pirouetted and then drew it close about her body, slender as a child now while the cold room filled with the warmth of her rippling laughter.

Three Apples

Pickapple placed three apples on the table.

"One of these is mouldy inside," he said. "One of them is sour and one of them is sweet."

"They all look the same to me," said Mullops. "How can you tell?"

"You can only tell when you eat'em."

"You ain't ate any of these. None of them's bitten. How do you know?"

"I been gathering apples for years," said Pickapple. "Only have to look. Only have to shake'em. See if the pips rattle."

"You said you had to taste'em."

"No - you have to taste'em. I have to shake'em."

"So which is the sweet one?"

"I ain't telling you. You have to taste one and find out."

Mullops looked at the apples again. He scratched his head.

"They all look the same."

"Look the same to you, but not to me. Bite one and see."

Mullops bit an apple and screwed up his face.

"This un's the sour one," he said.

"Got that right," said Pickapple.

"So one of these is mouldy and one of these is sweet."

Pickapple nodded.

"Need a sweet one to take that sour taste away," Mullops said.

He took up another and bit it.

"Pah!"

He spat it out.

"This un's as sour as the first. Taint mouldy though and taint sweet. That's two sour apples you got there. Give me the last one. Must be sweet, don't look mouldy at all."

Mullops took a great bite and spat it straight out.

"This un's the sourest of the lot! Pickapple - you tricked me. Weren't no sweet one at all. Wait till I get you..."

But Pickapple was gone, way down the track, too far for Mullops to catch as he flung the half-bitten apple after him.

THE HANGED MAN

Now Elmskin came to the place where the four winds meet. A hard ground strewn with jagged rocks where nothing grew and no birds sang. From the shadows of a thorn bush stepped a tall haggard man. Elmskin turned but there was nowhere to hide. The man strode towards him, his eyes blazing wild. They faced each other but neither spoke. As the dust whipped into Elmskin's eyes the tall man stretched out a hand.

"You have come to find me," his voice rasped harshly.

Elmskin shook his head.

"I don't know who you are."

The man's gaze was piercing.

"Then know this!" he snarled, ripping aside the blood-red scarf which swathed his neck.

Elmskin peered at the scars, like as if a rope had been knotted there.

"Who are you?" he asked.

"I am Gloathren. I am the Hanged Man," came the reply. "I was hanged for taking the breath from the wind, the laughter from the stream, the blossom from the bushes, the wit from the vixen as she crossed the field. Any deed that happened, it was me that stood the blame. They hung me once, they hung me twice. They hung me a third time and then they let me go.

"Now I can do anything I choose. They can never hang me. I can steal a sheep. I can drown a child. But now that I've been hanged, I don't want to do any of these. I want to help the sick and the lame. I want to help wifen and little childern. But they run away. They say I scare them. Look into my eyes."

Gloathren stared at Elmskin.

"Do I scare you?"

"N-no," Elmskin faltered, glancing this way and that.

Gloathren grabbed him by the throat, gripping tighter, squeezing till Elmskin staggered, gasping for breath. Then he let go as dark rooks circled in the smoke grey sky, their voices loud in Elmskin's ears. But then every hue of every colour on the distant hillside seemed to grow brighter and the howling wind dropped to a gentle breeze.

"There - that's how it feels," Gloathren grunted. "Now you feel like I feel. Near throttled, but you can breathe again. Breathe the clean fresh air. Listen to the birds. Smell the soft sweet rain. Don't that make you feel good?"

"Y-yes," Elmskin agreed, his knees so weak he nearly toppled.

Gloathren clapped an arm about his shoulders and tugged a noose from the depths of the pocket of his greatcoat.

"Carry it with me all the time, to remind me," he whispered as he pulled back his collar to show the scars again.

"I was born this way. My mother near strangled me. Come out backwards with the cord wrapped round my neck."

Elmskin stared at him, trying to catch his breath.

"Hanged at birth! That's me. Born for the gallows tree. But I escaped and escaped again. I'll escape again now. Look and see."

He flung the noose about a branch and hauled himself up. Then he dropped. Elmskin watched as he dangled there, his eyes bulging, his lips turning blue. Then he slipped from the rope and sprang to the ground..

"Want to try for yourself?" he demanded and handed Elmskin the noose. Elmskin ran the rope through his hands. Could feel it coarse and rough. Looked up at the bough of the tree. Then he shook his head.

"Not today," he said.

"Not today, but maybe tomorrow..." Gloathren muttered as he thrust the noose back inside his coat.

"Let me walk with you a while," he continued. "That way the rope is always with you. You never know when you may need it... or the rope may need *you*..."

Elmskin and Gloathren travelled on until they came to the bank of a deep dark river, then followed a path down to the edge of the water. Elmskin clutched the rail of a rickety bridge and they swayed back and forth above the swirling current then leapt into the mud on the other side.

Elmskin plunged on into the darkness of the woods till sudden he stumbled into a clearing where a woman sat beside a pool, her long knotted hair tumbling over her shoulders and down to her waist. As she heard them approaching, she turned.

"Who is there?"

She stared at them. She had a slit in the middle of her forehead like as if someone had cut it with a knife. Through the slit there shone a gleam.

"She has three eyes!" Elmskin exclaimed.

Gloathren stared hard at the woman's upturned face.

"She has three eyes, true as true, but each one is white as the moon. All of them are blind."

The woman smiled.

"I am Tormentil. I am blind but I can still see you. I can tell who you are, where you have come from and where you will go. Step closer."

She held out both her hands.

Elmskin took one. It was pale and cold.

"Come," Tormentil beckoned. "There are two of you."

She reached out towards Gloathren. As his hand found hers, she shivered.

"What are you?" she said. "What do you do? I know that you are there, yet not there at all.

"This one I cannot reckon," she muttered as she released Gloathren's hand. "His hand is colder than mine. It is as if he has been dead for year upon year. And yet he is here. I can taste his breath. I can sense his huge hulk as he blocks out the sun."

Before she could stop him, Gloathren seized her hand and thrust into it the length of rope he always carried. Tormentil looked anxious, shaking her head, her blank eyes staring this way and that. She drew it nervously through her fingers, fretting at the knot and the twine.

"Tis a noose," she said at last.

"Tis a noose, true as true," Gloathren nodded. "Now tell me what it tells you."

"Can see your mother," Tormentil sighed. "Can see her clear, cleaning a home for you, making your meals. Can see her watch you grow, out in the fields. Can see her face as they led you away. Can see her watching as you stood at the gallows..."

"Can you see how she birthed me?" Gloathren demanded.

Tormentil shuddered.

"Can hear her screaming, the blood and the tears."

"That was her. What of me?"

"Can hear you gasping to take your first breath. You had the chord wrapped around your neck. Can feel how they shook you, blew the air into your lungs. They said you wouldn't live, but you did. But from that day on, nothing you could do was right. Everything was topsy-turvy, everything you touched would break. Your mother's brewing jug, her tallest vase. But she loved you all the same. You were her only son – and even as a child you would hang from the bough of a tree gazing up at the stars."

Gloathren sat quietly. Tormentil let the rope play through her hands, then paused before she spoke again.

"Your mother's mother was named Skemdyke. She lived in a cottage all nestled in the moss. Its roof was bent and broken, laced with ivy all about. The walls were dark and cold and running so with water it was like a stream flowed through. And in the walls could hear a tiny linnet, fluttering and calling.

"When your mother was a child, only a tiny girlen, if ever she did any misdeed, why then Skemdyke would make her climb inside a box and fetch down a great key from the shelf. But before she locked it she would take out the linnet which lived in the walls and place it in the box alongside her. And then she would close the lid on them both and lock it with the key.

"And the linnet would flap and flutter all around your mother and there would be a crying and a wailing and a tearing out of feathers and a raking of the flesh of your mother's arms.

"When old Skemdyke died, your mother never went back to the cottage, but she left the linnet all locked in the box along with Skemdyke's cruelty. But the cruelty followed her anyway and forced her to beat you for your clumsiness and your wanderings. Then she left you to the mallen-crones, the lollards and the toss-pots, the dung-swills and the scald-wives so that you could be hanged.

"Mayhap she reckoned that when you were gone, the

linnet in the box would cease its calling, its beating and its fluttering that she heard every night in her dreams. But I know it is there still. One day you must go back, open the box and set it free."

"Linnet will be dead," Elmskin said.

Gloathren shook his head.

"It's like me. It cannot die. It lives on in the darkness. When I set it free, then it can die. Then mayhap, I can die too."

Elmskin leaned forward.

"You have to help Gloathren," he whispered to Tormentil. "You have to help him find old Skemdyke's cottage so he can set this bird free."

"Can only help you if you help me," she said, turning about and about.

"How can we help you?" Elmskin asked.

"I need a knife."

"What do you need a knife for?"

"Need a knife to help me see more. Need a knife to cut a new eye. This one here is near worn out."

She pointed to the slit in her forehead.

"Need to cut a new eye, maybe here..."

She raised the palms of her hands.

"Or here."

She gestured towards her belly.

Elmskin raised his eyebrows, but Gloathren shrugged and drew a knife from his belt.

"We all have scars," he muttered as he pressed the handle into Tormentil's palm.

She twisted it about, feeling the shaft, touching the blade. Then she let out a cry, jerking her head backwards and forwards before tossing the knife away.

"This knife cannot help me. It is stained all with blood. This knife has done unspeakable things!"

Elmskin cast a glance at Gloathren, but he just shrugged, bent down and retrieved the blade from where it had stuck in the turf. He wiped it on the back of his sleeve and placed it in his belt.

"You must go," hissed Tormentil.

"Tell us where," Elmskin pleaded.

"You must go to the cottage I told you of, the cottage covered all about with ivy. You must cross the river again and take the road towards the mountains..."

Elmskin and Gloathren hurried away, glancing round to see Tormentil sitting where they had found her, her face turned up towards the sky. It was growing dark now as they blundered on through a maze of twisted trees. Their boots were sodden with the brackish water which oozed between the roots. Elmskin's teeth were chattering as they plunged on through the mire. Then they broke out through the bushes, nearly stumbling into the water as they found themselves at the edge of the river. A grey goose clattered its outstretched wings and swooped into the air.

"This way!" said Elmskin suddenly as he caught sight of the bridge.

As they swung their way back across the cradle of planks a scrabble of starlings shot up from the treetops and a chorus of crows croaked in complaint.

"I will walk at night," said Gloathren as he strode away into the darkness, the noose still about his neck. "That way I can't hear no birds singing, for their voices are filled with all the sorrow my mother's mother ever brought me."

Elmskin pushed open a rotted oaken door. They had come to this place, just as Tormentil had told them - a cottage deep in a coppice all nestled in the moss and tangled over with ivy. Gloathren stood beside him and gazed into the gloom. In the middle of the floor stood an open chest. They approached it slowly and stared inside, but they could see nothing more than cobwebs and darkness.

In the wall a stone was missing. Gloathren peered into the cavity, and sniffed at the musky smell, the scuttle of spiders and hard-backed beetles. He thrust in his arm, scrabbling around, dragging out fistfuls of dust, a clutch of withered roots, a bent coin and a rusted nail.

"What are you looking for?" Elmskin asked.

"The linnet, it is gone," Gloathren replied. "At last it is over. Now I can die... "

"How will you die?" Elmskin asked.

Gloathren looked at him darkly.

"You will have to kill me," he said at last.

"Ain't never killed no-one," Elmskin recoiled. "Wouldn't know how."

"If you won't kill me," Gloathren growled, "then I will kill you."

Elmskin made to scramble back out through the door, but Gloathren grabbed him quick by the wrist and pulled him to sit beside him.

"I will kill you right now where you sit..."

Elmskin sat quiet on the bench and closed his eyes. He felt the world a-spinning, heard waterfalls and Rimmony's voice calling. Heard the sound of a linnet song. Felt Gloathren's hands around his neck.

Elmskin began to shake.

He could smell Gloathren's breath up close, a reek of onion and rotted meat. Sweat began to glisten on his brow. And then Gloathren let go.

Elmskin opened his eyes.

Squinted at the big man sitting beside him. Saw his

hands were trembling. Saw a tear in his eyes.

"Ain't no-one going to die." Gloathren's voice was a low hoarse whisper. "Ain't no-one going to die..."

A Wondrous Shell

Pickapple cradled a shell in his hands and stared at the loops and whorls which wound it around and around.

"What's that you have there?" asked Mullops, coming up behind him.

"Why," cried Pickapple, "tis the most wonderful shell in the world."

"Why so wonderful?" Mullops grunted. "Tis just an old snail shell you found on the path."

"Tis nary a snail shell," Pickapple declared. "Tis a shell which holds a tiny bird."

"How can a shell so small hold a bird with her wings and her feathers?" Mullops demanded.

"It is because the bird is small. Smallest bird you ever known."

Mullops shook his head in disbelief.

"Let me see," he said, reaching out for the shell.

Pickapple handed it to him gently.

"Be careful," he said, "or you will disturb the bird."

Mullops peered inside.

"I can't see no bird," he complained. "Can't see nothing at all."

"I told you the bird was small," Pickapple explained. "She's so small that no-one can see her."

"If no-one can see her, then how d'you know she's there?"

"Why, I know she's there because I can hear her sing."

"What song would come from a bird so tiny?"

"Listen," said Pickapple.

He took back the shell from Mullops and held it to his ear. A smile spread across his face.

"She is singing now - I can hear her. It's the most beautiful sound in the world. So tiny and so sweet, like a drop of rain falling in a meadow."

"Let me hear," Mullops begged.

Pickapple handed him the shell and Mullops held it to his ear. He screwed up his face and turned this way and that.

"Can't hear nothing at all..."

"That's because the song is as tiny as the bird. Have to be a clever man to hear it. Those that's not clever can't hear it at all."

Mullops tipped his head to one side and listened again.

"Well, now I can hear it as clear as day! Sounds like rainbows brushing your face."

"What did I tell you?" Pickapple grinned as he capered back and forth. "Told you was the most wonderful shell in the world!"

He twirled around and watched as Mullops peered inside the shell again, muttering -

"I can see her now, tucked away in the shadows, tiny as you like and so beautiful too!"

Pickapple stopped his frolicking and suddenly looked serious.

"What will you give me for this wondrous shell?"

"But Pickapple, I'm sure you want to keep it for yourself."

"No, no - you like it so much you should have it. Just tell me what you will give."

Mullops hesitated, searching through his pockets.

"Ain't got much," he said. "All I got's this old key. Don't even know what it opens no more."

"That's perfect!" cried Pickapple. "Give me the key."

Mullops thrust the key into his hand and hurried away, the shell still clutched to his ear.

Around the corner of the track, Pickapple met with Littleberry.

"Oh, Pickapple - whatever's the matter?" she asked. "Let me wipe those tears from your eyes..."

"I lost my wondrous shell," Pickapple sobbed, "the one with the tiny bird who lives inside and sings to me all the day long."

Littleberry shook her head.

"But Pickapple," she said, "thought that was only an old snail's shell you used to trick everyone."

"Well, now the trick is on me," said Pickapple ruefully. "All I got's this old key."

"Pickapple..." said Littleberry playfully, "now you have this key - who knows what lock it will turn?"

But Pickapple still looked sad.

"It is old - it is rusted. Won't fit any lock that I know. Whatever can I do?" he wailed.

Littleberry put an arm around him.

"Oh Pickapple, don't take on so," she said and kissed him quick upon the cheek.

With that Pickapple leapt up and pranced all around her, waving the key in the air before capering away.

"Oh Pickapple, where are you going now?" Littleberry called.

"This key is the most marvellous key in the world," Pickapple replied. "It has unlocked the door to your kisses... and now I go to see how many more doors it will open!"

THE POND OF SORROWS

Old Tarragon clutched a kettle in her apron as she scuttled through the forest, through the darkness of the night. Shadows shivered and their gnarled roots clawed and gripped, but the old woman skittered on between fox hole and badger set. Then a cold hand gripped her shoulder. Tarragon spun around, dropping the kettle as she stared up at a tall gaunt-faced man. Before she could move, he bent and picked up the kettle.

"Who are you?" she gasped, her eyes darting this way and that.

The tall man placed a finger to his lips.

"I am Mardyke," he replied, his voice a rasping whisper. "I sweep the leaves, I snare the birds."

He dangled the kettle before Tarragon's eyes.

"What have you here?" he asked.

"Tis a kettle," she stammered. "No but a leaky old kettle that's brought me nothing but trouble this year past."

"Could be fixed," Mardyke mused. "Could stop the holes. Could still boil water..."

Tarragon shook her head.

"It's not the brewing as bothers me. It's the trouble that it brings."

Mardyke leaned closer to listen. His coat was matted with dirt and feathers, his boots were riddled with holes.

"Tis a curse on me, this kettle," she wailed. "Tis a curse. Each time I boil a brew of nettle tea, why the smell of it makes it seem so my husband's standing there. He used to pick me the nettles with his own bare hands, but I put him in the ground a long year ago and no tea ain't never tasted right again. And now this kettle leaks half the water out afore it's even boiled. It's going in the pond - I tell you now!"

Mardyke raised one eyebrow.

"What pond is this?" he asked.

"Tis Raglin's pond, deep in the woods. No-one can see it till darkness falls, but when it does, then you can go there to cast away the sorrows that cling to whatever vexes you. Come the morning, pond is gone and all your sadness too. I've been down there many a time. Took a broken pot that was cursed by that lad Lurpin, came troubling me for money. But then I pitched the pot in the water and he didn't come back no more."

"Best you have this then," said Mardyke, handing back the kettle.

Tarragon clutched it to her belly and walked on. As Mardyke followed he dragged behind him a broom and a length of netting.

"Tell me of yourself," she said.

"I built my dwelling down by the brook," Mardyke replied. "Built it of branches and stones and a weave of moss and clay. When I wake I set snares for the rabbits and sweep up the leaves from all around to light me a fire. And then I set out to trap birds..."

They trudged on through a mire of mulch and mud till they came at last to a pond. A pale light shimmered across the water cast from a basket that a tall girl cradled, like as if she held the moon. But not the moon but an old tarnished lantern which she raised above her head to see who came shambling out of the shadows.

"Tarragon," she greeted the old woman.

"Raglin. What has been pitched in the water this

night?"

Raglin swung the lantern to show that drifting in the pond was a twisted, tarnished candlestick caked in blackened wax, a straw doll with one shrivelled eye staring blindly at the sky, a blunted sickle stuck with tufts of downy hair and a fiddle lacking all its strings moaning a tuneless melody in the thin grey wind. Tarragon pitched her kettle into the water, muttered a few words and then scurried away. Mardyke stepped forward then, out of the shadows. Raglin swung her lantern, the better to see his face.

"Who are you?" she challenged. "Have you brought a sorrow to cast into the pond?"

Mardyke said nothing as he regarded the cluster of trinkets that Raglin had gathered about her at the edge of the water.

"What happens to them?" he said at last. "What do you do with them all?"

"You will only see them till dawn," Raglin explained. "And then they will gone - and all the sorrows that cling to them, vanished away with the pond."

"Don't you keep any?" Mardyke asked her.

Raglin shook her head.

"They are worthless to me," she sighed. "Some nights I look at what's in the pond and I wish for a necklace such as my father will never let me wear, for he locks me away in the tower of the windmill that sits high on the hill where he has lived since the night my mother died. Now he is sick, but I cannot help him. I will not help him, for he has never helped me. All I wait for is a necklace to set about my throat, but no-one has brought one yet."

Mardyke sniffed and turned away from her, then gazed again at the trawl of baubles glinting at her feet.

"I could use them for snaring up of birds," he said.

Raglin looked at him askance.

"Until dawn you may take from the pond whatever you want. Take what you like, it is worthless to me - all bits of broken playthings and tarnished old mirrors, no necklaces at all. Just tell me, what will you do with them? How use these pretties for trapping birds?"

"I would not keep them as they are," Mardyke muttered, "for they are foolish things. But I can pick them all apart and anything that shines I hang them from the trees by the dwelling where I live. And there the jackdaws come to peck at them while I wait still and quiet. When they are all gathered then I throw a net about them. A jackdaw's flesh is sweet and its feathers dark and fine. I pluck them out to make my bed so I may sleep in a pitch-black night till I wake again each dawn."

"But what of their beaks, their claws, their eyes?"

"I bind them into garlands for any girlen passing by, for anyone who wears one will dream that they can fly. And as they fly they will see their life as it might be - their lummen-boys all waiting in the sky."

Mardyke paused and gazed into the pond, then spat into the water thoughtfully.

"Hold your lantern higher," he urged, plunging his hands through the slime on the surface to dredge up a fistful of dark dripping moss from the depths beneath.

Raglin watched as he scooped it into a bottle which he pulled from his pocket.

"What will you do with that?" she asked, her red hair hanging loose across her pale face, hiding the leaves that were tattooed on her cheeks like as if they were tears. But Mardyke said nothing as he buttoned up his coat.

"Soon it will be morning," Raglin warned him, "then the pond will be gone and I go then too."

"Where d'you go?" Mardyke asked abruptly.

"At dawn a pale bird comes," Raglin whispered, "and wakes inside my head. It stretches its wings and raises them till they beat inside my skull. Its beak pecks and harries behind my eyes as it turns and turns again, birthing through my mouth into a scream. And the scream spills out, piercing and raw till is not a scream no more..."

"What is it then?" Mardyke grunted, his hands still puddling in the thick ooze of the pond.

"It is my own self born again in the shape of a boy. All day I walk the lanes, gathering sticks to make me a shelter, gathering twigs to light a fire, pulling tatties from the fields to bake and feed my belly. Till night comes, then I am as you know me, as you see me now - the tall girl who holds the moon in a basket beside this pond's dark water."

Mardyke shrugged.

"As you please. I have what I came for. Mayhap you will find the necklace you wish for deep down in the water. It is nearly dawn now."

As he walked away, Raglin doubled over, clutching the sides of her head, her body racked in a silent scream.

In the dark wind, silence sang sullen as sorrow. Only the sound of Mardyke's boots trudging through the mulch of leaves and the drip of grey water from the overhanging trees.

Then a clatter of wings through the branches. Mardyke raised his arms to shield his face as a pale bird flew blind, near striking him. And he grabbed it, held it in his heavy hands. Could feel raw blood beating in its chest. Could feel breath caught in its craw. And then he squeezed. And then he twisted. And then a flurry of feathers fluttered to the floor. From deep in the wood where he had seen the pond, Mardyke heard a cry. But then he walked away, on through the mists of the morning till he reached the cold damp welcome of his dwelling.

Outside were lines hung with starlings and blackbirds, their wings hanging limp, their claws dangling down. All about were swept mounds of rotting leaves, their slow mulch oozing into the ground.

Inside he snapped the white bird's wings with a crack. Stripped the feathers from the breast then sliced with the flickering flash of a knife and stuck the flesh in a pot. Covered it over with a murk of water and a fistful of herbs. Then he reached for the bottle inside his coat and tipped in a drizzle of the rank slimy moss. He watched as it boiled all together, a brew of dark blood and the pond's bile of brackish sorrows.

He sat a while, drinking nettle tea, then he poured the broth into an old tin jug and set off down a rutted lane to where the windmill sat high on a hill, just as Raglin had told him. Crows and jackdaws swooped about its ragged sails and the roof was a patchwork of broken slates with a flurry of weeds sprouting in between.

As Mardyke knocked, the door opened and there stood Raglin's father, tall and haggard, tattooed all about with leaves. He peered at Mardyke with eyes of cloudy grey that had seen the rising and setting of more suns than he could ever number or forget.

"What do you want?" he asked.

"Brought something for you," Mardyke replied, holding out the jug of broth.

Raglin's father eyed it suspiciously.

"Heard you been sick," Mardyke said. "Heard you might be missing your vittles."

"Who told you this?"

"Plenty tell me plenty down in the forest."

Raglin's father took the jug and shuffled back inside, perching himself on the edge of his narrow bed.

"Drink it all," Mardyke urged him, then closed the door.

Raglin's father watched as Mardyke walked slowly down the hill, away from the windmill's lengthening shadow, like he was an ant crawling off to vanish into the darkness of the forest.

The setting sun shone through the slatted window so the linen all glowed red and Raglin's father sat up then and watched in his bed till a wind blew in across the fields and turned the mill sails round and he stretched his arms to welcome the creaking sound. And then the leaves tattooed on his body faded and fell to the ground and he sprang from the bed not an old man no more but a boy still lithe and young. Same boy as ever Raglin became when she walked the lanes by day.

He looked around, hungered by the change as the sap flowed through his veins. He cast his eyes about till they lighted on the jug which Mardyke had left standing on the table.

He grabbed it up, his fingers trembling as he supped on the dark rich brew, his nostrils twitching to an aroma he had never smelt before. Pigeons rattled through the windows high up in the tower, showering their droppings down into the darkness as the sails groaned around. The broth tasted bitter, like as if it was filled with rancid dreams which twisted and snarled inside his head as he drifted slowly back into sleep. As he slumped back on the bed, his eyes staring empty into the glowering sky, the jug slipped from his grasp and fell to the floor where a jackdaw hopped down, pecked at the spillage and flew swiftly away, beating its wings and shrieking a warning.

That night Mardyke came to the pond to find it all in darkness. No light was cast by the moon and none from the lantern inside the basket as Raglin lay still and pale amongst the broken reeds. Mardyke looked about. The pond was empty. No-one had yet cast their sorrows into the water, though through the trees he heard a muttering and a shuffling as if there were those who waited there for the light to be lit.

And so Mardyke lit the lamp and hung it inside the basket. He swept a pile of leaves all around Raglin's body and covered her over. He took the shawl that she had been wearing and pulled it over his shoulders and wrapped it about his face. He sat and watched the water, till one by one the shadows crept out of the trees and one by one cast their sorrows into the depths of the pond.

Mardyke licked his lips and opened up a sack into which he scooped the trinkets, a bracelet and a neck stud, a casket and a ring, the silver and the gold. And then there came one girlen dressed all in grey who pitched away a necklace such as Raglin had always dreamed of. Soon as the girl was gone, Mardyke fished it slowly out of the water, out of the dark green slime, and placed it on top of the fading pile of leaves under which Raglin lay.

As dawn approached, he scraped back the leaves to reveal not the tall girl but a young boy with his eyes all closed. Then as Mardyke raked away the last of the leaves, the boy shrivelled down to an old man and the leaves were tattooed all about his arms, with the bones of a pale bird strung about his neck.

As the sun rose, Mardyke walked slowly away. The moment he was gone, Tarragon scuttled out of the bushes, hauling a two-legged stool behind her. She looked around for the pond, but all that she saw through the rising mist was a bed of dank moss, scattered with white feathers. Then she caught sight of the necklace laid on top of the leaves. She peered about slowly, squinting this way and that, then snatched it up quick and scampered back into the trees.

CHUDDERS

As Rimmony ran, she could hear them behind her. She dared not look around, but she knew they were there. They followed her everywhere - in the shadows, behind walls, nestled in the crooked branches of trees. She could hear their voices, a low muttering rising to a crescendo, then falling away. But whenever she looked round there was nothing there. And yet she could sense them close behind her, touching her hair, brushing up against her sleeve, blowing cold breath on her cheek. Once she felt as though one of them tried to kiss her, but there was no-one there, only air.

She stumbled wildly, this way and that, nearly tripping into a ditch in the darkness. The blood was beating in her temples and voices screeched all around her.

And then she stopped. And listened. And all she could hear was the wind and the far off cry of an owl. She raised her hand to her face where a trickle of blood ran down her cheek. Her sleeve was ripped. It felt as if she had stumbled through a thorn bush, but she could not remember.

She looked back. The path behind was dark and silent. The path ahead was just the same.

And so she slept. Dreamt a raddle of voices, cries and screams and half-glimpsed figures, prodding and pointing, jostling and harrying. She woke to a dawn draped in misty drizzle. As she rose and rubbed her eyes she felt someone touch her shoulder. Lightly. She turned quick to see no-one. Nothing but the shadows of the forest.

She shook her head, thinking it must be the dream again. Then a little way off she heard a flute calling to her, soft and low, merging with the stuttering chorus of birds. And a drum tapping a rhythm, steady and beckoning. As she followed, she fancied she caught the drift of smoke, the smell of meat turning slow on a spit.

Then the touch on her shoulder again, urging her on, though still she saw no-one. Rimmony shivered. The path was slippery beneath her feet, dark mud oozing, crawling with snails and sticky with their silvery trails.

The drumming grew louder and the flute swirled and soared as she turned a corner into a clearing. A low fire was burning, smoky and smouldering. Then a figure appeared beside her out of the drizzle, lumbering and awkward and then suddenly dancing, its head jerking franticly from side to side. Then the touch on her shoulder again. She turned to find another, almost the same. Hair wild as straw tossed in the wind. And a grin. And a grin. A grin fixed and gritted and eyes that just stared.

Rimmony stared. The figures bowed. And then she saw the strings. And up in the trees a hunched silhouette squatting in the branches, his hands clutching a cluster of sticks and pulleys that led to the strings.

Rimmony smiled. Then she laughed and she curtseyed and held out her hand to touch one of the figures in greeting. The puppet's hand swung forward. Rimmony gripped. And felt skin.

Horny skin, weathered skin. Skin that had been out in the wind and the rain. But skin all the same.

Rimmony gasped. She looked up. The head of the puppet nodded forward. For a moment she thought that it winked. But the cheeks and the brows, same as the hands, creased and crinkled, wrinkled - but skin. Skin same as hers, same as any breathing person.

But not breathing. Dancing and jerking to the drum's twisting rhythm. Writhing and lurching to the flute's leering call. But not breathing. Not breathing at all.

The figure in the tree dropped down beside her. As he did so, the puppets crumpled to two heaps on the ground. Rimmony looked around. More puppets dangled all about the clearing, suspended from the branches of the trees. The piper and the drummer ceased their playing and shuffled across to the fire, their hands in their pockets, kicking out divots of earth.

The puppeteer was squat and wiry, his eyes quick and darting. He moved almost like a puppet himself, jerking and grinning, running on ahead of Rimmony to lead her to the clearing.

"Come," he said, "sit with us. I am Chillpicket. This is Skantwindle," - he nodded towards the piper. "And the drummer is Noonsacks. He cannot speak."

Noonsacks waved a greeting to Rimmony as his teeth ripped into a shank of meat, fresh killed and still dripping with blood. Rimmony squatted on a make-shift bench, eagerly grabbing a hunk of raw-cooked flesh, tearing and gnawing and chewing, her fingers sticky with grease.

Chillpicket rubbed a dry stick around his gums, leaned back and spat. Skantwindle and Noonsacks shuffled away to wander round the clearing, inspecting the puppets. But soon as Chillpicket wasn't looking they fell to slyly slapping them and punching them, sticking dried grass and acorns into their mouths and spinning them round and round. Soon as Chillpicket turned, they stopped. He turned back again to stare long and hard at Rimmony.

"What is it you do?" he said at last, picking up an old

shirt and threading a needle to lace up a tear.

"I'm a seamstress," she replied, watching his handiwork. "Can make fine dresses for anyone. Britches too. Make'em from anything."

Chillpicket sucked his teeth.

"Can you dress these sad sacks of skin you see hanging here? They ain't had no decent vestments since last Gatherer's Moon and gone."

Rimmony looked at him carefully, then she paused.

"When I touched them..." she said.

Chillpicket's eyes narrowed.

"Touch was same as a brother or any other boy."

Chillpicket nodded.

"Tis true. I can make them dance in ways they have never danced before. I make them sing in voices they have never heard. I make them speak the thoughts they never dared to utter. I can make the sad happy. I can make the proud humble. I can make those who have only crawled in the dirt stand and walk and fly... All this while Skantwindle plays upon his flute and Noonsacks beats his drum. And me, I sit up in the tree and when I pull the strings, then they live again."

"Where do you get them?" Rimmony asked.

Chillpicket shrugged.

"I find'em," he said.

"How? Are they washed up by the river? Are they trapped in a thorn bush?"

The puppeteer turned away and continued with his stitching. He drew a breath then bit through the thread with jagged teeth.

"I find them," he repeated. "Or else they find me. Walk through the night to lie at the door of my tent."

"Do you call them?" Rimmony asked. "Does Skantwindle lure them with a tune on his flute?"

"Don't know if he does or no. I'd be asleep. Up to Skantwindle what he does through the night. I just open the tent flap on a rainy morning and they're there."

"Are they...?"

Chillpicket grunted.

"They're ready to be sewn," he said. "They're ready to be stitched, each to each to make another. They're ready to dance again!"

Rimmony stared wide-eyed, glancing across at the hulking carcasses that hung all about the clearing.

"Call them my chudders," Chillpicket continued. "We tak'em from town to town, village to village. Barn to pond-side. Any place we can stop. I make'em dance while Skantwindle plays and Noonsacks bangs his drum. Folk come and watch. Give us shelter. Give us vittles. Give us shillen if'n we're lucky."

Rimmony picked at the hem of her dress.

"What can you do?" Chillpicket asked abruptly.

"Told you," said Rimmony. "I can sew, I can cut. I can shape a coat from most anything."

Chillpicket pointed.

"See that'un over there? Needs a new coat. Needs britches too. Maybe a hat. Never had a hat, but his hair's falling out by the handful. Hat'd cover it over."

He paused. Rimmony looked over at the puppet dangling gawk-eyed from a tall oak tree.

"Reckon you can do it?"

Rimmony nodded.

"Get to it then," Chillpicket grunted, tipping the slops from his cup into the fire. Then he paused, standing abruptly.

"Wait. Afore you start, best know what you are stitching for. Come and see our show. Come meet Tuppen and Snard. Come see my chudders dance."

Rimmony followed him to the other side of the clearing where two puppets swung gauntly side by side from a harness strapped at the top of the tree. Chillpicket shinned up the trunk to take his place among the pulleys and the strings.

"Let the show begin!" he bawled.

Rimmony sat on the grass and waited. Nothing happened.

"Let the show begin..." he called again.

Rimmony heard a scuffling and kerfuffling from behind a tree, then suddenly Skantwindle and Noonsacks appeared, walking haphazardly and playing out of time.

Chillpicket rained curses upon them.

"What kind of show is that?" he railed. "We have an audience here. Our very own seamstress. Do you want her to sew costumes as ill as you play? Go back and start over again."

Skantwindle and Noonsacks shuffled away, shamefaced. Rimmony settled herself down then looked up at the two puppets. It seemed to her that one of them winked. She blinked and looked again but now all was still as it had ever been.

A thrush trilled its song. The sun appeared from behind a cloud. Chillpicket bawled his greeting again and this time Skantwindle and Noonsacks came marching out smartly in step, wheeled in a circle and came to a halt, still beating and skirling in front of the two chudders, Tuppen and Snard.

Chillpicket jerked a string.

Tuppen twitched one finger.

Then another.

Then another.

Then his head turned towards Snard. She raised her chin and looked away. Tuppen's head fell dolefully. His shoulders drooped. His hands twisted awkwardly. Skantwindle teased out a plaintive tune, while Noonsacks set up a plodding rhythm. Snard turned back and the two puppets set to dancing slowly, lumbering and stumbling, and in raw raucous voices they sang:

> *Hop we may*
> *and stop your play*
> *and chase your pain and tears away.*
>
> *Loll-head and tumble-down,*
> *we go from town to town,*
> *follow the season round,*
> *Loll-head and tumble-down.*
>
> *Dance we can*
> *and chance again*
> *and laugh and fall and stand again.*
>
> *Loll-head and tumble-down,*
> *we go from town to town,*
> *follow the season round,*
> *Loll-head and tumble-down.*

They stood face to face and slapped their palms clumsily. But then Snard turned away with her back to Tuppen who sagged again. He waited long and melancholy as the flute played on. But then he raised his hand in a gesture of delight and bent to pick flowers, daisies and buttercups, snatching them up one by one. His huge gawky fingers moved deftly, knitting them together into a chain, a skein of silver and gold.

Rimmony watched, her mouth wide open as he tip-toed

up behind Snard, tapped her on the shoulder and as she swung around he placed the garland around her neck. Now she smiled and clapped her hands and threw her arms about him.

And then they kissed.

Long time and slow while the pipe played on and Rimmony watched and began to wonder whether Chillpicket's strings had gotten tangled together, so twined had his chudders become.

Then the music stopped and Tuppen and Snard stood staring out into the middle of the grove. Rimmony swung around to see where they might be looking, but all was the same as it had been before, a plume of smoke rising from the campfire.

She held up her hands to start clapping, thinking the show might be at an end, when out from behind the tree cavorted a great massive bear. Rimmony sprang up, ready to run, though she knowed this weren't no true bear, but a chudder same as Tuppen and Snard. She sat back down and peered close, wanting to learn from Chillpicket's craft.

The bear was hung from a pulley and stitched together all this way and that, from bits of dog and ferret scraps, skin of goat and donkey's hide.

Tuppen was still gazing way across the clearing and Rimmony cried out to him -

"The bear is coming!"

Tuppen stared at her, confused. She called again, waving her arms but at that moment the bear placed its great paws on Tuppen's shoulders. Tuppen swung about and gripped the creature in his arms. They grappled like as if they wrestlers, each heavy and blustering, striking out blows. But the bear was too powerful and bore down on Tuppen till he turned and ran to hide behind the tree.

All this time Snard had been standing and watching and now the bear turned to her and grabbed her with his paws. Rimmony cried out, thinking the bear would fight her too, but no, they took up in a dance while Noonsacks and Skantwindle played a jig for their capers.

A-kissing and a-hugging they circled back and forth till the bear loosed his grip and beckoned Snard to follow him. The music played louder as he led her away and just for a moment the clearing fell empty. Rimmony raised her hands again, thinking she should clap when there came a great roll on the drum and Tuppen reappeared, looking all about.

"They went that way!" Rimmony pointed, but he did not seem to hear.

Instead the drum roll stopped and the flute played a mournful air. Tuppen bowed his head and then began his song:

> *Gone, gone, gone.*
> *Now alone am I.*
> *The grey rain falls,*
> *The dark rooks fly,*
> *The thunder calls,*
> *The flowers die.*
> *Gone, gone, gone...*

Tears rolled down Rimmony's cheeks, but then Tuppen bowed and the bear and Snard returned and they bowed too, and Noonsacks and Skantwindle led them all in a furious caper till Chillpicket dropped his strings and the chudders collapsed in a heap on the ground.

Now Rimmony clapped till her hands were sore and Chillpicket clambered down from the tree.

"Never seen nothing so real," she cried, "and yet so

like a dream!"

But Chillpicket busied himself picking at the knots of his tangled pulleys and strings.

"Good enough," he shrugged. "Be better if them two could only play in time and keep to the tune."

Noonsacks and Skantwindle made to scuttle away, but Chillpicket stilled them.

"Come back you two, there's work to do.... and you."

He summoned Rimmony.

"Take this bear and fold him good. See he fits into that basket!"

Rimmony gritted her teeth then gripped the mesh of skins as tufts of grizzled hair fell away, stinking beneath her fingers.

"Mark well," said Chillpicket, "where it needs patching. That's work to do another day."

Rimmony tip-toed slow around the clearing, peering up at the chudders that dangled from the trees. The branches creaked as they swayed, their limbs hanging loose, heads lolling sideways. She measured with eye, with thumb, with length of stick, darting quick from one to another till she came at last to Tuppen.

He seemed to gaze at her.

Rimmony blinked.

"What d'you fancy?" she asked. "Make you all smart so that old Snard won't run off with no bear. An overcoat? A waistcoat maybe? A pair of new britches... you could do with new shoes."

She touched his cracked leather boot, sending him spinning and clutched at him quick, afeared he might fall. Then she sprang back. He was warm to hold, like a lummin boy. Rimmony coughed, looked at him again. The spinning had stopped and he was just hanging there, eyes staring nowhere, into the air.

Rimmony turned away.

"A coat, I think, before all else. Now what colour shall it be?"

Tuppen said nothing. Rimmony hurried off and spent the morning rooting through a sack of rags stashed at the back of a cart with the rest of the troupe's possessions. She plucked out russet and green and ochre, cut them up deftly with the scissors which she carried in her belt. Then she pulled out a little bag of needles and set to sewing, and the coat took shape as she patched the pieces together under her hands. No pattern needed, she had done this before so many times as the needle flew quickly and she snapped the thread between her teeth.

And then she sang. Softly at first, then louder and louder till Skantwindle and Noonsacks, who were sitting stringing beads out under a tree, took up the tune. The clearing echoed and when they stopped she turned around and fancied she saw that Tuppen was listening. Watching her with his steady eyes. But the moment was broken by Chillpicket, who strode into the centre of the grove, clapping his hands slow and deliberate.

"You make a fine noise," he said, "now let's see your sewing."

Rimmony spread the half-finished coat before him on the grass.

Chillpicket scratched the back of his neck.

"It looks well," he muttered grudgingly. "Weren't expecting such bright colours. Old Tuppen here has always been hung with a mantle of grey."

"But he looks so sad," Rimmony protested. "And if he looks sad, who'd want to come see him? Want to make people happy - else why would they give you vittles and shillen?"

"Why indeed?" Chillpicket reasoned.

He looked back at the old puppet.

"Sure, he's had that coat so long its colour is the dust of the long weary roads. Can't recall now what colour it was when I first stitched him into it."

"Let me try it," said Rimmony, "for size."

She walked slowly over to Tuppen, while Chillpicket watched. She stood in the puppet's shadow a moment and paused, then reached up and peeled away the old shabby coat and laid it beside her on the ground. Then she stood up on tip-toe and draped the bright patchwork of russet, green and ochre about his shoulders. She patted and tugged, mapping out nips and tucks with a cluster of pins which she clenched between her teeth. Then she stood back.

Chillpicket was still watching. Again he clapped his hands, slowly, but then turned and walked away.

"It'll do," she heard him say as he went.

Rimmony looked up at Tuppen. She fancied he was smiling as she patted him again, ran her hands down his back to be sure of the fit. Then she took off the coat and folded it up. His weathered skin was only covered by a ragged white shirt that flapped in the breeze.

She touched his hand just a moment and then shivered.

"Better cover you up," she said and hoisted the old grey coat back around his shoulders.

As she walked away she felt so he was watching her, but she did not want to turn and look.

Next day she sewed slowly, shyly watching Tuppen where he hung dumbly on the other side of the clearing. Chillpicket came over once in a while to see what she was doing.

"Can't be all day on one coat, you know," he grunted

gruffly, then walked away.

Rimmony sewed a hem of leaf patterns about the bottom of the coat.

"Don't mean nothing, I know. Who'll ever look that close?"

But she wanted to make it fine as she could for poor Tuppen who had suffered his rain-grey garment for so long.

The drone of bees and flitting flies made her head loll sleepily in the afternoon sun but she was roused by a sudden roll on the drum and a skirl of high-pitched notes as Skantwindle picked up his flute.

Rimmony dragged the patchwork from her knees and rose to her feet, setting off across the clearing to stand before Tuppen. The harness which held him creaked in the wind. His face was creased in a twisted grin. He seemed to move to help her as she peeled the old grey overcoat from his back.

"There," she said, "now you can feel the warmth of the sun."

Tuppen nodded as his head swung down and he gazed at her face with his deep-set eyes. Rimmony reached up to touch his cheek, but just at that moment Skantwindle and Noonsacks came up behind her with a flourish of flute and drum.

"Mind he don't bite," said Skantwindle while Noonsacks smirked and twirled his sticks.

Rimmony looked flustered.

"I've nearly finished now," she said, tugging the new coat across Tuppen's shoulders.

"Fits well enough," said Skantwindle.

"Shall I leave it on him?" Rimmony asked.

"No," said Skantwindle. "Keep it for the show. Chillpicket says we move on soon to get to the Lithan

Fair."

"How soon?" Rimmony enquired, fidgeting with her belt of needles and thread.

"Day or so. Day or so more. Meantime, Chillpicket wants you to fix up the other chudders. Can't have one looking dandy and tuck and the rest as bedraggled as a sparrow with no feathers."

Noonsacks laughed raucously, rattling his sticks, his sharp eyes burning into Rimmony's face.

That evening after supper, Rimmony sneaked back across the clearing and sat down by Tuppen, who lolled as if he was sleeping.

"Wake up," she said with a giggle.

And he opened one eye.

Rimmony blinked.

"Sorry to disturb you," she said.

"Ain't asleep." A deep voice rasping slow from the pit of his stomach. "Never sleep... never wake. Just waiting..."

"What are you waiting for?" Rimmony whispered nervously.

"Waiting till Chillpicket make me jump. Make me jig. All to make childern laugh. All for few shillen. Nothing for me... nothing for me."

Tuppen raised a hand to his face.

Rimmony looked at him.

"Thought you couldn't move without Chillpicket's strings and pulleys... thought you couldn't speak, cept with his voice..."

"Can do a lot of things he don't know."

"He made you?"

"Made me, true. Don't mean he know me. Don't mean he know half what I do."

Tuppen swung down slowly, the branches creaking, to stand swaying clumsily on his legs. He rested his hand on Rimmony's shoulder to steady himself. She felt his cold weight and shivered as she moved away quickly, but Tuppen followed. Rimmony glanced back and saw him stumbling. He tottered and she ran to catch him. His face crumpled into a smile and his bulk against her was not heavy.

"Only a bag of skin and rag," she reminded herself.

They plodded on side by side till they came to a dell and there they sat. Tuppen grunted and gazed around. Rimmony watched him, not sure what to say. The sun was setting behind the trees and dark birds flew silently home to roost. Rimmony reached about, plucking at flower heads, and though they were closing over, strung them into a chain.

Tuppen stared at her nimble fingers, then gazed at his own massive hands. Rimmony smiled as she nipped the last stem then flung the garland around his neck. He grinned and she kissed him lightly on the cheek. Tuppen raised a hand and touched where her lips had brushed.

"Soft," he said.

Rimmony nodded then turned away.

"Do you like your new coat?" she asked.

Tuppen grunted, then tugged at the old one that hung from his shoulders.

"Keep it on," Rimmony told him. "Night is coming. You'll get cold."

"Not cold," he said. "Not warm. Not sleep. Not wake. Not hungry. Tuppen is chudder now. Just do what Chillpicket tells me."

"He didn't tell you to come here."

Tuppen laughed, dull and aching as a bruise, rolling round the dell dark as thunder till the birds rose again and clattered away.

"Chillpicket don't know," he said at last.

Next day Rimmony visited Tuppen again where he hung same as ever from the tree. She greeted him with a smile but his face did not even flicker.

"Don't want to know me now?" she teased. "Don't want no-one else to know we stole off together in the trees?"

She paused and waited then looked up, sure she saw him raise one eyebrow. She shook her head and looked around. Skantwindle and Noonsacks had come to sit a distance off. She watched as their hands flickered and flurried, making signs to one another. Noonsacks clapped Skantwindle on the back and doubled up in laughter. Then they began to play.

As their music filled the clearing, Rimmony spoke to Tuppen again, her voice soft and low.

"You should leave here," she said. "You do not belong. There's more to do than jerk and stumble at Chillpicket's bidding."

She looked around.

Noonsacks and Skantwindle were still wrapped in their rhythms.

"Come away with me," she whispered, leaning forward. "I can make you new shoes. When they're finished we can leave."

Tuppen nodded slowly, so might just take it his head was bobbing in the breeze. But he smiled. And Rimmony smiled back. She talked on excitedly about where they would go and what they would do till her voice grew louder and she did not notice Skantwindle had stopped playing and walked away. But Noonsacks was still sitting there, watching every move of her lips, reading the flutter and flurry of her tumbling words.

"Today I will finish your shoes," she told Tuppen. "I will come and lace them onto your feet. I will wrap your new coat about your shoulders and then you must wait till the moon is high and come to find me all out in the grove where we walked before."

Tuppen nodded as his hulk swayed slowly. Rimmony touched his hand briefly, but did not notice Noonsacks scurry furtively away.

That night Rimmony seized up the shoes she had spent all day long making. Bits of bark and scraps of leather stitched and gathered all together. She folded the coat of russet and green and slipped through the shadows round the edge of the clearing till she came to Tuppen's tree.

He seemed asleep. Rimmony nudged him. He let out a long low sound, somewhere between a sigh and a snore. Rimmony put her fingers to her lips.

"Shshsh..."

Quick as quick she slipped the old grey coat from his shoulders and hung the new one in its place. Then she unlaced his boots so his feet dangled free. She ran her fingers across his great bulbous toes then eased on his new shoes, neat and trim. Tuppen stirred as if he was about to drop from the tree and free himself from his harness.

"No," said Rimmony. "Wait. We must not be seen together. Come to the glade when the moon rises full from behind the cloud. I will be there."

As Tuppen watched Rimmony slip away, a troubled look flitted like a shadow across his face.

She sat in the glade and waited. The moon it slid from behind the cloud. Rimmony turned around, waiting for the sound of Tuppen lumbering out through the trees. But only a scuttling of night birds. Only a rustle of leaves. She sat and she shivered and she watched as the clouds swallowed up the moon again before scudding on. Rimmony felt the damp of the grass beneath her as the night dew crept all around.

"Come Tuppen," she whispered. "Come and we'll journey together across hill and stream and dale. And you will never need dance no more and I will never be alone."

She looked around, but there was no-one. Then she heard, soft, a padding of feet and knew sure it was Tuppen, wearing the shoes which she had made. He came out of the bushes, stumbling and slow, swathed in the coat of russet and green.

She waited, arms open, as he approached through the darkness. As he loomed in upon her, Rimmony looked up sudden. He smelt of damp shadows, of burnt leaves and stale leather. But not like Tuppen at all. For was not Tuppen at all. Was Noonsacks, the drummer, all swathed about in Tuppen's clothes.

Rimmony ran. Ran pell-mell and headlong, plunging through bushes, legs lashed by thorns. She dare not look round but could hear Noonsacks behind her, his voice cursing wordlessly as he struggled through thickets.

Rimmony switched quickly to another path. Stopped to catch her breath and listen. She peered out, peered all around. She had lost him. He was gone.

She picked her way slowly to the edge of the wood, then burst out through undergrowth to see a figure before her, blocking her way. Tuppen. He was naked, stripped of the clothes she had made.

Rimmony gazed upon his skin, each stitch and scar, each weald half-healed. She held him then and kissed him, but Tuppen turned away.

"You forgot," he said. "Noonsacks may not speak, but he can listen. He knew our plan. He stole the clothes."

Rimmony reached for Tuppen's hand, so cold and soft.

"Come with me," she whispered.

Tuppen shook his head.

"No - Noonsacks tricked us. But there was purpose. Chillpicket made me. I am his chudder. I have to stay. I dance his dance. I follow his cart."

Rimmony held him close again, but he pulled away.

"My legs are weak. My breath is faint. I am only chudder. I must go back."

He coughed then stumbled away between the trees. Rimmony watched him go. She stood a moment as the moon disappeared behind a cloud and the darkness wrapped around her. Then she turned, scanning the shadows that crouched between the bushes, that perched high in the branches of the trees. She could feel them close behind her, touching her hair, brushing up against her sleeve, blowing cold breath on her cheek.

She stumbled wildly, this way and that, nearly tripping into a ditch in the darkness. The darkness which grew denser all around her. But then she stopped and she listened. From far off in the forest she could hear the mournful echo of the flute and the dull thudding beat of the drum.

And then Tuppen's voice, gruff and low:

> *Gone, gone, gone,* he repeated.
> *The grey rain falls,*
> *The dark rooks cry,*
> *The thunder calls,*
> *Alone am I.*
> *Gone, gone, gone...*

Rimmony walked slowly on, her voice keening in harmony:

Gone, gone, gone.
The flowers die.
Alone am I,
Alone am I...

...gone...gone...gone.....

Nowhere

Pickapple lay on his back in the meadow, following the river of the sky, the tranquil blue, the banks of grey and the frothing foam of white; the birds and fowl which swam and trawled and plunged. He dived on, heading for the stars which rode the night into day, close as little kittle stones, yet shimmering far away.

"Where have you been?" asked Littleberry who was waiting for him down by the bridge.

Pickapple smiled. His eyes spun like planets. His hair was knotted with twisted weed.

"Been nowhere," he said.

Littleberry sat beside him.

"What did you do in Nowhere?"

Pickapple rubbed the back of his neck.

Shells and sand fell from his hair.

"Nothing," he declared. "I didn't eat no goose-feather pie, I didn't ride no one-legged duck, I didn't lie in no treacle bed."

He closed his eyes.

Littleberry gripped his arm tightly.

"Next time you go to Nowhere to do Nothing," she said, "you must take me with you."

Pickapple nodded as Littleberry swung her legs over the edge of the bridge and gazed down at the stream below.

"Why, thank you!" she cried.

"Be careful," warned Pickapple, grabbing her by the waist. "If you fall in, the water is deep and you will get wet."

"Do not care if I be wet," Littleberry retorted. "But do care if this dress be wet for Rimmony made it for me special."

Pickapple drew her back from the edge.

"If you fall," he said, "I know you cannot swim and no more can I and you will surely drown."

"But if I drown," said Littleberry brightly, "then it won't matter one jot if this dress be wet or not!"

THE WHALE IN THE MOUNTAIN

Elmskin met the old man, just as he came in sight of the mountains. He was sitting at the edge of a field where cobwebs clung to the brambles and the berries hung rich and full.

"There are more tales to be told," the old man said, "than I can hold in my head. Let me share one with you..."

Elmskin sat down to listen. He always liked a good tale.

"Let me tell you," the old man continued, "once there was a traveller much like you. He had walked many miles and many miles more. He had seen sights such as no-one had ever seen before. He had crossed high mountains and stared down to the bottom of a bottomless well. And he knew stranger tales than any I could tell. But the strangest tale of all was the tale of the whale that he found in the mountains."

"How can that be?" Elmskin interrupted. "I have never seen a whale, but from all that I have heard, a whale only lives in the sea."

"And so it does," said the old man. "But I'm telling you what I have been told."

Elmskin stood up and gazed at the rolling clouds.

"I must be on my way before darkness comes."

"Where is it you're going?"

"I'm travelling to the mountains and there I may find many things, but I know for sure won't ever see no whale."

Elmskin walked on and on until his feet were sore. He walked and he walked until night fell and then he knocked upon a door. An old woman opened it and invited him inside. She told him her name was Shendel and she had lived up in the mountains all her life and more.

"Not many travellers come this way," she told Elmskin. "In fact the last that came he stayed and stayed. Stayed so long I had to marry him."

Elmskin looked around.

"Where is he now?"

He could see no sign of her husband's hat nor any boots propped up against the fire.

Old Shendel shrugged.

"Soon as we was married his feet itched to leave. Said he couldn't stay now, he had to go. So off he went."

"Did he never come back?"

"Come back nearly every year. Brought me presents..."

Old Shendel's gaze scanned the mantelpiece. A mermaid's purse, the eye of a dove and the tail of a snake, all set in glass.

Elmskin blinked.

"Never seen the like of these before."

"Best of all," said Old Shendel, "he gave me this..."

She pointed to a brooch pinned to her shawl. It was engraved in the shape of a whale. Elmskin peered close.

"What is it?" he asked.

"It is a whale," Shendel explained.

Elmskin shook his head.

"Never seen a whale before," he said. "Truth to tell I only ever heard of 'em in stories. Stories such as one I heard not so long ago."

Old Shendel smiled.

Elmskin squinnied the glass ornaments again.

"But where did he get them?"

"He was a sailor."

"How could that be ? We're up in the mountains far from the sea."

The old woman stared at him.

"That's all you know. Which way did you come?"

"Come up from the valley."

"Nothing down there. Went there once when I was a girl. Climbed all the way down and looked around. Everything was flat as flat and so I came back."

"Then where is the sea?"

"You want to see the sea? You have to keep on climbing. Have to climb higher than you ever been before."

Elmskin yawned.

"I cannot climb the mountain tonight. My legs are too weary and I am too hungry and the night is too dark."

Old Shendel looked at him.

"You can stay here," she said. "I will cook you supper. You can sleep down here in the straw on the floor. May not be a bed, but at least you will be warm. But soon as morning comes, then you must be gone."

Elmskin nodded gratefully and sat down on a chair. Soon enough Old Shendel brought him a bowl of broth and placed it before him on the table. Billows of steam wafted from the bowl and at first Elmskin could scarce see the broth at all, never mind taste it.

He glanced across at Old Shendel. She was already tucking in, spools of broth dribbling down her chin. Elmskin waited a moment, took a spoonful and blew. And then he saw that the broth was bright green.

"What's this?" he asked.

Old Shendel smiled.

"Tis seaweed," she said. "Seaweed and sea snails."

Elmskin peered through the steam.

"But the sea is far from here."

"What did I tell you?" Shendel replied.

Elmskin took up his spoon. He ladled a mouthful of bright green broth and blew on it slowly. Took a sip. Lowered his spoon. The old woman watched him as he ran his tongue around his lips.

"Well?" she asked.

"Well," he nodded. "It tastes of salt and the wind... and dreams."

Old Shendel nodded.

"So we shall see."

Elmskin drank quickly as the broth began to cool. As his spoon scraped the bottom of the bowl he looked around to see if there might be any more, but the old woman was already heading for the door.

"Sweet dreams," she said, nodding to the straw bedding strewn upon the floor.

Elmskin lay down. His limbs felt weary but his eyes seemed wide awake. Then the room began to rock as if he were on a boat. Elmskin tried to sit up, but his arms and legs were too heavy to move. He lay still as still, watching the glass ornaments all along the mantelpiece, the trinkets the old woman said her husband had brought her home from the sea.

The eye of the dove seemed to be watching him and the room pitched and tossed like as if a gale was blowing across an ocean outside and he swore he could hear the wind in the rigging and the creak of the mast as they sailed.

Then he heard a knocking from up above and supposed it must be Shendel checking if he was asleep. He tried to call out but no words would come and the voice that he heard, if he heard a voice at all, was raw and raucous like a mariner who had been before the mast for many a year.

The storm seemed to lull. Mayhap they were reaching a harbour. And then he sat up, for now he could feel his limbs moving again. He hauled himself to his feet, gripping on to the table, and made his way to the door. He twisted the handle, though he felt sure that Shendel would have locked it against the night, but it flew quickly open and he found himself standing on the mountain top, nothing about him but darkness.

But not just the darkness of night. As he stood he knew that this was the darkness of water. He could hear the waves rolling, and the lost howling wind that had woken his slumbers. He turned once more to find the door, but the cottage was gone. Only the dull creaking of timbers as a boat hauled out to sea.

Elmskin called after it, but the wind took his words and whipped them away. He looked around. He was standing on a spit of shingle, though he knew that just before this had been the top of a mountain. And where there should have been sky and cloud was a rolling ocean and the cry of lost gulls.

Elmskin shivered. He walked a few steps, wishing he was lying on the floor of Old Shendel's cottage, wrapped all about with fistfuls of straw. Then he stumbled against a small rowing boat tipped up on its side and gratefully he nestled down under it to shelter from the wind and the tide. There he sat and he watched till dawn crept in - a thin silver line where the sea met the sky.

Elmskin stood up and let out a cry. In the mist he saw nothing but grey shingle, stretching on and on. No mountain, no cottage, no trees. And before him lay the vastness of the sea.

He righted the boat and dragged it down to the water's

edge then set it afloat and leapt in, grabbing for the oars. He started to row, clumsy at first for he'd never been in a boat before. But then steady and true, heading out towards the horizon.

In the far distance Elmskin spied an island and rowed on towards it. He'd heard stories and more of what he might find on a far distant shore. But paddle as he might, the oars kept on slipping and it seemed he was just turning round and around and the wind it blew fierce and the waves they lashed high.

"I'll get no closer to that island like this," Elmskin grumbled, leaning on his oars.

But when he peered through the walls of water he saw that the island had come closer to *him*.

"Mighty peculiar," Elmskin muttered. "I heard stories about islands before, but never heard of one that could *swim*!"

He gritted his teeth and clung on tight. His clothes were soaked through and his boots they were sodden as the waves crashed all about, then the sudden silence before they sucked back and rolled in again. Elmskin looked up. The island was here. The island reared above him. Except weren't no island at all but a whale.

Salt water poured down from its back as it rose from the depths of the darkness. Elmskin glimpsed barnacles clinging to raw flesh then closed his eyes as he felt his small boat tossed up like a cork. He grabbed for the oars, clutching them tight as water whirled all around. But the whale was gone.

Elmskin spun around and around. The boat bucked backwards, tossing him down to lie gazing upwards in the sluice of stale water. He hauled himself up and there was the whale again, riding before him, heading on towards the shore.

Elmskin sat tight in the boat, struggling to catch his breath and waiting till the whale was beyond him then slowly and slowly he began to row back to dry land.

By the time the keel of the boat scraped across the shingle, Elmskin had completely lost sight of the whale. He staggered up the beach, wet and exhausted. He clambered up and away from the roar of the ocean just as the sun broke above the horizon. He saw that he was back in the mountains again and wandered around, wondering whether he might find old Shendel's cottage or whether he should just curl up and sleep. As he rounded a bend in the track he heard a voice singing, mournful and deep. It seemed to be calling him and so he followed the sound until he saw at last it was the whale, lying on its side on the ground.

He tiptoed forward and the song continued, but as Elmskin stood, not sure what to do, the creature rose up again and floated, like as if it was swimming, up and up into the morning clouds heading onward towards the sun.

Elmskin sank down and watched it go, listening as the mournful song seemed to fill the sky, and he felt its vibration flow through him, filling his bones and his belly with warmth, till at last he fell asleep.

When he woke the sun was shining bright. Elmskin shook himself and then felt his shirt, his britches and his coat had all dried. He looked up to see if the whale was still floating, but there was nothing in the sky but clouds.

Elmskin turned about and about. A butterfly skittered across his path and he followed till suddenly it flitted away and he found himself standing at Old Shendel's cottage, just as he remembered it, nestling in the hills.

He knocked upon the door. All around the sun was shining and birds were singing in the trees. No sign now of the crashing ocean or the lurking storm or the whale that rose like thunder.

The door opened slowly and Elmskin expected that Old Shendel would welcome him as she had done before, but instead a young woman stood there, a smile on her face.

"I've come back," Elmskin explained.

The young woman looked puzzled.

"How can you come back if you've never been here before?"

Elmskin stroked his chin.

"But this is the cottage. I came here last night."

He peered inside.

There were empty bowls left out on the table, as if they were still there from the night before. But then his eye caught the mantelpiece. Where the mermaid's purse, the snake's tail and the dove's eye had been, there was nothing there at all.

The young woman stared at him and smiled.

"Did you see me?"

Elmskin shook his head.

"If I seen you I would have remembered."

"What do you remember?"

"Remember an old woman, then a sea, then a storm, then a whale..."

"There's no seas here. We are high in the mountains."

"But the whale came here..."

Elmskin pointed up the track, then his gaze landed on the brooch the young woman was wearing, same as the one Old Shendel wore. The brooch engraved with the shape of a whale.

The young woman noticed him looking.

"There's a tale to tell about that brooch," she said. "A tale to tell and more."

Elmskin was shivering. He looked beyond her into the

room and saw the warm glow of the fire.

"Let me come in," he pleaded. "Let me come in and let me get warm, then you can tell me how you come to wear this brooch and what became of the whale."

The young woman smiled again.

"I told you before, there was no whale."

"Let me come in," Elmskin begged. "Let me stay a while and a while."

She opened the door a little wider.

"I can let you in," she said. "I can let you in and tell you my tale, but if you stay longer, why then you must marry me."

"There are more tales to be told," said Elmskin, remembering the words of the old man he'd met at the foot of the mountain, " - there are more tales to be told than I can hold in my head. And I cannot stay and marry you, for I am a sailor just back from the sea and soon enough my ship will sail and I will be gone to fetch you strange treasures."

The young woman smiled a smile of sadness and looked at him wide-eyed.

"But the sea is wild and the sea is rough," Elmskin cried as he backed away from the cottage towards the path. "I will face many dangers on my journey. Who knows if I will ever return!"

THE FEATHER IN THE SACK

Rimmony walked slowly down the long stony road. In the distance she saw a speck of dust moving towards her. Then the speck was a shadow flickering in the sun. But when at last it came up close, why the shadow was a man, though his face was little more than a shadow, his clothes were covered all in dust and across his back he bore a sack. From the weight of his tread Rimmony sensed that this sack must be heavy.

"Tell me what are you carrying that makes you walk so slow?"

The man paused and looked at her.

"I carry a sack," he said.

Rimmony smiled.

"A sack itself is not heavy. Tell me what is inside it that wearies you so?"

The man lowered the sack carefully to the ground.

"Why, in this sack is a precious thing."

"And what might that precious thing be?"

But the man shook his head so sorrowfully that she did not want to ask more. Instead she plucked at his burden.

"Let me carry it for you and lighten your load as you walk along this dusty road."

The man said nothing, only shrugged and looked sadder than ever before. Rimmony swung the sack upon her back, but to her surprise it was not heavy at all.

As they walked side by side she quizzed him.

"Tell me, what makes you seem so sad?"

The man stared down. He looked at the road, at his

care-worn boots, then up to the sky where the clouds scowled down with a muttering of rain.

"Wifen is gone," he said at last.

Rimmony looked at him.

"I'm sorry to hear that. Did she pass quick," she asked, "or did she die slow? Did you watch through the night for her final breath?"

The man shook his head.

"Not that at all. She rose one night when a storm was come down and walked out into its fury, crying 'I want to hold the thunder in my arms. I want the lightning's flash to sear my eyes. I want to cleanse my skin with every drop of rain and drown my body in darkness till the dawn light comes again.'"

As Rimmony stood and looked at him, he made a grab for the bag and clutched it to his chest.

"Tell me," she cried, "what it is you carry that's so precious? What is it that's so heavy and yet weighs nothing at all?"

"It is a feather," said the man.

"How is a feather so heavy?" Rimmony asked.

"It is a feather from the pillow that we shared," the man said.

Rimmony nodded.

"That would make this feather very precious to you indeed."

"But more," said the man. "Every feather in that pillow was gathered from the dead birds who flew through the village each night, their voices crying like lost children, their eyes still staring, their beaks still gaping, their starving feathers falling from the bones of their wings. My wife and I would walk the streets and pick them up at dawn and sew them into a pillow. The feathers carried the dreams of all that the birds had seen as they flew across the skies while they lived. Now every dream is gone. My wife took them with her out into the storm."

"Mayhap she will come back," said Rimmony brightly.

The man shook his head and poked at the sack.

"This is all I have," he said.

"Well then, another wifen may come your way!"

At this the man grew more down-cast than ever before. Rimmony looked into his face.

"But first you must smile. What wifen would want a sorrowful man?"

"Don't want another," he wept. "Just want my own wife to return."

"But she is lost to the storm."

The man gripped the sack tightly but Rimmony reached out and snatched it from him.

"You cannot cling to your sorrows," she said.

One dark feather floated to the ground as she ripped the sack open. But then she turned it inside out to find that the fabric was woven with bright shining colours, swirling and coiling, bright as every sky that the birds had flown, but hidden in the darkness of the bag. Quick as quick, Rimmony pulled her scissors from her belt and her needle and her thread, and she snipped and she cut and she sewed till she had made him a waistcoat all blazing and bright.

"With a waistcoat such as this you will find a new wifen for sure."

The man pulled it on and strutted about, then set off down the road, smiling and laughing with a carefree wave of his hand.

Rimmony looked down. There on the ground lay the feather. As she bent to pick it up, a bird landed beside her. Its wings were dark but its eyes were darker still and before Rimmony could move, sudden it snatched up the feather.

The light drained from the sky and all was black and white and grey, even to the blades of grass which trembled, the thistles and the briar bushes all along the way - all except for a scatter of tall purple flowers which breathed an odour of musk. The bird was bird no more but a woman who sat weaving nets of darkness into a gauze of dreams.

As the woman stood and walked towards her, Rimmony saw that her skirts were all made of the nets that she wove, layer upon layer. And in the nets she could see that men were caught, shrunken no bigger than new-born babies, wrapped and cocooned in the gauze. Some were smiling, some were laughing, some singing, some struggling, some sleeping. And some they seemed as if they were dead. By the moon's pale light, the woman began to unravel them, to kiss them, to play with them, to cradle them one by one to her breast. Then as Rimmony watched, she bound them up tight again and hid them in her dress so that no-one could hear their pleading and screaming.

The woman looked straight at Rimmony then and came towards her, skirts swirling and flailing, dark as storm clouds, her eyes wild as lightning, her face wet with rain. Rimmony stepped back startled, but the woman said, "Do not be afraid of me, for I have ridden to the heart of the storm."

Rimmony stood still then as the woman came close, wrapped her cloak around her and held her to her body soft and warm. Rimmony felt so she was melting as the woman rocked her through the depths of night till dawn's cool fingers touched them both.

And the woman was gone. Rimmony was alone again, back on the empty road. The feather lay beside her on the ground. As she bent to pick it up, a strong wind blew and swirled it away down the road, away beyond her reach. She watched until it became just a speck, but then that speck grew larger again, a shadow flickering in the sun, till she saw it was the outline of a man coming towards her from the mountain beyond. He stopped beside her and spoke, but it was as though he scarcely saw her.

"I was lost without my sorrow - but now I have another one. A girlen made me a waistcoat fine but now it has been ripped from me by the storm and I can feel the thunder in my arms, like as if it is my wife returned, with the lightning flash wild in her eyes and the rain beating down on us both."

JINTY CATCHPENNY AND OLD JELLIMUTTS

High on the wall of the front room of the cottage there was a little door. Jinty Catchpenny, the girlen who lived there, would sometimes look up at it and wonder what it was for. But most times she paid it no notice at all.

But if she'd ever looked, if she'd ever climbed on a chair and stood on tippy-toes and opened the door, she would have found a windy stair. And if she'd followed that windy stair on up she'd have come to a tiny room up top. A room so tiny you could hardly turn round, but there she would have found Jellimutts, the little old woman who lived there all alone with the spiders and the cobwebs and the mice.

Now Jinty did not know that Old Jellimutts would climb down those stairs each night and open that door down into the room and scratch around for any bits of food that might have been left on the table. Then she'd scamper back before anyone woke. And so the moons went on turning and nobody knew she was there.

Up in the room, Old Jellimutts would spend all day playing with the mice and the spiders and give them all names. And when the mice died she'd keep their bones and hang them up, white as white, on lines of string that she'd tied to the ceiling. All night long she'd play tunes on these bones with a silver spoon and Jinty Catchpenny would hear the sound, but she'd turn over in bed and go back to sleep, thinking it was only the rain..

But then one night Jinty lay in bed under the skylight,

listening to the rain beat down outside so loud she could not sleep. She tossed and she turned until it stopped, but then she heard it, the music that Jellimutts played on the bones of the mice in her little hidden room. And then Jinty knew it sounded different. It did not sound like rain.

Then the music stopped. Jinty sat up. She was wide awake now and could not go back to sleep. The first light of dawn crept in through the window when she heard a creaking and a scurrying and so she got up and went downstairs. There she found Old Jellimutts sitting at the table, picking at crumbs of bread and cheese left over from the supper.

"Where do you come from?" Jinty asked.

"Don't be afraid," said the old woman. "You've never seen me before, and I've never seen you - but we live cheek by jowl under the same roof."

She pointed to the corner and Jinty turned her head to look up at the door at the top of the wall.

"How do you come to be there?" Jinty wanted to know.

The old woman shook her head.

"Long time ago," she said, "I was out in the forest, picking primroses and singing free and easy as you like, when through the trees, in the shadows, I saw a Mardolf - and he came after me. I dropped my primroses and ran all the way to this cottage and through the door and hopped up high to that other door at the top of the wall. And then I climbed the tiny stairs that are inside and took myself off to the little room at the top. And there I stayed, though every night I heard the Mardolf come a-knocking at the window."

"There are no Mardolfs in the wood," Jinty Catchpenny said. "My mother told me that. What did he look like, this Mardolf you say you saw?"

Old Jellimutts closed her eyes tight. Her lip trembled,

her fingers clenched.

"Why, he was tall as tall, with long shaggy hair like it was a beard, though tweren't no beard at all. Wild staring eyes and great big hands, big as hams of meat, though weren't no hands at all. And he came scary after me, through the bushes right up to the door."

Jinty Catchpenny shook her head.

"Weren't no Mardolf at all. That just a man. And I know one just like the man you say. Tall man with a long handsome beard and twinkling eyes and big strong hands. Mayhap he's the grandson of this man that you saw."

The old woman opened her eyes and unclenched her fingers then laid her hand on Jinty's arm.

"You be careful," she said. "For your man ain't no man at all, but a Mardolf for sure."

Jinty Catchpenny tossed her hair.

"Why, I see him every day, all out in the wood. And he is safe as safe, and often he do sing to me and bring me primroses to take home."

She cupped her ear and listened.

"Fact, I think I hear him now. He's up every morning, soon as the sun rises like it is right now. I'll go out and find him and see what he has for me."

She stood and smoothed down her skirt and patted her hair. But Old Jellimutts grabbed a chair and dragged it beneath the little door in the wall and up she scrambled and away she went into her room as Jinty stepped out along the garden path.

She hastened quickly into the wood, her step was light, her voice in song until she came to the clearing where she saw the man with his beard so long and his hands so strong. She looked to see what flowers he had brought, but they were not primroses as before, but wild hawthorn which he pressed close in her hand, but then she felt the sharpness of the barbs and saw the blood begin to flow from her fingers.

As she pulled away, the man rose up, standing tall above her. His beard has longer than she remembered and his hands as he held her were more strong. And as he smiled, his teeth were sharp, like as if they would pierce her flesh.

"You are Mardolf, true," she cried, and before he could reply, she twisted and pulled away.

Away and away, back through the forest, back through the primrose beds, back to the cottage door. All the time she was sure she heard the Mardolf close behind her, his feet pounding, his breath hot, his strong hands reaching out to grab at her hair as it flew.

She fell through the door. Then turned and bolted it just as she heard a banging and kicking and saw a face peering in through the window. Quick as she could she pulled a chair beneath the other door, the high door in the wall. She pulled herself through and jammed it shut as she heard a knocking upon the window pane.

She turned to find the tiny steps and called out Old Jellimutts' name. There came no answer, only the rustle of cobwebs and scurry of mice as she clambered up to the top. There was Jellimutts' room, just as she had told her, with the mice bones hanging from the ceiling and the silver spoon. But the old woman herself was nowhere to be seen.

Jinty Catchpenny sat so quiet she could hear her own breathing as she listened to the knocking and the banging below. She heard the Mardolf go around the house and try the door at the back, but that was tightly closed. She listened to hear if he would scale the roof and try to climb down the chimney. But at last it fell silent and she knew that he'd gone.

She cast her eyes around the room again. There were stubs of candles, plates of crumbs, even rings and necklaces such as Old Jellimutts might have worn when she was younger. Even, Jinty noticed, a bracelet that was *hers*, been missing many moons and gone.

Jinty Catchpenny slipped it on, then idly picked up the silver spoon and began to tap at the tiny white bones all hanging from the ceiling. One by one the mice came out and scurried about, then sat and listened as she played on, the rain song that she heard at night as sleep drifted in though her window.

Then downstairs she heard voices, joining in. One she recognised was Old Jellimutts. But then a deeper tone. Who could it be, Jinty Catchpenny wondered. She put down the silver spoon and left the bones to rattle and chime as the mice all scurried away.

She crept down the tiny stair and pushed open the high door just a crack. There sitting at the table, was Old Jellimutts, except that now she looked young and decked out with even more of Jinty's own jewellery. She laughed and tossed a head of flowing hair and turned to take the hand of the man who sat with her. A young man, with a long beard, a willing smile and strong fingers.

"You are Mardolf," Jinty gasped, but the young man turned and shook his head.

"Not Mardolf," he said. "There have been no Mardolfs in the forest for years. Why did you run from me?"

"Come down," Jellimutts urged at Jinty peered through the crack in the upper door. "Come down and join us."

But Jinty sat where she was and stared, then turned about and shut the door and ran back up to the tiny room, picked up the silver spoon and began to tap out the tune like rain all on the hanging bones.

Arm-Wrestling

One hot, dry, dusty afternoon, Mullops and Pickapple were arm-wrestling, sitting each side of a wooden table outside of Pickapple's hut.

"I will easy win," Mullops boasted, "for I'm much bigger than you."

"You may be bigger, but I am more clever," Pickapple replied.

"What good's being clever?" Mullops grunted. "It's the strongest one as wins at this game. I think I got the beating of you."

But Pickapple held firm onto Mullops' ham-fisted grip long enough for Mullops to get hungry. Pickapple could hear his stomach rumbling.

"Why Mullops," he said, "if we are to sit here all afternoon, then at least we should have some vittles. Inside my hut I have the juiciest pie and a jug of fresh beer. Why don't you go and fetch them?"

Soon as he heard this mention of food, Mullops grinned and relaxed his grip - and quick as a blink, Pickapple pushed his arm to the table and rose to his feet.

"There," he said, "I think my cunning has beaten your strength."

"Mayhap it did," said Mullops, licking his lips. "We'll have another match when I've finished the pie and the beer."

"Ain't no pie nor no beer neither," Pickapple confessed. "That was just to trick you!"

THE HORSE IN THE WATER

Elmskin had travelled far beyond himself and far beyond the hills he knew. He came in the rain, a shadow shifting, and knocked upon the window, soft - but no-one heard him and no-one knew what words he whispered and no-one saw him go. But in the morning they found that ivy had been stripped from the walls and all the moss which wrapped the very stones was gone.

He gathered up armfuls of leaves and grass everywhere that he went, all though the night when everything was cast with grey. Wandered on all down the lanes and through the fields until he came to the river. There he knelt down and called, low and gentle. Nothing else was heard except an echo of his own voice in the mist and the drip of the willow branches all along the bank. But then a ripple in the water and a horse's head broke through, beaded with droplets.

Elmskin reached out and patted the horse's mane as its nostrils flared and its eyes blazed darkly.

"Lantern," he said. "All is well. See - I bring food for you, food from the land."

The horse reared up and turned its head and gazed on the pile of ivy and moss all gathered on the bank. Then it rose tall and stepped from the water, near as high as a house, towering over Elmskin till it fell to grubbing about in the stack of greenery as rivulets of water ran down its flanks.

As dawn broke, Lantern stepped back into the water which swirled all around him till only his shoulders and his neck and his head could be seen as he strode along, his feet on the bottom while Elmskin walked beside him on the bank.

They rounded a bend and saw a heron pacing the water's edge, stepping slow and deliberate, its shadow long and grey. It stopped to gaze about, its neck awkwardly graceful, peering this way and that, then continuing. As Elmskin called soft for Lantern to stop, the heron suddenly lifted, its wings beating the air as silent as cloud as it rose and arced away then wheeled back to settle again on a spit of sand along the bank.

Elmskin sensed someone behind him and turned to find a child dripping all over with water, her head wreathed about with river weeds.

"Who are you?" he asked.

"I'm Freemantle. I come from the river. I heard the horse walking and wanted to hide."

"Lantern will not harm you," Elmskin reassured her. "But what do you hold in your hand?"

Freemantle uncurled her fingers to reveal a small pink shell.

"What is this?" asked Elmskin.

"It is my sister," Freemantle smiled. "She talks to me when I get lonely. She tells me of her dreams."

"And what does she dream of?" Elmskin enquired as from the corner of his eye he caught sight of Lantern watching the heron suspiciously as it moved towards them slowly, step by step.

"She dreams of the cottage we lived in, back on the land. The poppies which grew outside the door, redder than any blood - and the biddy-hens which clucked and chattered in the yard, waking us every dawn."

The heron raised its head, staring at the horse as it rose from the water, while Elmskin continued:

"Why do you not live there now?"

"The cottage burned down. Our mother is gone. All that is left is my sister and me. We live in the river, deep under the water."

"What do you do there?"

"We swim with the fish. When we're tired of chasing them, we come to the bank and play with the otters as they frolic in the shallows."

"And you," said Elmskin suddenly, looking up to see the heron standing still and silent beside them, " - what do you dream of?"

"I dream of when the moon is crescent-new with its arms open wide, like as if it holds the old moon to keep it safe. Then I must come to the surface and peer up into the sky.

"I sit on the river bank and listen to the sound of wind rustling through the leaves of the trees that stand so dark and tall. It whispers like the rushing of water that flows through my hair when I dive back into the river. And when I'm deep below I listen to it flow because it reminds me of the shimmering leaves."

She stopped and looked at Elmskin, who was eyeing the heron which seemed to grow taller, tall as the horse which began to back away.

"Show me something from the river," said Elmskin, "to prove that is where you live."

"I have to ask my sister," Freemantle replied, and whispered into the shell.

She waited a moment then smiled.

"She says I can show you the Moon Sorrel."

"What is Moon Sorrel?" Elmskin asked, still watching the horse and the heron as they eyed each other warily.

"I gathered it from my mother's garden and now it grows underwater, so its petals are always dew-wet. It bids me to come here, to stare at the sky. And when I am here I smell again the smouldering smoke of our mother's cottage and hear her lonely crying. She dies again each time I return and calls for her daughters to come home."

"Let me touch the Moon Sorrel," Elmskin begged, glancing up at the heron's watchful eye.

Lantern moved slowly away as Freemantle smiled and nodded, stroking the petals with the tips of her fingers.

"Here - you can have it," she said, suddenly thrusting the flower into Elmskin's hand.

But before he could take it, the shadow of the heron plunged down, grabbing up the Moon Sorrel in its beak and then beating its huge wings to bear it away, out across the sand, out into the middle of the river, where it dropped the pale flower back into the water. Freemantle raced to the edge and dived straight in. Elmskin watched the ripple and a trail of bubbles, and then she was gone as the heron wheeled away into the distance.

Elmskin scrambled on along the bank, calling to Lantern who trod slowly through the water beside him. The path grew slippery and wet as they rounded a bend and Elmskin reached out to grasp at a knotted root to save himself from falling.

Before him stood another girl, awkward, gawkish and tall. Her eyes were cloudy grey, as grey as the heron's wing.

"What brings you this way?" she asked, glancing at Lantern who paced towards them along the river bed.

"I've been talking to a girlen who says she lives in the water. Said she had a mother who died in a fire in their cottage."

"What was this child's name?" asked the tall slender girl.

"Think it was Freemantle," Elmskin replied.

"Oh no," said the girl, "Freemantle is dead. She died in the fire."

"How do you know her?" Elmskin asked.

"Why - she was my sister," the girl explained.

"I thought her sister was a small pink shell," Elmskin puzzled.

"No - I am here. The shell is one that I gave her when she was a tiny child."

The tall girl turned to walk away with a long loping step.

"I must go to find my mother," she called.

Elmskin watched as she disappeared around the corner and then suddenly he saw the heron again, lifting up from the long grass, just where the tall girl had been before.

Elmskin and Lantern walked on until they came to a town. They rode the length of the high street where the baker set out fresh loaves to cool and the cobbler crouched over his last, hammering new soles onto a pair of boots that were neary worn away. While childern gazed up at the tallest horse they had ever seen, Elmskin peered in through the upper windows into rooms where wifen were plumping pillows and turning linen sheets and old'uns rattled rows of bobbins to make lengths of billowing lace.

Then at one grimy window Elmskin stopped to see a room where an old man sat and all about him from ceiling to wall, grey rain fell cold and drear while dark birds flapped and harried in the branches of a squat twisted tree. The man looked up in surprise to see a face peering in at him. He flung the window open, nearly pitching Elmskin to the ground.

"What d'you want here?" the old man demanded.

"Why sir," Elmskin replied, "I am on a journey on the

tallest horse you've ever seen. I did not mean to look in through your window. I did not mean to intrude... but I do not understand - your very bedchamber is set with more weather than if you ever lived out in the wood."

"What do you know of inside and outside? What do you know of wind and rain? We make our own weather as we go through life and here I have made mine, for I have lost everything that I had."

"What have you lost?" Elmskin asked, stroking Lantern's neck, for the horse seemed anxious to move on.

"Lost both my daughters and my wifen too. Lost them all when the cottage burnt down."

"But I have seen your daughters," cried Elmskin. "I have seen them true. One lives in the river and the other is..."

"... a heron!" the man exclaimed. "Why yes, she grew so tall, didn't know when to stop. Much like this horse of your'n, I reckon."

Lantern whinnied, shook his head and shuffled his feet. Elmskin steadied himself and peered through the window again. The rain had grown heavier and the man was coughing and sneezing. Elmskin reached across and climbed from Lantern's back, over the window sill and through the casement into the room.

"Follow me," said the man. "I am Sallowbriar."

And they walked on past the tree into a wood.

"But where is Lantern?" Elmskin cried, then to his surprise he saw the horse come cantering through the trees, his head brushing between the branches.

They walked on until they came to a cottage standing near the bank of a river. Lantern's nostrils flared as the dull smell of smoke hung in the air. He paused, his hooves treading warily in the soft silted mud of the track. The walls of the cottage were blackened by fire and the door hung open, its frame burned away. But Sallowbriar beckoned them on.

Inside they heard a woman singing and the rattle of pots and the bubble of a pan.

"Come in with you!" she exclaimed.

As they entered, Elmskin saw that the room was filled with sunlight, a fresh linen cloth on the table, and vases of bright flowers stood everywhere, filling the room with a sweet scent of nectar.

"This is Threndle, my wifen," Sallowbriar explained.

Threndle smiled and beckoned them in.

"Sit down," she said as she drew a huge pie from the oven and placed it on the table.

Elmskin eyed it hungrily while Lantern peered in through the window, munching on a fistful of straw.

"Help yourself," said Sallowbriar and Elmskin cut himself a generous portion of pie.

Sallowbriar was about to do the same when Threndle stopped them.

"Wait!" she cried. "Our daughters are not here."

Elmskin put down his knife reluctantly and sat staring at the pie as it slowly cooled on the plate. He waited longer, his empty belly famished. Lantern had become impatient outside and had wandered away to find fresh grass, but inside the room Sallowbriar and Threndle sat in silence. As Elmskin watched, their faces wrinkled and their bright eyes dimmed. Cobwebs gathered in the corners and dust settled thick across the floor.

Outside from the river, Elmskin could hear the voices of Freemantle and her sister, singing:

We dive beneath the water
As birds swim in the sky.

We are our mother's daughters
And we will never die.

In birds' cry and wind's breath
You will hear our song,
From dawning through to evening
And all the dark night long.

But you will never find us
If you search the water deep,
For we are wrapped in reedy beds,
There to take our sleep.

We are our mother's daughters
And we will never die.
We dive beneath the water
As birds swim in the sky.

Elmskin stepped outside, drawn by the thread of their voices. In the distance he saw that Lantern had waded into the river, away and away until his shoulders sank below the surface, then his neck until finally his head plunged down beneath the water. Elmskin watched and waited, but the tallest horse he'd ever seen did not come up again.

Behind him he heard a crackle of flames. The smell of smoke filled the air. The cottage was burning and Moon Sorrel glowed pale all along the path as he rushed towards the door.

Inside, Sallowbriar and Threndle were still seated at the table, singing:

In birds' cry and in wind's breath
We will hear your song,

*From dawning through to evening
And all the dark night long.*

*We are mother, we are father
And when we hear your cry,
We rise up from the ashes
And you will never die.*

OLD JESSOP

Old Jessop lived in a little hut, all on the far side of the forest. Her hands they were wrinkled now and her hair had turned white, though her eyes still twinkled merry and bright. All them that visited, they used to say how warm her hearth glowed and how her pot brimmed full with stew and her face it beamed always like she heard childern at play.

But when they had gone, Old Jessop sat alone and her hut it was cold for the roof it leaked and the walls they were damp and her pot it was empty and her hearth was filled with dead ashes which she raked over and over again.

Then one day young Binnie came wandering all through the groves and she happened upon Old Jessop's hut, which she had never seen before. She knocked on the door and before the old woman could answer, why Binnie swift she stepped in and saw Jessop sitting alone by the empty hearth, with the walls all damp and the roof all broken and nothing to eat in her pot.

"Come in!" cried Old Jessop and smiled her smile which could chase the shadows away.

Binnie sat down on a little stool and stared about the room.

"You are sad," she said at last.

Old Jessop shook her head.

"How can I be sad? How can I be sad, now that you are here? Childern have always made me happy, though I know not who you be."

"I am Binnie," said the girl seriously, "and I see that you are smiling but truth to tell, I see nothing here for you to smile about."

"Smile for memories," Jessop said.

"What do you remember?" Binnie asked.

The old woman stared at her.

"You look like my daughter," she said, "though daughters had I none. But you look just as I did when I was your age. And I remember I used to go out, all skipping through the woods and gather me a bowl full of berries and then I'd bring them back and sit just where you are sitting now, right on that very stool. And I would pluck up each berry betwixt my finger and my thumb and let it tingle all red and bright, right there on my tongue. And when I was done, why then I would sing the song my mother sang to me..."

"What song was that?" asked Binnie.

Old Jessop paused. For a moment it seemed as though she couldn't remember, but then she gazed into the empty grate and dropped her head and hummed a note and then she raised her head again and sang:

> *The shades of the forest are dark*
> *Where the juice of the berry runs sweet,*
> *And the shadows will dance you till dawning,*
> *Never knowing just who you will meet.*

> *But the juice of the berry*
> *Will kiss your dry tongue*
> *And make olduns' eyes sparkle*
> *Like when they were young.*

Binnie watched her and clapped her hands.

"That's beautiful!" she exclaimed.

Jessop nodded.

"There's more," she said, and as she raised her voice again it seemed for a moment that sunlight danced about the room and the hearth was filled with a glowing fire and the birds at the window took up the tune:

> *The rays of the dawning shine bright*
> *Where the juice of the berry runs sweet,*
> *And sunlight will lead you to evening*
> *When the toil of the day is complete.*

As Jessop's voice faded away, the fire that Binnie thought she saw was cold ashes once more and the shadows hung heavy all around.

"I must go," said the girl.

"Must you?" begged Jessop, clutching at her sleeve.

But Binnie nodded seriously.

"Yes - I must go and fetch something for you. I will be back..." she cried as she clattered out through the door.

Jessop sat and gazed into the empty fire, her tired eyes trying to shape the pictures that she would see when the coals were lit and glowing. But there was nothing there, only ashes and soot. A shiver ran through her and she turned to peer into the shadows and thought she saw a figure there, hunched in a threadbare cloak.

Jessop called a name, but there came no reply and so she looked again.

"Who are you?" she muttered. "Could be mother, could be daughter lost. Mayhap it is me, young as the child I used to be, come to see how I'm faring."

Jessop turned back to the fire and when she looked in the corner again, the figure had flitted away, quick as she'd come. The old woman tutted and took up a stick to prod at the cinders.

"Nobody there. Don't nobody come now. Even that girl Binnie, must have been born from the hunger of my dreams..."

Old Jessop slept then. For how long she did not know, but the next thing she heard was a-knocking and there was Binnie once again, standing at her door. Jessop's eyes opened wide and then wider again, for in Binnie's apron was a clutch of berries red, their juices all spilling to stain the white linen.

"Come in, come in," Jessop cried and Binnie hurried inside to empty the berries into a bowl on the table. Soon as she did, the cottage glowed warm again like as if the fire was lit and the birds outside they sang shrill as childern's laughter.

And Jessop and Binnie they sat side by side, taking turns to pick berries from the bowl. And each one they ate, their faces grew brighter and then they sang, soft at first then louder:

> *The juice of the berry*
> *Will kiss your dry tongue*
> *And make olduns' eyes sparkle*
> *Like when they were young.*
>
> *For the juice of the berry*
> *Holds secrets untold*
> *To make young'uns chase shadows*
> *Until they grow old...*

Jessop took the bowl then in her brown speckled hands and held it there in her lap, like as if it was keeping her warm. And her eyes drifted shut as Binnie looked on, and soon she was sleeping. Binnie watched a moment and then a moment more. Watched as the berries faded and shrivelled and all she saw was the ashes in the grate and the dust on the floor. And then she tiptoed slowly out of the door and walked away through the woods, not a girl no more, but an old woman too, singing:

> *The rot is in the apple*
> *And the blight is on the corn.*
> *The geese have fled the meadow*
> *And there's blood upon the thorn.*
>
> *The moon it is not silver,*
> *The sun it is not gold.*
> *The sky it is not velvet*
> *And the clouds hang grey and cold...*

MOON MOTHER

Some called her the Moon Mother, while others just called her Silverweed, for they had known her since she was a young'un, though that was many years gone. And many years gone she was driven from the village, some said for stealing sheep. Now anyone who sees her will tell you that she wears a sheepskin still, hung loose over her long grey smock. And silver moons festooned about her neck, shimmering at her wrist and gathered about her waist.

They will tell you that as a child she sat long nights under the turning skies till her own mother grew weary of calling her and left her to roam alone. When she was a woman grown she crawled out to the dung-mire and squatted down, there to give birth all under the moon that hung full and red in the darkness. But if you ask was this child girlen or boy they will shrug their shoulders and tell you -

"Twas a dog. A quivering cur, a slathering hound that slouched off into the shadows."

And Silverweed was left all alone to walk the lanes and the black stubble fields. Every village she came to, soon as they smelt her scent on the air, the dogs would set up a howling and a whining. Soon as she came there she would call to them, hoping one might be her child. But the dogs only snarled and bared their teeth and sprang at her till she ran.

She ran on into the arms of the darkness. A darkness where there was no moon. And each night she would light a fire and call the name of her child. But no voice came in return, though night by night the moon would rise, slow at first, just a sliver of silver till night by night its eye grew so bright it seemed to fill the sky and Silverweed didn't need the fire no more and she would sit and watch the slope of the fields that rolled on down to the river that shimmered in the valley below.

On empty nights Silverweed lurked in the mist, howling out for the child she had lost. Then she came to the mountain and she scaled to its craggy peak and from that day on she stayed there, for she could see all the land below and hoped she would catch a glimpse of her child, coming that way to find her. For every night she lit the fire to light the way when the sky was dark until the full moon rose again and she would stand a-top the mountain and call out her daughter's name.

The child did not come. But many others made their way all up the stony track that led to the top of the mountain. They shuffled slowly as if she had called them and they brought with them keepsakes and trinkets, old broken bracelets and rusted thimbles and the Moon Mother made them a-new. She took them in her blistered hands and tossed them into the flames that she kept burning night and day until the next moon came.

The baubles melted as they watched and Silverweed collected the molten metal in a pan and waited for it to cool. Then she fashioned out trinkets in the shape of the moon - earrings, necklaces, rings and bracelets - some a new moon crescent, some full moon bright, others the phases between, whichever moon shone in the sky on the night that she forged them with her hammer and her tongs.

Rimmony found her way to the mountain, following the

trail of travellers with their bags of broken baubles. Found her way to the top where Silverweed sat.

"What do you do here?" Rimmony asked.

"I make moons from scraps that would be thrown aside. Things that would be lost. Nothing should ever be lost..."

She peered beyond Rimmony way over the river that glinted between the hills.

"What have *you* lost?" Rimmony asked her.

And Silverweed told her. Told her of the child who was a dog. Told her how she ran off and never came back. Then she paused and slipped a silver moon into Rimmony's palm.

Rimmony squeezed it tightly.

"I will find her," she said.

She found her in an out-house at the back of a low-roofed tavern at the end of a sullen-tongued village beyond the glowering mountain. Found her cowering, gnawing at bones. Found her wearing the skin of a dog, loose across her back as she crawled, teeth bared.

"But not a dog," the creature snarled.

"No," said Rimmony, holding out one hand towards her but still glancing back at the door. "No, not dog. Not dog at all."

The creature stood up.

"I am Gressen."

She shook the dog skin from her back.

"When I was born I was dog. Now I am woman grown."

"Then you are daughter of Silverweed."

Gressen's face darkened.

"I will not go back to her. She threw me away. When she saw I was dog, she left me where I lay."

"She told me you ran from her. And still - she is your mother. She wanted you to stay."

Gressen scowled.

"So you have met her."

"Met her - yes. She gave me this."

Rimmony pointed to the silver moon which dangled from her belt. Gressen reached out to touch it but then started back as if she could still feel the heat of the fire which had smelted the glinting disk.

"Did not run," she protested. "I was taken by a young shepherd who treated me well. He set me to tend his sheep all out on the hillside. I would spend each day in the sun, running and chasing just as he bade me."

Rimmony smiled.

"You were happy," she said.

Gressen paused.

"Was happy, yes - till I bit a sheep. Stupid thing and stubborn. Would not move as I wanted. So I bit it."

"What happened?"

"Sheep died."

"Not from one bite?"

Gressen turned away her eyes.

"Wasn't one bite. Was more. And then more. Was the taste of blood, the rip of flesh."

Rimmony looked at her.

"What did the shepherd do?"

Gressen scowled.

"He threw me down a well."

Rimmony raised an eyebrow.

"He threw me down a well," Gressen repeated. "Left me there for dead."

"You had water to drink?"

Gressen shook her head.

"Well was dry. I howled like the dog I was. I jumped

at the walls, I scrabbled with my claws. But I always slid back. Shepherd was gone. I sucked on stones. Gnawed them till my teeth were sore.

"Then one night I saw the full moon shining bright above the well. I saw in its face my mother's face and knew that she was calling. So I turned then to a girlen and scaled the sides of the well. I gritted my teeth and clung till my fingers were raw. But then I hauled myself to the top and threw myself down on the ground. The sky was dark, the moon had gone and I remembered my mother didn't want me at all."

Gressen sat glowering at the silver moon that dangled from Rimmony's belt, then made a grab for it, but Rimmony pushed her away. Gressen shivered and howled.

"This is the face of the moon I saw when I gazed up from the well. It will keep me woman still and not turn back to dog."

"It was your mother who made this moon," Rimmony told her, "smelted out from metal."

Gressen raised her head.

"Then she shall make a moon for me. Hurry - take me to her."

Rimmony led her back across the slippery river and through the valleys of thunder and rain. Each time they came to a huddle of hovels, Gressen would cower and whimper like she was a dog again.

"Come," said Rimmony, "come. No-one will hurt you now. The night is dark and the road is long but we keep on walking and we'll meet with no harm."

Gressen growled and turned away, her eyes darting through the depths of shadows that Rimmony could not see, till the moon rose from behind the mountain.

"There," Rimmony assured her, "there is Silverweed calling to you. We will be with her soon."

"Then she will make me a moon," Gressen insisted.

"Have you brought something for her?" Rimmony asked, "so that she may make this moon. A twist of metal, something that shines..."

"I have this," Gressen replied and pulled a knife from her pocket.

"There - touch its blade. It is sharp," she said.

"Where did you get this?" Rimmony asked.

"Got it from a boy."

"What was a boy doing with a knife such as this?"

"Found him out in the woods one cold dark night, his hair all twined with snow white feathers. He was cutting twigs from a hawthorn tree. I asked him what he did with them. He said the berries would warm his blood."

"How did you come by his knife?"

"I tricked it from him."

"You tricked a boy's dagger on a cold winter night?"

Gressen nodded.

"Knowed it was more use to me than to him. He could get them red berries with his teeth. I asked him if I could look at his knife. He let me handle it long and slow. But when I gave it back, tweren't no knife that I gave him but an icicle broke from the bough of a low-hanging tree, shining sharp as silver all out under the moon.

"He said the blade was cold. And then he must have looked and seen. But I was already gone, running fast as the dog I was when my mother bore me."

They climbed the mountain slow, the mist swirling thicker as they reached the top, till the moon broke through, aching white in the darkness.

A low hut stood beside a flickering fire, the flames

reflected in the pools of burnished water. Silverweed stepped out, light glinting on the cluster of moons which hung about her neck. A low growl rose from Gressen's throat. Rimmony watched as she dropped to all fours and circled around Silverweed, circled round the fire, her belly low to the ground.

"Silverweed," Rimmony whispered soft. "This is Gressen. I have brought her back to you."

But Gressen bared her teeth, threw back her head and howled. Silverweed watched, then held out her hand. Gressen backed off, whimpering as Silverweed moved towards her. Then lay flat, her head turned away. Silverweed reached forward and stroked her hair. At that moment, Gressen let out a wild howl, sprang up and stood before her mother. Eye to eye.

The moon shone bright between them. Silverweed raised her arm and pointed, and at that moment, like as if she drew a curtain, a dark cloud blocked the light. Gressen still stood rigid, eyes blazing, silent.

Then she spoke.

"Make me a moon," she whispered, "to keep away the dark."

"You have something for me?" Silverweed asked, holding out her hand.

Gressen reached into her pocket and pulled out the knife. Silverweed ran her finger along the shining blade and looked at her daughter curiously.

"This knife can cut you vittles or chase away your foes. You wish to trade it for a glittering moon?"

Gressen's eyes blazed suddenly.

"This moon will keep me woman."

"As you wish," said Silverweed. She took the blade from her daughter and cast it in the fire.

At that moment the sky was lit again and Rimmony

stepped closer to watch. The metal of the shaft did not melt in the flames, but one by one the blood of hawthorn berries dripped from its tip. The hawthorn berries that it had been cutting when Gressen tricked it from the boy.

Gressen sprang forward and touched one, smeared it across her face. Then along her arms and down her legs and all about her belly. She threw her dog skin to the ground and stood before her mother.

"Now you are daughter," Silverweed said.

Rimmony made her way down the mountainside, leaving the two women circling warily, their voices howling, locked in an eerie harmony. Then a boy came towards her out of the mist with his hands cupped before him, holding the melt of a precious slither of ice. Flowers of blood sprang up behind him with every step he took.

"Where are you going?" Rimmony asked.

But the boy said nothing as he passed on by. His eyes were fixed on the moon.

A Necklace of Snails

Every morning Pickapple would stuff his pockets with fruit from the apple trees which grew around his hut. Sometimes they'd be springtime green, sometimes soft summer yellow and sometimes russet as the autumn leaves. Some were sour and some were sweet. Some were big and some were small, but Pickapple loved them all.

He'd keep them in his pockets and walk around the day, scrunching and munching and spitting out pips. Everywhere a pip fell, Pickapple would mark it with a pebble so he could come back there one day and find another tree growing.

"Then I will have to sew myself more pockets to carry all the apples that I'll pick."

Soon enough the woods were dotted with pebbles like the sky was filled with stars, but while he waited for the pips to grow, Pickapple still picked apples from the trees that he knew. Then he'd sit and gnaw and chomp.

"Got to eat apples or else I get hungry," he said to the sparrows that came hopping around.

Up in the branches the fat pigeons cooed and all about his feet the lop-eared rabbits scurried. Pickapple stopped and rubbed his midriff.

"Oooh - but too many apples gives me belly ache."

Then he heard a rustling and a scuffling in the bushes close behind.

Pickapple turned around but no-one could he see except he heard the trill of laughter a-hiding in the trees.

"Taint nothing," he said loudly. "Except it be one of them plaguesome squirrels come to steal my apples away."

For although his belly was full, Pickapple still had a sack full of fruit beside him on the ground. He paused for a moment, but then the laughter came again.

Pickapple scratched his head.

"Mighty strange squirrels to start laughing. Mayhap it's a woodpecker instead."

The laughter stopped suddenly and Pickapple stood root-still until he felt a tap-tap-tapping on his head.

"Why - tis a woodpecker, true," he exclaimed. "But a mighty strange woodpecker that thinks my napper is a tree... whatever can it be?"

He heard the rustling and a giggling while the tapping came on sharper until he reached out and grabbed and found he was gripping Littleberry's wrist. "I knew'd you was there!" cried Pickapple.

"No and you didn't," Littleberry retorted. "You thought was a squirrel and then a woodpecker, true."

"Squirrels never giggle and a woodpecker's beak is sharper than a twig."

"But your head is proper wooden," Littleberry cried, as she poked at Pickapple's bag with her toe to see what was hidden inside.

"Ain't that wooden," Pickapple smiled, turning round quick as quick. "I see what you're doing and there's nothing in that bag for you."

"Oh Pickapple, I seen'em. It's full of apples, true."

Pickapple scratched his chin.

"What am I to do? If'n I don't give you an apple then you will surely moan. But if I do give you an apple then you will get a belly ache - and that will make you moan even more. What am I to do?"

Littleberry pulled a sad face.

"Oh Pickapple - I won't moan."

"Anyways," said Pickapple suddenly, gathering up

the sack and knotting the twine at the top, "ain't no apples anyhow. This sack is full of eggs!"

"But Pickapple - I seen'em," Littleberry protested. "They be apples true, all green and russet and yallery gold."

Pickapple winked.

"Might look like apples to you. But I'm the one as picked them and I know where I found them and I know they all be eggs."

"What sort of eggs?" Littleberry demanded.

"All sorts of eggs they are. Some of them's donkey eggs and some of them's eggs from that big old oak tree and some of them's eggs that Old Granny Willowmist lays when nobody's looking."

Littleberry listened, frowning in disbelief.

"Old Granny Willowmist don't lay eggs," she objected.

"How d'you know?" Pickapple retorted. "How do you know what anyone does when nobody can see them? You don't know what I do all day in that hut of mine."

"You hang up mice by their tails and boil tadpoles to make tea!"

Pickapple shook his head.

"You don't know," he said, and then lowered his voice. "You don't know I spend all day stringing necklaces out of snail shells."

"Pah!" Littleberry exclaimed. "Who would wear a necklace of snail shells?"

"You would, for a start. These necklaces are so fine I sell'em to the Pedlar Man and he takes'em to all the girlen, all along the Track."

"But a snail is all slimy. Wouldn't want one round my neck." Littleberry pulled a face.

"Its shell is all shiny when you break it up and polish it. Why - all the girlen are wearing them now."

"Pedlar Man do have fine necklaces, that's for sure," mused Littleberry.

"And it's me as makes them," Pickapple reminded her. "But I can't see no snails here to make one for you. What am I to do? I know - let me go back to the hut and look what I can find."

Pickapple seized up the bag of apples but Littleberry grabbed him by the arm.

"Oh no, Pickapple," she said. "I know your game. You plan to steal the apples away and you'll go off to your hut and never come back and I won't have no apple at all and no necklace neither."

Pickapple dropped the bag.

"You got me there," he said. "You got me here, you got me there. But how'm I supposed to make your necklace if you won't let me go anywhere?"

"I'll keep this bag, Pickapple, while you go about in the bushes and find shells and berries to string into a necklace."

"Take too long to make a necklace," Pickapple declared. "But I can make you a bracelet."

He set about gathering stems of nettles and handfuls of thistles, his fingers moving so quick and nimble he couldn't feel the nips and the prickles.

"I'm watching you," he called. "See you don't touch them apples."

Littleberry laughed and danced a ring around the bag while Pickapple busied himself, fashioning a twisted wreath.

"Now close your eyes!" he cried, "so you don't see what I made you. A bracelet fine as ever you did see!"

Littleberry closed her eyes, stifling her giggles.

"Oh Pickapple, what have you made me?" she exclaimed as Pickapple slipped a slug down the back of her dress.

Littleberry wriggled and cried out, "Pickapple! - What's this all soft and squidgy?"

"Nothing but a snail that's lost its shell. How'm I to make a necklace otherwise?"

Littleberry shrieked and danced until the slug dropped down between the folds of her dress.

"Now hold out your hands," Pickapple instructed. "And keep your eyes tight shut. If you look upon the bracelet before I have tied it then it will wither all away."

Littleberry fell quiet as Pickapple bound her wrists around with the twist of nettles and thistle.

"It stings... it bites... it burns..." she writhed and cursed.

"Eyes shut..." Pickapple reminded her as he whipped up the bag and capered away, leaving Littleberry stamping and rubbing her wrists with dock leaves and spittle.

Then she looked upon the ground and saw something round and brown.

"Least I got one of his eggs," she smiled. "It must have rolled out of his bag. This be a special one all laid by Granny Willowmist in the darkness of the night. I'm going to take it home with me and sleep with it under my pillow. Then I'll hear my lummin-boy come knocking at my window..."

Then she slowly opened up her hand and looked again.

"Tis only an apple after all. Least though I can eat it."

She took a juicy bite, then spat it out.

"Pah - Pickapple is up to his tricks again. This apple is more sour than any snail he'd take to make a necklace!"

LANTERN AND TUMBLEPIP

Lantern held his hand to his head to stop his hat falling as he ducked beneath the low lintel of the door. He folded his limbs into a chair, his long arms almost touching each wall. He caught his breath from the effort of climbing the narrow winding stairs and then he rose and crouched over the eye glass which stood in the centre of the room. Through it he could look out of each window to gaze in every direction across the forest which surrounded this tall gaunt house.

It was dusk. In the distance he could see the white owls again, rising and gliding above the trees. They swooped towards him and then turned away. But then swooped back again until at last he saw one beating closer and closer, its wings hanging wide in the eye of the glass. Until it sat upon the window sill and Lantern raised his head to look at it. The owl gazed steadily then dropped a small bundle into the room. Lantern grabbed it quickly and turned again to the owl, but its wings were already spread as it lifted away into the gathering darkness.

Lantern picked at the binding that twined about the package. He opened it up to discover a lock of dark twisted hair which he stared at for a while, then placed it carefully on a low table alongside a line of other small gifts: a key, a ribbon, a small rip of cloth.

Below him in the house, high-ceilinged rooms echoed with the memories of dancing and laughter, but Lantern could not go there now. These were the rooms where he played as a boy, his footsteps criss-crossing through the dust that spread across the floors. This was where he grew. But Lantern grew and grew and he could not stop growing till he feared he would reach almost up to the frieze of plaster that ran around the top of the walls. And so he entered the attic room where there was space to grow no more and he could gaze out upon the world with his eye glass and watch the owls come and go.

But now they bore him gifts and he could scarce guess what they meant for he rarely left the house, excepting at night when no-one would see as he strode between the trees, his head butting up against the branches. He would take him to a cottage so small he could scarce enter in, but he ducked down his head and he slipped through the door. And then in the morning he would return to the tall house once more. There he would wait and the owls would come bearing messages he did not understand.

One day Lantern squinnied through his eye glass and saw a small woman coming from the woods, small enough to fit in and out that cottage door. Lantern watched as she walked towards the house, watched her stop and stare up at the towering walls. Watched as she scurried around and around, scratching her head and muttering as she went. He was about to go down the stairs to greet her when she turned and scuttled away.

Days passed and months and a year or two and a year or two more. The owls still came and Lantern's table was filled all up with trinkets though he never went back to the cottage again.

Then she came. Came marching her way out of the woods, straight up to the door. But not alone this time. She had a child with her, a tiny boy with long dark hair.

This time Lantern went down to answer her knocking.

"This child," she said, "is yours."

Nothing more.

She turned and walked away, leaving the boy alone on the step.

The boy was very small and Lantern was very tall. He looked down and scratched his head.

"Come in," he said, offering his hand.

The boy's fingers were like tiny petals as he clasped them in his palm.

"What is your name?" Lantern asked.

"Tumblepip," the boy replied.

"So, Tumblepip, this must be your home. Come - let me show you your room."

Lantern opened the door into the tall room. The high ceiling was cracked and there were holes where water leaked through. The plaster on the walls was peeling and smudged with smoke like as if there had been a fire. But it had been a grand room, Tumblepip could tell.

"Who lived here?" he asked.

"I came here when I was a boy as small as you," Lantern replied. "It was empty then. My mother put me in through the window where the glass was all broken. That much I remember. And there were pigeons roosting everywhere, but we soon chased them away. And I lived in this room and I grew and I grew."

He paused and looked down at Tumblepip.

"Happen we should do the same with you."

But Tumblepip wasn't listening, he was running all around the room, climbing over the soot-blackened chairs and hiding beneath the table where there were pigeon droppings still and a vase of yellow rain in which one dead flower still stood, its white roots writhing in the sludge at the bottom. Tumblepip dipped his finger into the spillage of stale water that festered in the moss clinging around the base of the vase. Then he drew a swirling line through the dust that lay on the table top.

"I like it here," he said. "My mother's cottage is so small. She said I could not stay, she has another babe on the way. Wouldn't have room for us both."

He climbed upon the table, spread his arms and flung himself to the floor.

"Look, I'm a bird!" he cried.

Lantern stroked his chin.

"Will you stay and play with me?" the boy beseeched.

But Lantern shook his head.

"I have my own room in the attic."

He closed the door and locked it, then paused for a moment and listened, thinking the child might cry, but no - all he could hear was the sound of Tumblepip's feet scampering all around the room.

From his window, Lantern looked out into the wood, drenched darkly in green, which cloaked the owls as their white wings beat silently through the leaves beneath the stooping boughs. They skimmed across the grass in front of his house, across the pale flowers brilliant in the dusk, to soar to his window and land light as snow on the ledge, there to drop the ribboned packages which he ripped open to find a small pair of shoes and a hat. Tumblepip's shoes and Tumblepip's hat.

Lantern placed them on the table beside his bed then unfolded his limbs to lay him down to sleep. He dreamt then of walking tall through the woods, ducking down to dodge the branches of the trees while the leaves brushed his face and caught in his hair. He strode on, seeking a track he had taken before, but each brought him to places he had never been, to a pond filled with kettles, to a marsh of dead crows' feathers, to a clearing where dogs roamed, their eyes wide as moons, who chased him as he ran on, tripping and stumbling till he came at last to the cottage he sought. Panting and sweating, he paused at the door before knocking. But it opened before he could raise his hand. And there stood the small woman, wearing an apron, a spoon in her hand and flour smudged all over her face.

"I am baking a cake," she said. "Come inside."

Inside she took off her apron. Inside she let loose her hair. Inside she left the oven still burning and led Lantern up the narrow rickety stair.

Next morning he woke, still in his own bed, in the tiny room atop the tall house. He heard from below a shrill voice calling and the sound of feet scampering about. Lantern sat up. And then he remembered.

"Tumblepip!" he said, scrambling down his own stairs to reach the tall room below.

Lantern paused in the doorway. Tumblepip stood stock still in the middle of the room. The vase of water on the table was spilled over to form a sludge of soot and dust, which was caked all over Tumblepip's fingers. The faded flowers were flung everywhere, their pale petals shrivelled, their dark seeds spilling across the floor. Lantern followed the boy's eyes to the walls of the room which were daubed all around with dark swirling lines like maps of great rivers winding down towards an ocean far away.

"What's this?" Lantern demanded.

Tumblepip hung his head and shuffled his feet.

"What have you done to this room?" Lantern continued angrily.

Tumblepip bit his tongue then suddenly chirped up:

"At night in my dreams I sail down these rivers."

Lantern frowned.

"I could not get out of this room," Tumblepip continued, "for you had locked the door. I had nowhere else to go. And so I escaped all down the rivers."

Lantern looked at the child's earnest face and smiled.

"And where did they take you, these rivers of yours?"

Tumblepip frowned and scratched his head.

"Don't know," he said. "Maybe tomorrow night I will go again. Then I can tell you."

"But how do you know of rivers?" asked Lantern. "There are no rivers for you to see, here in the forest where you live."

"Rivers here!" declared Tumblepip proudly, showing Lantern the veins on his hands and his arms that stood out thick and grumey.

"My mother told me my veins are rivers and streams, and so I do draw them on the walls so that I can sail away at night. She said they were same as her mother's and her mother before and if I followed the rivers then I was sure to find them."

"Come," said Lantern, holding out his hand. "Let us follow where the maps will take us. Let us find you a real river."

Tumblepip followed him and they walked out from the slate-grey shadow of the house into the dew-drenched morning.

They didn't find no river, though. Only the drizzle of a ditch. A dank ditch, a dark ditch. And down its runnel, owls flew, flapping their wings silent as secrets. Tumblepip held out his hands towards them, calling them by name. They wheeled and turned, dropping gifts as they came. Tumblepip skittered all about, picking up the packages and unwrapping tiny cakes his mother had made, a fistful of buttons all pretty colours and a dark stone that turned bright as the sun. Tumblepip gathered them and put them in his pockets, squealing and dancing as the owls flew away. Then he stood still.

"I have to go home," he said gravely and before Lantern could stop him, he ran off into the wood.

Lantern shrugged and stood a moment. In the distance he thought he heard Tumblepip's mother call from the cottage. But was not Tumblepip's name he heard.

"Lantern... Lantern..." she cried.

He lifted his head and was about to call in reply, was about to follow where Tumblepip had run, but then he turned away. The distant voice changed from Tumblepip's mother to an owl crying deep in the woods.

Lantern strode on.

"If Tumblepip will not come with me, I will find the river myself," he said.

The forest grew darker, full of oozing, slippery mud. Full of flies and insects calling. Lantern feared snakes and the slick of their tongues, a flick of venom in the shadows. Full of scurrying and hurrying and hidden cries. Full of twisted towering trees blocking out the sky.

Then a thicket. Then a meadow. Then the river, wide and deep. Lantern marched towards it, his long shadow cast across the mossy grass. He stood a moment on the bank, then took a step and another step more, sinking down into the cold dark water. He felt the slow tug of the current around his legs, around his waist, until his body was submerged, his shoulders and his neck. Until his head ducked under. Only a trail of bubbles on the surface.

On the bank, pale flowers bloomed, their petals white as the moon. From the distance, owls flew, swooping over the water and then away again.

A silence, as all the birds ceased singing and then the

light breeze died away. A moment and then a moment more and then a ripple in the water as a horse's head broke through, beaded with droplets, its nostrils flared and its eyes blazing darkly...

A GIRL WITH NO SHOES

In the shadow of a huddle of run-down cottages a scrawny woman stood. Her hair was tied tight in a knot on the top of her head and she pushed a tattered basket set on a pair of rickety wheels. In the basket sat a child, a child with pointed ears.

As she pushed, the mother sang:

A girl with no shoes,
A girl with no shoes,
What would you do
With a girl with no shoes?

Rimmony came then, down the lane and heard the woman singing her refrain.

"My girl has no shoes," the woman explained.

And indeed when the child stood up from the basket, there were no shoes on her feet which seemed too big for the rest of her, though her head it seemed too small and her eyes glared fierce as she stared.

"What is her name?" Rimmony asked.

"Call her Thrup," said the mother, before the child could speak. "Was Thruppence once, but she ain't worth that now. And I am Trimblenimb."

Rimmony gazed at the child, whose swollen feet were blistered and bruised.

"Been walking many miles," Trimblenimb explained. "Then she could walk no more and I had to push her in this basket of mine, though truth to tell she is heavy now."

"Shoes she must have," said Rimmony. "Let me make you a pair. I will go now to search out what will fit. Where will I find you tomorrow?"

"We will be here," said Trimblenimb. "We will not stray."

Mallow Musk lay in a dream of green. Green the light, green the rain, green the sun. Green the soft moss which spread beneath her as seeds lodged in her body and leaves grew from her hair, flowing from her fingers to merge with the forest that pressed all around, while she listened to the breeze, the sound of distant bird song, the falling of petals, the crawling of penny-ants in and out the grass.

Rimmony found her there, down by the river, sitting all alone at the pool, her mottled legs dangling in the water, her lips parted and back arched. As Rimmony approached, Mallow Musk let out a cry and from between her thighs birthed a fish into the water. She reached out to catch it, but it slipped through her fingers and flurried away, a flash of red in the chase of the stream.

Rimmony came up to her and put an arm around her shoulder.

"My little one is gone," Mallow Musk cried, and then sank back exhausted.

"I see it," said Rimmony. "It is there, it is there. Look - on the far side of the pool."

Mallow Musk's eyes clouded over and Rimmony raced away, reaching down through the reeds to try and catch the fish. But just as she made to clutch it, it rose up from the water, all feathered now with wings, and flew into a tree.

Rimmony followed after.

"You are you mother's little'un," she coaxed. "Come and see, come and see."

But the bird only few up higher in the tree and then away and away, swooping on through the wood, but all the time looking back to see that Rimmony followed, stumbling on through nettles until at last the red bird settled on the branch of a tall dark tree. Rimmony stood and watched, enraptured by its song, then once again pleading for the bird to return to Mallow Musk, its mother.

As the red bird sang higher and higher, Rimmony looked around at the leaves that were scattered on the ground. They were russet, they were brown, strong and supple as any leather. She wrapped one around her hand and touched it to her cheek.

"Could make shoes from these," she mused, "shoes for little Thrup."

And so Rimmony busied about, picking the broadest, strongest leaves till she'd quite filled up her bag. Then she straightened her back. The red bird had stopped singing. Rimmony peered up between the branches, but it had gone.

"Never mind," she shrugged. "Mayhap you were never meant to return to your mother. Mayhap you were meant to lead me to this tree so that I could make shoes."

And make shoes she did, sitting where she was right under the tree, cutting and stitching and tugging at the thread till she fashioned a fine pair of shoes which she tried against her own feet.

"Hope they're big enough," she said, "for little Thrup has great big feet, though she only has a tiny head."

Soon as she was done, Rimmony upped and away, traipsing back through the wood till she came once again to the cluster of cottages. There waiting just where she had left them stood Trimblenimb and Thrup. Thrup was still strapped inside the basket, wailing and complaining

and Trimblenimb was singing to her, same as ever before:
A girl with no shoes,
A girl with no shoes,
What would you do
With a girl with no shoes?

"I have shoes!" Rimmony exclaimed. "Look Thrup - you are a girl with no shoes no more."

She unwrapped the shoes and showed them to the mother and daughter.

Trimblenimb sniffed.

"Be sure they will fit?"

"Well - I made them best I could, but let's see!"

Trimblenimb unstrapped the basket and Thrup clambered out. Her feet seemed even bigger than Rimmony had remembered them, but the girl stuck out one foot and Rimmony knelt down and gently eased the shoe on over her toes and wrapped it around her ankles.

Trimblenimb watched the while, shaking her head and tutting, but a broad beam spread across Thrup's face as she held out her other foot. Again Rimmony eased on the shoe. Thrup stood for a moment, staring down proudly at her feet.

"Can't sing that song no more," she said to her mother. Trimblenimb looked on and nodded, saying nothing as Thrup jumped up and down and span around, hopping from one foot to the other. Rimmony smiled too, pleased that all her stitching had worked, pleased that the bird had led her to the tree that bore the leaves of leather.

Then Thrup stopped jumping and let out a wail.

"What now?" muttered Trimblenimb. "Can't you be pleased enough that someone you don't even know has gone to all the bother of making you new shoes?"

"Look," the child squawled, pointing at her feet.

Rimmony looked. The shoes were turning back to leaves. Brown leaves. Shrivelled leaves, like as if they had just dropped from the tree. Until all the leaves fell away and Thrup was just left with her two big feet pointing away down the road.

"What did I tell you? Now look what you done - you don't deserve nothing," Trimblenimb accused as Rimmony scuttled about, gathering up the fallen leaves.

"I'm sorry, I'm sorry," she said.

"Not your fault," Trimblenimb retorted. "It's this'un here. She don't deserve nothing, nothing at all. A girl with no shoes is all she is and what she'll always be!"

Thrup let out a wail, but Trimblenimb grabbed her by the ear and jerked her roughly back into the basket.

"Let me try again," Rimmony begged. "I'll go back to the forest and find the tree. The leaves seemed strong enough when first they fell. Must have been how I stitched them."

"Strong they may be," Trimblenimb shrugged, "but my Thrup ain't going to live all her life by the forest waiting for leaves to fall. No - a girl with no shoes is what she'll always be!"

Rimmony walked quickly away, the shrivelled leaves tucked in her bag while Trimblenimb spun the basket around and set off down the road in the other direction, singing loud as she went:

> *A girl with no shoes,*
> *A girl with no shoes,*
> *What would you do*
> *With a girl with no shoes?*

Back in the forest, Rimmony looked for the tree, but could not find her way again and so she sought the red bird who had led her there. But all the trees were filled with birds and she no longer knew which was the bird who was once a fish. And so she made her way back to the river.

There sat Mallow Musk, all by herself, cradling the bird to her breast. She looked up slow, as if she was in a dream, as Rimmony opened her bag and showed her the leathery leaves that had withered away.

"I tried to make shoes with them," Rimmony explained.

The red bird hopped about, pecking at the contents of the bag, but Mallow Musk scooped them up.

"Your bird child led me to a tree," Rimmony went on, "and the tree shed these leaves so leathery and strong I wanted to make shoes for a girl who had no shoes at all. Her mother sings at her all the day and pushes her in a basket..."

"My child was a fish," said Mallow Musk, "but no matter. This girl should have shoes."

And she began to eat the leaves, slowly one by one while the inquisitive bird looked on.

"There," she said when she was done. "Next time I give birth I will give you shoes."

The red bird flew off into a tree, squawking and flapping, but then came back to nestle again into its mother's breast.

Rimmony returned to the shadowy cottages. Trimblenimb and Thrup were there waiting, same as they ever had been before.

"Well," demanded Trimblenimb, "where are the shoes? You said that you would make more."

Rimmony told what had happened. Told what Mallow Musk had promised.

"Then we will wait," said Trimblenimb, "for my girl must have shoes."

And Rimmony waited too. Waited each moon and returned to the wood to see if Mallow Musk was close to her birthing. But each time she came, Mallow Musk was no closer though her belly swelled bigger as she gazed at her reflection in the water and played with her red bird there in the woods, stroking it and petting it and combing out its tail till broken feathers flew in a flurry bright as flames. Then as Mallow Musk slept beneath a low-hanging tree, one hand resting on her swollen belly, Rimmony exclaimed to the bird,

"Take me again all back to the tree, let me try once more to make shoes from those leathern leaves..."

The red bird cocked its head to one side, squawked once and then flew off, swooping low through the groves with Rimmony following close behind. The sun rose higher and still they continued but they came no closer to the tree of leathern leaves.

"Where can it be?" Rimmony complained. "You took me straight there soon as you were born."

The red bird lurched away and Rimmony ran after till they broke through the brambles and saw a tree standing all alone, its branches broken and its body blasted, its bark all blackened.

"Lightning and thunder done this," Rimmony muttered, looking down on the ground to see burnt leaves lying all around which turned to grey ash soon as she tried to gather them.

Then she looked up. The bird had gone again.

She walked back between the brooding trees, the sky bruised and aching. She could feel a rain that wanted to fall, she could hear a dark rumble of thunder, distant, calling as she ran on.

Rimmony came to the river then, and there on the bank sat Mallow Musk dangling her feet in the water, her hands across her belly clenched, swaying backwards and forwards. A cry rose up from inside her and at that moment lightning blazed wild across the sky and rain broke hot and sweet, pounding the dry parched ground. Mallow Musk held out her hands then and gathered each drop to rub across her face, her body and all down her arms. And then the thunder laughing loud. And then the birthing, spasming.

Rimmony watched as into the water slipped a fish. But not a fish at all. The rain stopped, and the thunder and the lightning and all was still. Mallow Musk's face smiled serene.

There in the water floated green, not fish at all but a pair of shoes, neatly stitched, that drifted to the shore. Rimmony bent forward and scooped them out carefully. Held them up and let the water run off in rivulets and then in tiny silver drops. She looked at Mallow Musk but she was sleeping, her eyes flickering gently.

"Thank you," said Rimmony.

Mallow Musk stirred a little and raised her hand but then slept again as Rimmony tiptoed away.

As she made her way through the wood, Rimmony peered at the shoes. They were embroidered all about with a pattern of yellow, almost as if they were flowers and inside were so soft as if lined with feathers. Above her the red bird was fluttering, swooping low and chirruping, looking at the shoes.

"I hope they fit," Rimmony muttered as they came at last to the huddle of cottages where Trimblenimb and Thrup were waiting, same as ever before.

"Look!" Rimmony cried, proudly holding out the pair of new green shoes.

Thrup seized them up in delight.

"I hope they fit," Trimblenimb sniffed, beating away the red bird as it swooped low about her head.

Thrup chuckled gleefully as she pulled the green shoes onto her feet. She danced up and down, waggling her tiny head back and forth.

"Stop that!" Trimblenimb cried, slapping at her daughter. "Tell the woman thank you and how much you like the shoes."

But Thrup ignored her.

"Now you can't sing me that song no more," she replied as she carried on dancing.

Just at that moment the shoes shrivelled up, same as the other pair before and Thrup herself shrank till she was a slippery fish flapping on the ground. Trimblenimb and Rimmony stood rooted to the spot as the red bird swooped down and picked up the fish and carried it off to the wood. Trimblenimb just stared as the bird vanished away into the trees, then she walked off down the long dusty road, pulling her basket behind her, singing:

> *A girl with no shoes,*
> *A girl with no shoes,*
> *What would you do*
> *With a girl with no shoes?*
>
> *You can hate her and hit her*
> *Till she's black and blue.*
>
> *You can feed her with plum cake*
> *And old turnip stew.*

*You can fill her with lies
Till she thinks that they're true,*

*But what can you do
With a girl with no shoes?*

*A girl with no shoes,
A girl with no shoes,
What would you do
With a girl with no shoes...*

A Little Bit of Bread and No Cheese

Pickapple sat atop one side of the well with Littleberry astride the other, whiling away the afternoon chucking beechnuts at one another.

"What's that yellow waistcoat you'm a-wearing?" she teased. "Look more like a yellowhammer singing 'little-bit-of-bread-and-no-cheese'!"

"Ain't nothing wrong with a little bit of bread and cheese," Pickapple replied, leaping back down to the ground.

He opened his kerchief, but found it full of crumbs.

"Must've ate it all... but I heard that song the other day when Old Binnock came a wandering down the lane."

"What? Old Binnock - she sang that song?"

Littleberry spun another beechnut into the air then caught it between her teeth.

"No - not her, but a yellowhammer true. Flew all about her as she walked on down the lane. Whistled in the hedges then came back again to perch upon her shoulder and peck all at her ear... 'Little-bit-of-bread-and-no-cheese'..."

Pickapple wrapped up the kerchief and tucked it in his pocket then started to flap his arms as if they might be wings. Littleberry laughed so much at his antics that she near toppled down the well.

"What was Old Binnock doing?" she asked at last, clutching her sides till the laughter subsided.

Pickapple shrugged.

"Doing what she always do, out in all weathers, trying to find her daughter."

Littleberry shook her head.

"Gone many moons ago."

"Then she reached in her pocket," Pickapple continued, "and pulled out an old buckle that glinted bright in the sun. Told me it used to be her daughter's. Told me how she used to stare at it so that she could see how her own face do seem when others looked at her.

"'This is a fine thing,' I told her. 'Why - ain't never seen my own face, cept in a puddle when the rain been falling and then it's so muddy you can't see much at all.'

"'Why yes,' Old Binnock said, 'my girlen she treasured it more than all her rings and ribbons.'

"'This buckle is so precious,' I said to her, 'I will give you three acorns for it.'

"But Binnock shook her head at this.

"'Well then I will give you four,' I said, but she shook her head again.

"'I will give you five and no more,' I cried, spinning all around.

"'You can give me nothing that will match the worth of this buckle,' she declared, 'for it is all that I have left of my daughter.'

"'Why then I will give you nothing!' I proclaimed - and plucked the buckle from her hand.

"At that Old Binnock's yellowhammer fluttered all about, pecking at my fingers and trying to snatch it back.

"'You're nothing but a thief!' Old Binnock screamed at me. But I shook my head.

"'No thief but trickster true,' I told her. 'Not even trickster, come to that. You said your price was nothing and nothing is what I gave.'

"Then the yellowhammer pecked me so hard it drew a trickle of blood and I dropped the buckle at Binnock's feet. It lay between us while I sucked at the wound.

"'Cursed bird!' she said. 'Are you hurt?'

"'Nothing that will not mend,' I said as I bent to pick up the buckle. I told Binnock it was rightfully hers, but she waved it away.

"'Truth to tell, I'm sick of it,' she said. 'Every time I look at it, just see my daughter's face. And I knows she ain't coming back, no matter how hard I look. No - you keep it.'"

"What good's a buckle to you?" Littleberry teased Pickapple as she chewed on a nut. "You ain't even got a belt. Your britches are all tied up with string."

But Pickapple held up his hand.

"I travelled on till I came to that village on the other side of the forest. Went down on the green and turned a few cartwheels and sang a few songs till they all gathered round. Then I took the buckle from my pocket and held it up for all to see. I told'em quick, I told'em true - 'Look upon this buckle,' I says 'and you will see how your face do seem when others look at you.'

"There was a clamour and commotion and a grabbing and a shoving, but I held them all back.

"'Only got one buckle. Only one can look.'

"Then a man stepped up as broad as two oxen. He slapped his neck then he slapped his belly.

"'My wifen do say,' he told them all, ' that I'm as lean as the day she first met me.'

"I can tell you," Pickapple winked at Littleberry, "there was quite a few gathered round who had to cover their mouths with their kerchiefs to hide their smirks and giggles. But this man he swaggered up to me and he took the buckle and he looked and he stared..."

"What did he see?" Littleberry's eyes grew wider as she perched on the side of the wall.

"He seen... a pig!"

"No!"

"Yes - I do not jest."

"What did he do?"

"This man he shook his head. 'This buckle must be bent,' he said, 'or else my wifen need a new pair of eyes.'

"But whilst they were all a-laughing, a girlen steps up and whispers, 'My sister always tells me that my face shines bright as the sun.' So I handed her the buckle, but then she thrust it back. 'Can't see no sun at all,' she cried, 'but only a raddled old rook.'

"Some of those folk they were slipping away. Didn't want to chance a look after all. Them that was left pushed an old man forward. His hair was white and his back was bent.

"'Let him look in the buckle,' they said, 'for he is the wisest for miles around. Any one of us who has a quarrel will come to him to solve it.'

"I handed the old man the buckle and he held it in his shaking hands."

"What did he see?" Littleberry spluttered, her mouth full of bits of broken beechnuts.

"This wise old man," said Pickapple slowly, "peered into the buckle. And what did he see? - He saw a donkey!"

"'This cannot be true,' the people said. 'The buckle must be twisted. Or if not, then must be a dream.'

"'If'n a dream,' I told them, 'then this dream it must be true, for a pig and a rook and a donkey indeed you be!'

"For in that moment, that's what they were. The man as broad as two oxen was gone, and the girlen whose sister said she shone bright as the sun and even the old man too, and in their place there stood... a pig and a rook and a donkey!

"Them three beasts made so much commotion, people came back out their cottages again. And still they wanted to look at their faces in Rimmony's buckle, like it was a game. I couldn't stop'em, try as I might. Soon enough there was a whole herd of creatures all lowing and crowing and bleating and cawing."

"What'd you do with them?" Littleberry exclaimed, spitting a beechnut to the very bottom of the well.

"What'd I do with them? What would you do? I took'em to the market to sell'em all. Herded'em off down the road. But you should've heard the racket they made. Couldn't make them stop howsoever I shouted, howsoever I cursed, howsoever I begged. The noise went on all night long, grunting and barking and cooing. I couldn't get no sleep.

"'It's all this buckle's fault,' I says and pulled it from my pocket, thinking if I looked on it myself, I'd turn into a creature just like them, be it sheep or rabbit or warty old toad. Then at least I could talk to them and they might listen to me."

"Whatever did you see? Think you might be a squirrel or a ferret, running quick as quick. Or mayhap even a goose!" Littleberry laughed so much the well near swallowed her up.

Pickapple shook his head.

"Nothing. I saw no creatures at all. All I saw was me. Other people got a creature hidden away inside them, but me - I'm only me. I am what you see. So next day I carried on along my way and took'em into town and sold'em in the market, every last one of them and that night I set off back home with my pockets all a-jingling with silver shillen."

"Where is the silver? Show me!" Littleberry clapped her hands. "You can buy me ribbons plenty from the Pedlar Man!"

But Pickapple ignored her and carried on.

"I hadn't gone too far when I heard a great commotion down the road. I looked back and what did I see but the man as broad as two oxen, the girlen bright as the sun and the wise old man and all the rest besides a-coming after me!"

"They weren't beasts no more?"

"No - not at all. They'd all changed back. And worse than that. After them came the market folk who gave me all the silver, all chasing after me, all down the road."

"What did you do?"

"What did I do? I hopped up in a tree and stayed there quiet as quiet till they all gone running by. When the dust had settled back in the lane, down I drops again, then who should chance by but Old Binnock with her little yellowhammer flying about her still.

"I rushed up to her and give her all the shillen that I had in my pocket."

"What you do that for?" Littleberry wailed. "What about my ribbons?"

"Didn't want to keep it, it was weighing me down. Sides, Old Binnock deserved it more than me. If it hadn't been for her daughter's buckle my pockets would be empty still. And sure enough my belly was - empty as a bucket of nothing. So I thought Old Binnock might have a scrap of food in exchange.

"'All I got,' she said, 'is a little bit of bread and no cheese, just like my yellowhammer.'

"So we sat in the hedgerow and she shared her bread with me then I weren't hungry no more. And I was so happy I gave her back the buckle. Told her she should keep it to remind her of her girlen."

"Pickapple, you're a fool," Littleberry told him and she flicked the last beechnut to hit him on the nose.

"If I am a fool, then I am a wise fool," Pickapple retorted, "for that buckle was more trouble than any pocket full of shillen."

"You know what?" said Littleberry. "I don't believe you. Don't believe there ever was any buckle, nor any pocket full of silver shillen!"

Pickapple paused.

"But there was a donkey, for sure. I can show you where it kicked me on the backside."

"I don't want to see your backside," Littleberry declared. "And sure that could be any donkey that kicked you. I reckon you've been a-climbing in the paddock again."

"If I been climbing in the paddock, sure it was to get you these beechnuts," said Pickapple as he emptied out his pockets to find the last few husks.

There in the lining, wrapped all tight in another kerchief, was a little bit of bread. But look as he might, he still couldn't find any cheese.

COPPEN AND THE CROOK-BACKED DANCERS

The crook-backed dancers gathered in the forest, rattling their sticks and spitting bitter gall. A dark dove came flying and landed among them and they beat it with their staves till it was no more. But from that mess of feather and bone an old crone rose. She danced crabbed and crouching, her elbows raised, her knuckles cracked, her black skirts hitched around her knees.

She was Coppen and she gathered the dancers all about her and hobblefoot she came them to the gate of a city where the watchman sat waiting. She passed her hand across his eyes and he smiled and let them enter.

"Come Guzzer, come Grymswitch, come my bully boys," Coppen cried.

And they swept through the streets, rapping at windows and rattling the locks and beating out a rhythm on the black greasy cobbles. Then the steep winding streets they climbed till they came upon a doorway where a girl-child sat, no more than but a bundle of rags.

"Help me, please," the girl implored. "I live on gutter milk and sparrows' eggs."

As the child held out her hand, Coppen made to spit in it, but then tilted back her head.

"What ails you, Little Bird?" she said.

The girl flinched back from Coppen's piercing gaze.

"Please, they call me Mizzle and it is my mother who is ailing. She lies a-bed sick up these stairs."

"Well, Mizzle my little bird, let me see."

Coppen thrust the girl aside and strode up the stairway, leaving the crook-backed dancers clustered in the street, greeting passers-by with curses and insults.

In a garret room the mother lay, pale as death with scarce a whisper of breath.

"Mother," Mizzle trembled, "I have brought..."

"Coppen. I am Coppen, little bird. Let me see."

She pushed the child out of her way and gripped the mother's wrist. Then she prodded at her face, clawing back her eyelids with one yellowed finger.

"What can you tell me?" Mizzle implored as her mother gave a groan.

Coppen gripped at the wrist once more then dropped it again.

"She will die."

Mizzle burst into tears.

"She will die unless you give her this."

Coppen poked inside her cloak and pulled out a potion bottle, filthy with grease.

"Just a drop," she rasped, "on her tongue."

She prized the mother's lips apart and let one tainted drop fall into her mouth, then stroked her face and spun around.

"There, she will sleep mow. Watch her well."

As Mizzle clung close to her mother's side, Coppen swept about the room till her eyes lighted on a pair of dull leaden candle sticks which she seized up and plunged in her pocket. With a clatter of boots she rattled down the stairs to join her company on the street outside where they were dancing once more, carrying a pig's head impaled on a pole.

All night Mizzle sat at her mother's side. Watched as her breathing grew more shallow, her cheeks paler still in the flicker of moonlight that crawled through the window. Then the breathing stopped. Her limbs did not move.

"Coppen has killed her," said Mizzle as she laid on the pillow beside her.

At dawn she woke and washed her mother down with a screw of ragged cloth mopped around a drizzle of water at the bottom of a cracked earthen bowl.

"Mother," she cried, "didn't mean you to die. Thought Coppen's potion would save you, but..."

But her mother rose up then, straight in the bed, her grey robe slipping from her shoulders, her pale eyes staring through the windows to the sky.

And then a strange cry arose from her throat and Mizzle watched as her mother was mother no more but a goose, her wings spreading wide, flapping franticly in the trap of this attic. She beat Mizzle back against the window, her neck swinging and jerking as her webbed feet flailed, struggling to grip the stained twisted sheets of the bed.

"Mother," said Mizzle and the great bird calmed.

"Mother, come with me."

And she led the wild creature down to the street to sit on the doorstep beside her as she begged for pennies from all who passed by.

A wild wind wailed around the winding streets as Mizzle looked up to see Coppen and her company coming towards them, their faces grotesque, cloaks billowing black, their sticks beating rhythm on every door. Soon as she heard them, the goose rose up, her eyes dark as fire, her wings stretched wide. But Coppen pushed her back.

"You have killed my mother with your poison," Mizzle accused.

Coppen stared down at the goose that crouched in the

doorway.

"Not poison at all but *potion*," she said. "See - she lives. A changed life is better than no life at all."

"Where are the candlesticks?" Mizzle challenged. "I know you have stole them."

"Took them, true. Took them to sell for bread for my crew."

Coppen turned and gestured at the dancers who were circling around, passing the pig's head pierced on its pole from one to the other.

"So you have all eaten and I have nothing," Mizzle complained.

Coppen tweaked her cheek.

"Saved the best for you, Little Bird. Saved the best for you."

She unwrapped a package of greasy paper and showed Mizzle a pie, still warm and steaming. Mizzle hesitated, then grabbed it up quickly and bit through the crust soft as butter with a lick of salt. The juices they ran out dark as blood as she gobbled the sweet moist flesh.

"There," whispered Coppen, "your belly is filled."

But the girl was asleep, nestled close beside the goose which still sat silent in the doorway. As she slept, Mizzle dreamt she was with her mother walking all down to the meadow by the river. There they stood and called the geese till a great flock came flying low across the flats and landed beside them, shuffling and snorting. And Mizzle and her mother, just as they always had, threw crusts and scraps, while the geese wheeled around them, around and around till they stood right in the very middle of the flock, their boots sunk deep into the mud.

Mizzle woke then to find she was still in the doorway with Coppen standing over her and the crook-backed dancers ranged all around. Mizzle rubbed her eyes and smiled.

"Thank you for the pie..." she said.

But before she could continue, the dancers gripped her arms and tied a rag around her eyes, then bound her tight.

"Come, Little Bird," Coppen hissed. "You must come with us now - we will teach you to fly."

They led her then with a beating of drums and a rattling of sticks as Mizzle felt herself prodded and shoved and pelted with rotted apples and showered in spittle. As she shuffled forward she could feel the cobbles slippery with filth beneath her bare feet till they stopped at the gatehouse. The gatekeeper stepped forward, mauling at her roughly and poking her with his stave. At last Mizzle heard Coppen whisper something to him again and then he stepped away.

"You may pass," he said and the crook-backed dancers led her through the gate and out into the fields where she tripped and stumbled through a mire of cow dung, mud and mulch, the drums beating louder all around, first behind her, then in front.

Then silence. Mizzle stood, listening. The rustle of trees. Soft leaves underfoot. And then birdsong rippling gentle as a stream.

A rough shove in the back.

"Move on."

Mizzle moved, fast as her clumsy feet could blunder. Till they stopped again. She felt hands grip her, unpicking the bindings till she stood in a glade in the forest. Coppen circled round her, skirts hitched high, her finger pointing as all about dark feathers lay in a flurry on the ground.

"Now Little Bird, you must dance!"

And the drummers pounded out a rhythm so loud that all the birds in all the trees started up and flew away and the crook-backed dancers beat their staves as they capered slow about and about then faster yet and faster still, till all was a blur and Mizzle spun on her heels around and around and Coppen screeched and the dancers yelled then they fell sudden down to the ground.

Mizzle watched as their limbs jerked and twisted till they turned to dark doves, Coppen and the dancers. Then above them in the sky, she saw one solitary goose swooping towards them, plummeting down, its wide wings hammering in a mesh of feather and bone as the dark doves rose and scattered away.

When the goose landed beside her, Mizzle gently embraced the stretch of its neck.

"Mother," she said.

And mother she was, just as she had always been before the sickness came. She took Mizzle tenderly by the hand.

"We must go," she said.

"Back to the city?" Mizzle asked.

"No," said her mother, "never again. We must go far away from here."

MANDRAKE PETALS AND SCATTERED FEATHERS

Mizzle scurried after Skellyknox, out from the forest and onto the long hard road.

"Where are we going?" she asked again.

But her mother said nothing as she strode on ahead towards the distant hills, holding out an impatient hand.

"Never mind where we're going. Never mind why we go. Just try to keep up," Skellyknox snapped, leaving Mizzle to sink down and sit defiantly at the side of the road.

"What are you doing there, child? Can't beg no more the way we used to. Nobody comes this way."

"Then how will we live?" Mizzle wailed.

Skellyknox clapped her hands in despair.

"Never mind *how*. We *are* living," she said. "Before Coppen cured me you thought I was dead."

"Cruel cure," muttered Mizzle, shaking her head.

"Get up!" snapped Skellyknox, kicking at her shins. "All you been good for is sitting all your life, out on that cold damp step."

"You put me there," Mizzle retorted, clambering slowly to her feet. "You put me there and told me to tell everyone you was sick."

"Well, I was."

"Don't look too sick to me now..."

Mizzle ducked as Skellyknox swung a crack to the side of her head, then suddenly hugged her.

"Come, daughter, come. We are all that we have. The

road is long, but let us walk on."

But Mizzle did not walk. She would not walk. She could not walk. She sat by the roadside and watched as her mother marched away and away along the winding road. Then she sat all alone and wept for the cold narrow streets of the city which she had hated all her life. Wept for the rat-catchers, the lamp lighters and the night-walkers. Wept for the urchin-scrats, the quick-fingers and the grubby faced errand boys. Knew that she would never see them no more on this road of shadows and hunger.

The night was long, the night was harsh as blind winds sucked across the echoing darkness. Mizzle scarce slept and wished she was back shivering on her step with the walls of the city to shield her. Then a boy stepped out of the dawn and touched her on the shoulder.

She sat up sudden.

"Who are you?"

"I am Elmskin. Let me sit with you."

He crouched down beside her.

Mizzle still shivered. She gave the boy a sidelong glance.

"Got any crust?" she asked him. "Got any cheese? Got any coin to help a poor girl?"

"Got no coin," he said, peering out into the swirling grey mist. "What good is coin here? Nothing here but stones and thorns."

Mizzle threw her arms around him.

"Please good sir, will you help a poor girl?"

Elmskin pulled away and Mizzle sat back, tucking her arms snug under her shawl as she fingered the necklace she had filched quick as quick from deep inside his pocket.

"Please good sir, my mother is sick."

Elmskin peered about.

"Where is your mother?"

Mizzle lowered her eyes and shook her head.

"My mother is gone."

"If your mother is gone, then how can I help her?"

"Can help her poor daughter. I am still here," Mizzle pleaded.

They sat a moment in silence as the mist slowly lifted to show the road before them, stretching away up into the hills. Elmskin rose to his feet and paced up and down.

"Don't go," Mizzle begged. "Stay here by me."

Elmskin took her by the arm and raised her to her feet and they walked on slow, side by side, struggling against a blustery wind until they saw a figure ahead of them on the track. Mizzle looked up suddenly.

"Mother!" she cried, running towards her. "You came back."

Skellyknox shook her head.

"The night was dark," she said. "There was no moon, there was no stars. Only shadows, shadows and cold. And I lost me on the road, if road there was, just a track, just a scatter of stones. And then twere gone. And I wandered through mud and the rain it came, driving in my back, stinging at my face... till I heard a voice."

"Whose was it?"

"Thought it was you, child. Thought it was you. Thought it was my daughter lost out in the cold. Thought mayhap you'd followed and got lost just like me."

Mizzle shook her head.

"Disbelieve you may," Skellyknox continued. "But I heard it true. And I've known your whining long enough. So I followed it to see if you were in peril. Just as the first light of dawn was breaking, I came upon a cottage then, all nestled in the moss. Its roof was bent and broken and laced with ivy all about. On the ground outside lay piles of ragged clothes, folded up neat and tidy like they were waiting to be sewed."

"But what of the voice?"

"Voice was still calling from inside the cottage. I shouted out, said - 'your mother is here' - and it echoed back, 'I am here mother, I am here - but I am trapped, oh please come and fetch me.' So I slipped inside where the lintel had fallen and a rotted door hung half open, and there sat a young girlen-woman clad in a dress picked all about with acorns and leaves.

"'Where is my daughter?' I cried. 'Do you have her hidden here?'

"The girlen shook her head and then she spoke again, but this time her voice was alike to an old crone, so cracked I had to stare in her face to see she had not turned old. But then as I peered close, the voice was an aged man who croaked, 'Stay away from me...'

"I watched as the girlen's lips moved and there in her mouth sat a tiny linnet. Then I knew it was not her voice at all but the voice of the bird I heard. I gazed into the girlen's eyes and saw her beseech me, 'Take this creature away.' I thought of every cunning I needed to play. My mouth is well-skilled, my fingers nimble-quick and so I kissed her full on the lips. And then I twisted and teased with my teeth and stroked her throat gently until out popped that tiny linnet in a flurry of feathers and flew all about the damp mossy walls, till it sat on the window ledge, whistling and staring.

"I looked at the girlen then, as she sat there shaking.

"'Who are you?' I asked.

"'I am Rimmony,' she replied."

"Rimmony!" Elmskin exclaimed. He came rushing over. "Where is she now?"

"I left her in the cottage," Skellyknox replied. "She told me she sat there each day to mend the clothes of travellers who came passing that way. Had a belt hung with scissors, needles and ribbons all dangling from her waist.

"Said one day she heard this linnet singing at the window. She picked it up and held it to her lips as if to kiss it but quick as quick it hopped inside her mouth, speaking in voices she had never heard, shouting at strangers to lure them or trick them, though there was none who could save her till at last I happened along."

"Take me to her," Elmskin implored.

Skellyknox sank down upon a rock.

"I'm proper wearied," she declared, then turned to her daughter.

"Where'd you find this'un?" she asked, jerking her head towards Elmskin who was shuffling away, kicking impatiently at the heads of straggling thistles.

"Tis a boy, mother," Mizzle replied. "Taking the same road as us."

Skellyknox sniffed and looked him up and down.

Elmskin returned her gaze.

"Your daughter told me you were sick," he said.

"Sick of *her* more like," Skellyknox retorted before turning back to Mizzle.

"Can he beg?" she demanded. "Can he filch?"

"Don't beg from no-one," Elmskin declared. "I make my own way."

"And what is your way?" Skellyknox quizzled. "Where are you going?"

"Going to find Rimmony, the girl you saw in the cottage. Please take me to her."

Skellyknox spat and pulled her shawl around her.

"The sky it grows dark and the wind it blows cold."

Elmskin strode off, pacing up and down the road, as Mizzle slipped her hand inside her pocket and sidled up to Skellyknox.

"What you got there?" her mother sniffed.

"Tis a necklace," Mizzle answered. "A curious thing."

Skellyknox twisted it about and about.

"Tis tawdry and tattered. Not worth a jot. Where'd you filch it?"

Mizzle nodded towards Elmskin.

Skellyknox raised an eyebrow.

"Where was it?"

"In his pocket."

"That all he got?"

Mizzle nodded.

"If that be all he got, must be precious to him. Best give it back girl, it's no use to us. But if he finds it gone, it's *you* he'll blame. Put it back..."

Mizzle twisted the necklace between her fingers and sighed.

"Twas a pretty thing."

"Twas twisted and shrivelled. I can teach you to make better. Look - see what I got from that girlen in the cottage."

Skellyknox opened the flap of her bag. Nestled there inside was a pair of scissors, a clutch of needles and a fistful of ribbons.

"Mayhap you can be a seamstress and earn an honest living."

Mizzle arched one eyebrow.

"Ain't no honesty in working," she retorted. "Long nights and squinty eyes, just to make a kerchief."

"Here he comes now..."

As Elmskin walked back towards them, Skellyknox nudged her daughter and the necklace fell to the ground.

Mizzle bent to retrieve it, but Elmskin stopped her.

"How do you come by this?" he demanded.

"It must have fallen from your pocket," she whispered. "My mother bade me keep it safe for you."

"I keep it safe for *Rimmony*," Elmskin cried.

Mizzle pressed the necklace into his outstretched hand, then kissed him quickly on the cheek. Elmskin turned away.

"Take me to the cottage," he said. "I need to see Rimmony again."

They walked through a wind of blossom and petals, a wind of sharp knives and hard bitter sorrow till they came to a copse beside of the road, and there in a hollow nestled the cottage, all knotted with tangled ivy just as Skellyknox had told them.

"I know this place!" cried Elmskin. "I have been here before..."

He gazed at the empty window and thought he saw a figure sitting there.

"Rimmony!..." he called, but there came no answer.

Mizzle was scratting at the rags that were stacked up outside. Skellyknox watched her as she slipped a scarf, a shawl, an old tattered shirt, into the depths of her bag.

"Rimmony!..." Elmskin called again.

Skellyknox shook her head, but at that moment, Elmskin heard Rimmony's voice singing soft from where she sat at the window. He rushed across the clearing, pushing open the half-rotted door.

Inside the walls were daubed with dark blood and scattered feathers. In the corner a noose swung slowly from a beam. Beneath it sat a stool surrounded all about with the lurid white petals of mandrake flowers which sprang from the damp earthen floor.

By the window he saw Rimmony, hunched, her back to the door, as if she was sewing.

"Rimmony," Elmskin whispered breathlessly.

The singing stopped.

Rimmony did not move.

She did not speak.

Elmskin crossed the room towards her.

He placed a hand upon her shoulder.

Then she pitched forward, a sack of straw, toppling towards the floor. Elmskin grabbed her, to stop her falling, turned her face as if he might kiss her and found himself staring into the open beak of the linnet where it sat wedged in the slit of the mouth of a head stitched together from cloth that felt so soft, almost like skin to touch.

Elmskin made a grab for the bird, but at that moment it rose up and fluttered out through the window. He followed its flight and watched as outside Mizzle still scavenged through the rags on the ground while Skellyknox cradled the linnet in her hands where it cried like a baby and then called out in the voice of her daughter:

"Please help a poor girl..."

Skellyknox stared at the small ball of feathers in her hands.

"I think this fowl can help us," she mused. "I think we can train it well."

As Elmskin walked away from the cottage, he cast his eye ruefully back to the empty window where he'd seen the figure he thought was Rimmony. But Rimmony was not here. Rimmony was gone and he had to journey on, plunging deep beneath the shadows of the trees. Then he caught his breath. He stared around. From far off he heard a sound, a hammering of drums, a rattling of sticks as through the trees dark figures came, hunched and crook-backed, circling round him, spitting and cursing and calling his name.

He twisted round and round and around again, his head a-spin amid the din. Till the drumming stopped and all was silent. Leering faces pressed about him, masked and grimacing. One prodded at him with a bony finger, then another, then another more.

Elmskin held his ground, staring each one down. Then above the stooping trees, a tiny linnet rose, singing in Mizzle's plaintive voice and leading the sullen figures away along the winding path towards the waiting cottage.

THE WAITING STORM

All about Elmskin heard rustling of leaves and cracking of twigs and voices of dark birds calling. And he called too, called Rimmony's name, but no-one replied. And he walked on still, till the wood was ended and came he then to an empty place where the dull wind wailed and if he called out, all his words were borne away. Away to where a mountain rose, swathed in a shrawl of cloud.

Elmskin began to climb, foot before foot and hand over hand, till he glimpsed where stooping shapes hunched like waiting strangers, but as he scrambled closer, saw were twisted shrubs and stunted trees. Shadows slipped between shadows, slithering and sudden, till he turned to look down and saw only the mist, swirling round and around, choked in the throat of the valley.

He called again, called Rimmony's name, but his voice was lost in the silence which clung to the grey looming rock. His legs ached now with the longing for her, a stone rolled heavy in his groin.

Then a smell of smoke.

Elmskin stopped.

He looked up.

He was near at the top.

And at the top there squatted a cave, the drizzle of a fire lit inside. A bent figure scuttled to tend it, half hidden in the shadows, but Elmskin caught a glimpse of her clear grey eyes through the curtain of smoke, heard a snatch of her voice singing dark and low, and knew that this was Rimmony true. She squinted suspiciously as he took a step towards the mouth of the cave and soft he spoke her name.

Rimmony flinched back.

"How do you know me?" she demanded.

"I am Elmskin," he said.

She shook her head.

Elmskin reached inside his jacket and drew out the necklace he had kept for her. Rimmony snatched for it quickly, running the shells and the berries through her fingers so roughly the frayed string almost snapped. She cradled the necklace a moment then squinted out at him.

"I made this to wear for Flax Wing," she said.

Elmskin nodded.

"I am Elmskin," he repeated. Forgotten words hovered on his tongue. "I tried to save you. I came to find you again."

Rimmony turned away inside the dusk of the cave.

"You've found me now," she said, "but truth, I do not know you."

"I followed you to Lowden's Beck."

Rimmony shook her head.

"I never saw you," she said.

"And yet I followed you every day, watched your every step."

"Maybe I saw a shadow," Rimmony shrugged. "A shadow and a cough. And some sort of rustling. Never saw you."

"But I called to you. Other days - back on the Green."

"Never heard you. Only heard the trilling of the linnet that led me to the waterfall. Then all I heard was the plunge of the river. And another voice calling."

"Who did you hear?"

"Flax Wing. It was him. Heard him call from the mountains, from the echoing sky."

"What did he say?"

Rimmony shook her head in the shadows.

"Called my name."

"Nothing else?"

"Didn't need to say nothing more."

"Might have been me..." Elmskin muttered. "Might have been me you heard call."

Rimmony turned away.

"Could not be you, Elmskin, for I never heard you at all."

"Did you find him, this Flax Wing you were running after?" Elmskin demanded.

Rimmony paused.

"Yes - he is here."

Elmskin peered into the darkness of the cave, expecting to see a tall figure waiting in the shadows. But there was nobody there.

"He is resting now," Rimmony explained.

"How did you find him?" Elmskin asked.

"Found him in the sadness of a boy with the head of a gull. Found him in the tender touch of a puppet all sewed together from skin. Found him in the loss of a man burdened down by the weight of a feather. Found him in the courage of a moon child - in the smelt of the hot white metal. Found him in the joy of a birthing when leathern leaves slid forth from a mother.

"Found him but did not find him at all, for though I heard him calling me, I never glimpsed his form. Found him in a cottage long way from here all tangled about with ivy. And now he spends each day always close by my side."

"Where is he now?" asked Elmskin.

Rimmony stepped out then from the mouth of the cave.

"He is sleeping," she said, "beneath this blanket I

stitched for him, same as I stitched this gown that I wear."

Elmskin stared at her, for garments wore she none. Rimmony returned his gaze. He scarce recognised her now, her hair it was all hacked away and her face marked about with a swirl of tattoos, like as if they had been made by tiny claws. She pulled back the cover then, that kept Flax Wing warm and there Elmskin saw, not a man at all but a cluster of bones. And not the bones of a man, but a bird, a tiny linnet. Then as Elmskin looked, he saw that the walls of the cave were hung all about with feathers.

Elmskin stared at Rimmony as she hunched and shivered.

"You need to make more clothes," he said.

"My needles, my thimbles, my scissors and ribbons, they were stole from me."

"Who took them?"

"Sorrow took them. Sorrow and storms. Sorrow and a snitch-eyed vixen. Sorrow and a scurry-rat lived behind the wall."

"You still have one thimble," Elmskin pointed. Rimmony slid it from her finger and held it up to the sky.

The thimble filled with lightning. The thimble filled with thunder and rain. And the rain it ran thick as blood, which Rimmony drank, its sweet salt kissing her lips.

She smiled.

"It is the blood of every finger-prick that I have suffered sewing garments day and night."

One drop spilled to the ground, where it glistened, red as any berry.

"Red as the berries of the necklace you made," Elmskin reminded her, stepping forward to fasten the string around her throat.

Rimmony pushed him from her.

"Let me tell you," she said, as she scuffed the bright

red drop into the dust with her heel, "- you want me for the girlen I was, but I am woman-grown. The berries they are faded now, shrivelled, lost and gone..."

Elmskin turned and walked away into the arms of the waiting storm.

BACK AT THE CROSSROADS

*Back at the crossroads, Pickapple stands,
a drum and a candlestick, one in each hand.*

*Mullops and Littleberry lie fast asleep,
as down the twining pathways he begins to creep.*

*So fasten your windows and lock up your door,
for if Pickapple comes a-knocking
you will never sleep no more.*

*Down the twining pathways he begins to creep,
as Mullops and Littleberry lie fast asleep.*

*A drum and a candlestick, one in each hand,
and back at the crossroads,
an empty gallows stands.*

Also by David Greygoose

Brunt Boggart: A Tapestry of Tales
Hawkwood Books: 2015
Pushkin Press: 2018

"Conjures a magical, poetic world of tricksters in an ancient village."
THE OBSERVER

"In Brunt Boggart, David Greygoose conjures a rich, primordial dreamtime from sullen hedgerows and fields... a wonderful excavation of the story traditions that our ancestors huddled around for warmth, and highly recommended."
ALAN MOORE: 'V for Vendetta'

"These are utterly wonderful new-old tales. In his bones, David Greygoose understands the rhythms of great storytelling, with its incantations, repetitions, knowing asides and snappy dialogue, and he has a frankly marvellous ear for the music of language. This tapestry is inventive and witty, dramatic and moving, and deeply earthed in the superstitions and folk beliefs of old England. Now that I've stepped into Brunt Boggart, I know that part of me will never leave it."
KEVIN CROSSLEY-HOLLAND: 'The Arthur Trilogy'

"David Greygoose is a master-storyteller, creating the visceral netherworld that is Brunt Boggart. Greygoose draws deeply on the riches of Britain's folklore to conjure up dark and whimsical tales of an imagined village. I found myself lost in the wildflower meadows, mossy hollows and wolf pits of Brunt Boggart."
EMILY PORTMAN: BBC Folk Awards winner

"Brunt Boggart is a skilfully crafted collection of timeless tales which connects the reader on a visceral level. Each is as true a tale as ever was told. Just as a great sculptor sees the divine form within the slab of granite, Greygoose has stripped away all that is extraneous exposing the primal folktales which lay buried in us all."
JOHN REPPION: Graphic comic writer, 'Wild Girl' and 'Albion'

"It tastes fabulously medieval, it smells uncanny, it looks like the roots of half-forgotten herbs, and it sounds like verbs of thunder and earth."
JAY GRIFFITHS: Author of 'Wild'

"A fascinating book by a storyteller immersed in the dark folktales of another time."
BRIAN PATTEN: Liverpool Poet: 'The Mersey Sound'

"Brunt Boggart is a totally unique and entrancing book... a carnival cavalcade of misfit performers tumbling over and over... troubadour-tellings that take one step beyond imagining... as loaded with dream-stuff as the golden-brown poppy seed... these are stories with the moon in their eyes and the wind in their hair."
ANDREW DARLINGTON: 'Eight Miles Higher'

"Real storytelling stuff – a bit like coming across a newly-written Odyssey."
MARY MEDLICOTT: 'Storyworks'

"Folklore and nature collide in Brunt Boggart. Greygoose's inventive language makes these tales a joy to read aloud - in true storyteller style."
ANTONIA CHARLESWORTH: 'The Big Issue in The North'

"Brunt Boggart is a beautifully written lyrical novel by a master of language. Rich in imagery and poetic in style, it captivates from the first haunting words and never lets go its hold until the last magical lines. Let me tell you, this is a book once read, never forgotten."
THE FAMULUS

"[A] many faceted, finely crafted and genuinely enjoyable book... a piece of work that can be enjoyed equally by aficionados of fantasy, of folk horror and of fairy tale and folklore."
GREY MALKIN: 'MOOF' magazine

"An exceptional book, truly original and startling. Greygoose's prose is unique, with more than a passing nod to Dylan Thomas' Under Milk Wood. It is a tapestry, heavy woven with rich spangling threads, and embellished with wondrous gee-gaws and trinkets... surreal dreamscapes, wonderful dream snippets and glimpses into a quasi-medieval past."
XPHAIEA: 'Goodreads'